~ DISSENT

With good wishes!

Liz Hutchinson

Frome 2020

'Hunger Lane, Frome,' by Steven Jenkins

# DISSENTERS

Conscience and Corruption
in 17th-century Frome

a Novel
by
LIZ HUTCHINSON

HOBNOB PRESS

First published in the United Kingdom
by The Hobnob Press,
8 Lock Warehouse, Severn Road, Gloucester GL1 2GA
www.hobnobpress.co.uk

in association with
Silver Crow Books, an imprint of Frome Writers' Collective

© Liz Hutchinson, 2020

British Library Cataloguing in Publication Data
A catalogue record for this book is available from the British Library

ISBN 978-1-906978-83-9

Typeset in Doves Type 13/15 pt
Typesetting and origination by John Chandler

Front cover illustration of 'Hunger Lane', Frome, by Steven Jenkins
www.hogweedart.co.uk

JAMES BAILY'S
MAP OF FROME
1668

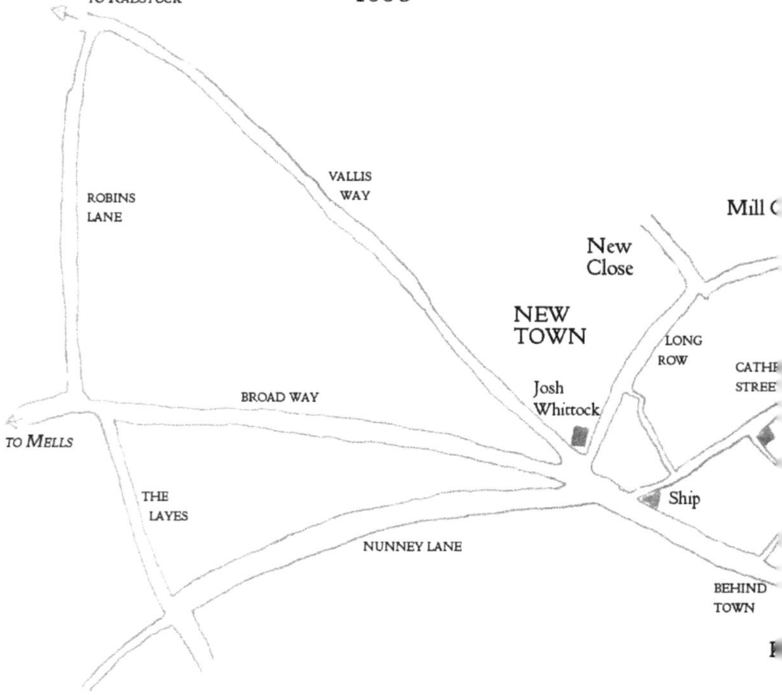

TO RADSTOCK

VALLIS
WAY

ROBINS
LANE

Mill (

New
Close

NEW
TOWN

LONG
ROW

CATHE
STREE

BROAD WAY

Josh
Whittock

TO MELLS

THE
LAYES

Ship

NUNNEY LANE

BEHIND
TOWN

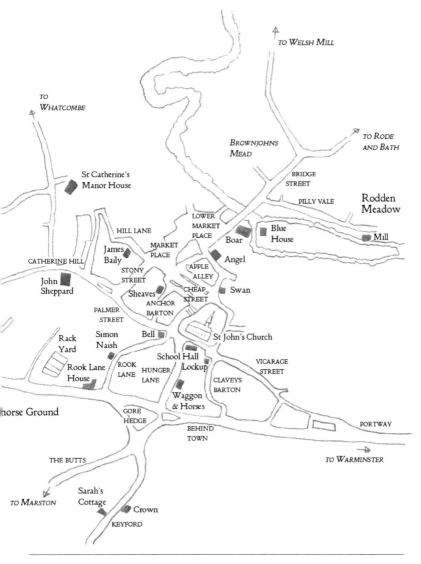

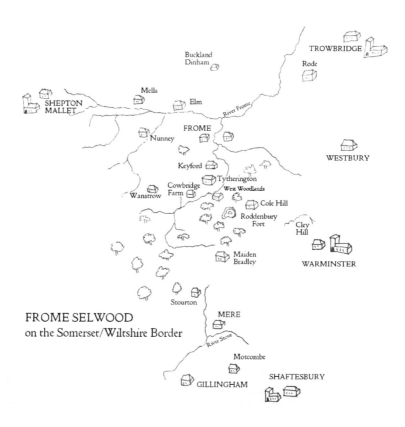

TROWBRIDGE

Buckland
Dinham

Rode

Mells

SHEPTON
MALLET

Elm

River Frome

FROME

Nunney

WESTBURY

Keyford

Tytherington

Cowbridge
Farm

West Woodlands

Wanstrow

Cole Hill

Roddenbury
Fort

Cley
Hill

WARMINSTER

Maiden
Bradley

Stourton

MERE

FROME SELWOOD
on the Somerset/Wiltshire Border

River Stour

Motcombe

GILLINGHAM

SHAFTESBURY

## FOREWORD

S INCE COMING TO live in Frome in 2011, the author has been fascinated by the history and buildings of the place – the ghosts, the very stones, have wonderful tales to tell if you just close your eyes and let your imagination run loose. Anecdotes related by new friends and acquaintances provided a rich source of inspiration for *Dissenters*, whose plot and characters are, it must be emphasised, wholly fictitious.

Liz Hutchinson graduated from the University of Kent at Canterbury in 1974 with a degree in Economic and Social History. It was almost forty years before she made full use of her studies, immersing herself in the life of 17th-century England to create this novel. By contrast *Sigura*, the first book in her *Daughter of Byzantium* series – is set in 15th-century Greece.

# FROME ~ MARCH 1666

## CHAPTER 1

NATHANIEL CROUCHED LOWER in the gulley, his nostrils full of the smell of leaf mould: rot and decay. Papery leaves disintegrating to skeletons crumbled under his fingers. There was a sheen on the surface of the mouldering beech leaves as the crescent moon glittered on a light dew. He was thankful for the recent spell of dry weather; his boots were too tattered to keep out the mud and water this ditch often held.

The hand pressing his head down eased up and he just caught Ben's whisper above the sigh of the wind: 'Slowly, slowly. They got their backs to we. Can'st see what they doin'?'

Nathaniel raised his head above the gulley's rim. His eyes were accustomed to the almost dark of the night, and the group on which they spied had positioned a pair of lanterns at their centre, illuminating the hands and faces of some and drawing silhouettes of others. His throat tightened as he took in their tall, wide brimmed hats and swirling cloaks. He slipped back into the ditch; he and Ben might be hidden by the darkness and as silent as the dead rabbits in their sack, but the figures he had seen suggested unearthly powers of observation.

'My God! Be they witches? Is it one of they covens?'

The whites of Ben's eyes caught what little light there

was. 'Seem like it to me. Let's get out of here before they sees we. And if the justices come after them, we don't want to be caught hanging around with this.'

Between them the two lads hefted the weighty sack, a bundle of wires, and a roll of tools in sacking, and crept cautiously along the bottom of the ditch that circled the ancient fort. Beech trees, stripped of their auburn leaves by the bitter wind, had colonised the hilltop and camouflaged the earthworks, while holly bushes made a dense curtain around the lower slopes. Using the countryman's skills passed on by their forbears, the brothers could walk over the twigs, leaf litter and ankle-turning slopes of Roddenbury as silently as the animals and birds they hunted.

'Last thing we want is witches gathering on our patch,' Nathaniel said as they closed the cottage door behind them at Cole Hill. 'Draw the magistrates down on us for sure, that would. Mebbe it's time we look to get a living other ways.'

Ben kicked off his filthy boots. 'I hear they wants strong lads what works by night, for something in town. Joshua was sayin'.'

'One of his "ventures" is it? I don't mind givin' it a go.'


'You boys been underground afore now?' Joshua tapped the bowl of his clay pipe to settle the tobacco as he stretched his feet to the blazing hearth of the Swan Inn, two nights later. 'No? Well I s'pose night work in the woods isn't too bad a start. This'll need your night eyes too, and strong backs, and muzzled mouths.' He drained his mug of ale and looked at the brothers over the rim. 'Anyone that hints, whispers, or even winks about our game can expect a knife in his guts. Un'erstand me?'

The pair nodded solemnly in unison.

'Meet me top of Catherine Hill, midnight tomorrow. No hobnails. Dark coats and shirts. It's a shilling each for a night's work.' Joshua pushed himself up from the stool. 'Any gossip, I knows where your sister lives. You don't want her coming to harm on a dark night . . .'

The candle flames shuddered in the draught as he slammed the tavern door behind him.

'I hopes you knows what you've got us into,' Nathaniel muttered to his elder brother. 'I don't like him threatenin' our Molly-Ann.'

'Best watch your tongue then.'

'Can't be lookin' out for her all the time.'

'Just his talk, but don't risk it.'

A log fell in the fire, and sparks rushed up the wide chimney.

A pair of suspicious eyes was the only visible feature of the muffled figure who beckoned them through the yard gates at the top of the cobbled hill the following night. Law-abiding citizens had been in their beds for two or three hours and even the town drunks had found a shelter for the night by this time. The eyes followed them with a penetrating stare, as though verifying their identities, then flicked to the left, indicating a low door. The light was dim, but it showed a short flight of steps that led down to a stone paved cellar. Within stood a dozen small barrels, rusted iron hoops girding the old oak staves, and a gleaming copper still. Joshua hammered in the last bung. The air was moist, with a distinctive sweet smell that the brothers instantly recognised.

'Cider making is it?' Nathaniel couldn't help himself from

asking. 'What is it you wants us to do here? And why at night?'

'Less you knows, the better for you,' Joshua snapped. 'You're just the transport. And recall what I said about your Molly-Ann. I'd be glad of a reason to get to know more of her.' The lantern light shone on his wolfish leer. 'Right. These barrels to be rolled down to the Sheaves. Use the ropes to check their speed, you'll find how heavy they be soon enough. Any breakages, it's Molly-Ann will pay for it.'

The big man turned and unbolted an iron door. A waft of stale, dank air enveloped Nathaniel, and his stomach heaved.

'God! Stinks like something died.'

'Here: miners' caps and candles.' Joshua held the headgear out to them. 'Take a flint with you or you'll never find your way out when the lights blow. And keep an eye for the fairy folk once you're down there.'

His hoarse laughter was cut off by the clang of the iron door.

Bracing himself against the weight of the anker barrel, Nathaniel held firmly to the rope looped about it and around and over his shoulders. The cask slid away from him down the steeply sloping tunnel, and he fought against gravity to moderate the speed of its descent. The feeble light from the candle pegged to his cap brim danced across the barrel as it made its way down the passage, bumping over irregularities in the natural stone floor, grazing the rock sides of the tunnel as it sped along. His skin burned as he fought to hold the rope, and his muscles ached with the prolonged strain upon them. Behind him, he could hear a second cask begin its rumbling descent; if the rope snapped or Ben lost his footing, that thing would crash into him with deadly force.

After a few hundred yards, which seemed never ending, the ground began to level out, and the speed of his burden slowed. Nathaniel drew a deep breath, they had made it down without mishap; even his candle was still burning. He freed himself from the ropes and wiped his sleeve over his face; it was another cold March night up above, but sweat was running into his eyes and down his back. He looked about him, peering into the darkness. The passage had opened into a brick-built chamber festooned with cobwebs and carpeted with a thick tilth, into which his boots sank. The stench of the tunnel seemed to come from this rotting mat of decaying refuse. Ben's barrel came to a stop beside his own; the dense litter evidently served as a brake or cushion.

'Now what?' Ben's eyes flickered over the walls and Nathaniel was conscious of his older brother's nervousness. It wasn't like Ben to get scared. Superstitious he might be, but he was always up for an adventure. This hurtling plummet had clearly rattled him, however.

'Bit of a door there.' Nathaniel nodded to his right at an opening, partially blocked by a couple of splintered planks. 'Shall I look?' He pushed against the mouldering wood which gave way and admitted a haze of lantern light.

'Hoy, that you, Josh?' A disembodied voice came through the doorway.

'We got two of they barrels 'ere from him,' Ben responded hesitantly. 'D'you want 'em through there?'

He stepped back as the lantern was thrust towards him; after the thick gloom of the tunnel its light was dazzling.

'Ah. Careful now, boys. That's valuable stuff there.'

'What, old cider?'

'No, lord love 'ee. Our Josh's found how to turn that into a pretty drop of spirits. That's best apple brandy in there. Put a fire in yer belly that would.'

Encouraged by the apparent talkativeness of the man,

Nathaniel asked: 'So why by night and underground? Be they stolen?'

'Nay, that's Josh's own, I've said. Just don't want no pryin' eyes seein' where it goes, do we?' The man clammed up. He'd evidently remembered Joshua's insistence on secrecy, if rather late. 'Now, there's another ten to come by my reckoning. You'd best get aloft there and bring they down.'

Ben had started back up the tunnel but Nathaniel turned. 'What do Joshua mean about the fairy folk down here? Be there spirits or ghosts or something?'

The man sniggered. 'Only apple spirits! But he puts it out there's fairies or will o' wisps to explain any lights or noises, if so be watchman or constable come by. Try and make them afeared, they might keep away.'

By the time all twelve of the anker barrels were safely stowed in the Sheaves' lower cellar, the night was almost over. Joshua was back in the top yard deftly tacking up his bay mare as Nathaniel and Ben staggered up the steps from the tunnel entrance. The horse, hitched to an iron ring in the wall, looked around at the interruption. Joshua delved into his drawstring purse, pulled out two coins and handed them over.

'Remember, lips sealed about my business. I may have another job for you Thursday night. I'll get word to you.' He pulled himself up into the saddle. 'Close the gates behind as you leave.'

Nathaniel held the shilling in his blistered fist as he made his way down the hill towards St John's church, then up Hunger Lane and so towards Keyford. The coin represented the assurance of bread for a week and even a piece of cheese; he tucked it away carefully in an inner pocket of his coat before he risked losing it. All the way home to Cole Hill he would dream of crusty bread and a nice strong bit of cheddar. The cock was crowing and the first dawn light had touched the horizon over Roddenbury when the brothers at last reached the farmhouse, climbed the steep stairs, and fell into their beds.

His feet were blocks of ice, his fingers stiff, and his nose stung with the cold the next morning. There was no warmth to be found in the threadbare blankets. He wondered when spring would come; it had been a long winter this year. Nathaniel opened his eyes to the dull grey noontide light. He knew he had to get a fire lit, get something warming inside him, but it took an effort of will to rise from his bed and to clamber down the steep stairs into the kitchen. His back and arms ached from last night's work but the silver shilling was a warming thought, and maybe more where that came from.

The place was a disgrace. Dirty cups and plates stood abandoned on the table; mud was smeared across the floor from the door; the ashes on the hearth were as cold as snow and no sticks in the basket. He pulled on his still damp boots and shivered his way to the backhouse. They'd have to go a-wooding today, there was scarce any firing left. He looked round the yard despondently: a slick of slurry ran from the pigsty into a scummy pool, the few remaining hens pecked at the midden, hunting maggots and worms, and beyond the fence the rich fields ran up towards the forest wall. Not their fields now. When their father died, heavily in debt, the last life on the copyhold had fallen and they had no way to pay for a new lease on the land. They were lucky to have been able to rent the dilapidated farmhouse but the fields had been taken back by Lord Weymouth into his own demesne. The beasts had gone too, apart from the pig.

Nathaniel sighed. Nothing much left now for the brothers

and Molly-Ann. He and Ben would have to hire themselves out as labourers for the foreseeable future, they'd never have the capital to farm on their own account. Wage slaves they'd be for the rest of their lives, selling theirselves to the likes of Joshua. It was a desolate prospect.

By Thursday the weather had changed. Nathaniel knew better than to believe spring was here for sure but there was warmth in the sun and, out of the wind, he could feel his blood thawing. Ben had agreed to help him clean up the yard but he was still nowhere to be seen as Nathaniel drew the first bucket of water from the well. As he stood upright, he glanced across the field below Roddenbury and noticed a bent figure in dark clothing ambling slowly along the hedgerow. She stooped and plucked something from the ground then moved on.

'Old Sarah?' Ben had appeared silently beside him. 'Her've survived the winter then.'

'Aye. Looks like she's out foragin'. I doubt she'll find much today.'

'Mebbe a few early primy roses. Some nettle shoots.'

'Poor old soul.'

'I heard she's taken in a lodger, Reverend Silcox. His rent'll keep her in food and fuel.'

'Let's hope.' Nathaniel turned the windlass to raise a second bucketful. 'Why's he need to lodge? Don't he have a vicarage?'

'Haven't you heard? He's turned out of his living at Wanstrow. Lost his roof an' all. Something to do with the new king; 'ee don't like the look of some vicars, turfed 'em out of their parishes altogether. That's why Silcox's come to Frome, to be minister to they puritans, and king's got a new fellow at St John's.'

'So how do this Silcox make ends meet? What's he doin' for money?'

'Going to start up a little school, they say. Penny a day each nipper. Alright for them as can spare it.' Ben sighed. 'We can do without book learning. Brings more problems than it's worth, I reckon.'

'S'pose mother might have learned us if she'd lived. She started teaching Molly-Ann her letters when we was babbies, didn't she? I think the girl still knows them.'

'She allus were brighter than we.'

'Needs to be.'

'Didn't get her so far, though,' Ben said. 'Cook and serving maid at the Boar.'

'Least she's got a dry roof and a warm bed and good food.'

'She works hard for it, and puts up with that slimy landlord all over her. We might need to sort him out afore long.'

'Could cost her the place though.'

By the time Nathaniel looked again, old Sarah was nowhere to be seen.

Joshua's message arrived as the brothers finished the scraping then washing of the yard. The pig was snuffling happily in her fresh straw and the hens had lined up on the low wall as if to keep their feathers out of the wet. Ben scratched his head as the urchin who had brought the message trotted away. 'Meet him at Cowbridge Farm at eight,' he said. 'Fair enough, doesn't sound like it's in the tunnels this time. We better take some bait with us, might be a long night. What we got?'

'How about a couple of they big potatoes, baked?' Nathaniel said. 'Take 'em hot, they'll serve as hand-warmers before we eat them.'

The windows in the few neighbouring cottages were dark as the brothers slipped silently through East Woodlands and onto the track to West Woodlands where Cowbridge Farm lay. The farmhouse door opened and lantern light spilled gold into the yard. They made their way towards it and the chained dog began to bark a warning before it was hushed by a deep voice. 'Josh is in the barn there. He's waiting for 'ee,' it continued.

Joshua had his broad back to them, his arms full of springy white wool that he was stuffing into a canvas bag. He spoke over his shoulder: 'Grab a couple of sacks and load the fleeces in, six to a bag each time. Strap 'em up tight.'

Nathaniel could see that the wool was of the finest quality: long staple, silky, well cleaned. 'This to go to the clothiers, Josh?'

Joshua shot him an angry frown, 'None of your business where it's going. You'll keep your mouth shut and follow my orders. I'm coming with you tonight, guide you on the route and vouch for you. Show you the ropes as the sailors say.' He wrenched the strap hard. 'If all's well, you might get a reg'lar call. I've lost a couple of men, need to fill their places.'

He brought a string of pack mules round to the barn, and together they loaded the sacks, one on each side of the animals, Ben and Nathaniel working together to lift the unwieldy bags. Each man took the lead rein of a string of three mules and they set off into the night, heading south down the Maiden Bradley road.

The night was clear and still, the moon would not rise till near dawn, and the mud on the road had frozen. The starlight was bright enough to show the way and the mules kept up a brisk pace. Josh had tied sacking bags over the animals' feet to deaden their hoofs when they encountered stony surfaces, and the group was able to proceed almost noiselessly. Nathaniel held his potato in his pocket with his free hand. The warmth cheered him and he was almost enjoying the "venture" when Joshua veered off the road and into a stand of trees by the county bridge. The brothers quickly followed with their mules, then stood silently, listening intently to the sounds of the fields and woodland. Nathaniel heard it after a few moments, a regular hoof beat approaching from the south. Josh must have very keen hearing, he thought. A single rider trotted briskly towards them, then past their hiding place and on towards Frome. Nathaniel drew breath. The mules had remained as quiet as the men; the only sign of life the clouds of steam from their nostrils. With a pat of approval, Joshua led his string back onto the roadway. There were no further alarms on the rest of the journey, and they passed through Maiden Bradley and close to Stourton. No lights showed anywhere.

Soon after crossing the highway with its fingerpost to London, they entered the little town of Mere, and Nathaniel could just make out the hands on the church clock standing at nearly three. A lantern shone in the stable yard of the Cock Inn and Joshua led them under the broad archway. Immediately, a figure emerged from the stables, held the door wide and beckoned them in. The mules blew down their nostrils, as if they knew that a rest awaited them.

'Unload the packs,' Joshua ordered. 'Stack them behind there.' He pointed to an empty stall. 'We'll give the animals a breather then we can ride back to Frome. Be in bed by sunrise.'

'Where's the fleeces goin' to then?' Nathaniel asked.

'How many times?' Joshua scowled at him. 'Less you knows the better. If you're going to make an owler, you got to learn the basics. Do as you're told and ask no questions. Got it?'

'Sorry, Josh. Yes.'

'Right. You two could be useful to me, but rein in that curiosity.' He went off to speak with the man in the muffler.

'What's an owler?' Nathaniel asked his brother, quietly.

Ben wasn't looking too pleased. 'Kind of a smuggler,' he muttered. 'Takes goods down to the coast to send to France and Flanders. I doubt they have a long life. I heard gov'ment's crackin' down hard.'

Nathaniel bit into his potato, his stomach had been rumbling for the last hour. 'Must be money in it for someone. S'long as we gets our shilling, I'll take my chance.'

As if he had heard them, Joshua returned and handed over the night's pay. 'Next time you can come without me. I've just vouched for you to Matt there. That'll mean a bit extra pay for you in future. Now, mount up, and we'll soon be home.' His words may have been cheery, but it was a cold, penetrating stare that he fixed on the brothers.

# CHAPTER 2

MOLLY-ANN TIPPED the bowl of scummy grey water into the drain that led down to the river below; it was a useful arrangement that kept the Boar's yard dry and easily scoured of filth. The April sunshine sparkled on the river, prettifying what she knew to be a fearsomely dirty stream that carried away the effluent of the town: waste water from the fulling mills and the dyers; sewage from the townsfolk and their animals; scourings from breweries and slaughter yards. It didn't bear thinking about, so she didn't anymore, and stepped back into the tavern's kitchen. As she dried her hands on the coarse apron that she habitually wore for the dirtiest work, a shadow fell across the back doorstep, followed by a large wicker basket and a little old woman.

'Mornin' Sarah,' Molly-Ann said with a smile. 'I've missed your visits over the winter. Have you got something for us, now that spring's here?'

Old Sarah lowered her basket to the stone flags and slowly straightened her back. 'Aye, first ramsons of the year, and a good mixture of green stuff to go with them if you've a mind to make spring soup: nettles, cleavers, dandelions, bit of sorrel, all young and tender. Onion and a couple of 'taters and you've soup for a king.'

Molly-Ann's eyes lit up. 'Just what we want. I was wondering what I could make that's different today. Fed up with dried peas and salt pork, we are. Wild garlic soup, some new bread, and cheese, and even old Grimwade'll be happy. I'll take the lot. How much d'you want?'

As Sarah emptied her basket onto the kitchen table, Molly-Ann sorted through the coins in the moneybox. 'Skinflint's not left me much. Will thruppence do?'

Sarah sighed. 'Aye. Can I bring you anything else? I'm just bottling up some cough syrup: thyme, liquorice and elderberry – last of the year – or there's primy roses for a tea for rheumatics?'

Molly-Ann's lips parted in a grin. 'I'll suggest it to the mistress. She was moaning about the stairs being too steep for her knees. Make sure you charges her a good price.'

Joe Grimwade, the landlord, filled the doorway both widthways and heightways as he entered the kitchen. He tucked his thumbs into the arm holes of his jerkin and frowned at the women. 'Gossiping again? What you want here, Mistress Sarah? You're interrupting Molly-Ann's work.'

'She's bringing fresh herbs for my soup, Joe,' Molly-Ann said. 'The smell of this will bring in the customers, don't you worry.'

Sarah picked up her basket. 'I'll be off then. G'day to 'ee.' The look she gave Joe Grimwade as she passed through the back door would have curdled new milk.

Joe advanced upon Molly-Ann, his eyes shining, but his mouth a tight line. He towered over her, then one hand seized the nape of her neck and with the other he started to fondle her through the fabric of her bodice and shift. He bent down to kiss her on the lips. With a mighty shove she pushed him back; caught off balance he bumped his backside against the corner of the table and grunted with pain.

'Leave me be, Joe, I won't stand for that sort of thing. Touch me again and you'll have the mistress to answer to.' She side-stepped away from him keeping the table between them.

'You needs this job, Molly-Ann. Show me a bit more friendliness and I'd reward you. Wouldn't take much to keep me happy.'

Molly-Ann's shudder should have made it clear to Joe just what she thought of his offer, but he persisted, trying to catch her arm.

'Bugger off, Joe, or I'll tell my brothers too.'

'More respect, girl, or you'll be out on yer ear.'

Joe finally backed off in response to strident calls for service from the public room.

'Christ 'a mercy, such a crowd.' Betty the landlady emerged from the tap room, her hands gripping a stack of dirty plates and bowls. 'Joe should be happy with the day's takings. It may be market day and the sun shining, but I've never seen such a busy noontide 'afore.'

Molly-Ann looked up from the tub in which she was scouring half a dozen pewter bowls with sand. 'Reckon they smelled the soup all up the Market Place. Must put that on again, and twice as much next time.' She laid a bowl to drain. 'Had to run up to the bakehouse for more bread too, it was so popular.'

'Well after you've done these dishes you go up for a rest, you've earned it. The room's emptying out. I'll clear up and set to for this evening. Then you can come down while I puts my feet up for a bit.'

Molly-Ann nodded. 'But I might go out rather than rest. I wants to go and see what my brothers are a doin' of, and I could stop by at old Sarah's, order more ramsons for later in the week while them's popular.'

Molly-Ann's straw mattress in the attic held little appeal, other than when she was dog tired after a busy evening. And on such an inviting spring afternoon she didn't want to stop at the Boar, especially not if Joe was on the premises for the afternoon.

She pulled shut the door of Sarah's Keyford cottage, after giving the old woman her order for the green stuff, and glanced up at the window in the gable end above. The cottage was sturdily built of the local limestone, forest marble the masons called it, a greyish yellow colour, not the glowing honey of Bath stone, and generally used in irregular chunks rather than neatly squared off. It was a tiny place, one room and a lean-to wash house downstairs, with an attic bedroom above. A movement behind the thick glass caught her eye. The swirls and imperfections in the glazing distorted what she could see, but she was sure it was a man's face, framed in black cloth, with a flash of white below. What, she wondered, was old Sarah doing with a man in the house? Sarah had always said she'd no family; first the church and now the chapel seemed to be her true family, and of course she was widely known about the town for her help at births and deaths, as well as her herbal medicines.

A family: Molly-Ann might still have her feckless brothers, but she pined for a real warm family. Her father had had a heart of stone, and her own dear mother was a hazy memory now, but one that still influenced Molly-Ann's sense of values. Mother had been a devout churchgoer, and Molly-Ann had attended Dr Humfry's services at St John's with her as a small child. Master Silcox had taken a keen interest in the family in his turn and given both his spiritual and practical help when the parents died. Years later, he'd been her main support when she'd found herself pregnant following a rape by one of the Boar's customers. Her reputation had been lost as a result, and now she had little hope of finding a respectable husband. Were it not for Gideon Silcox, she might by now have been a fallen woman. As it was, the vulnerability she had felt had instilled in her a greater caution towards men, resilience, and a determination to fight back with all her strength, if a liaison wasn't on her own terms.

The face had gone from the window and she turned down through Keyford to Feltham Lane, and on to her brothers' home. She would just about have time to get there and back before Betty and Joe needed her again in the tap room. She pulled her thick woollen shawl more tightly over her shoulders; the spring winds were keen despite the sunshine.

Molly-Ann's throat tightened a little as the old farmhouse at Cole Hill came into view. It was quite large, three storeys high, but the stock had shared the ground floor with the family in recent years, bringing damp, destruction and smells; it was decades since there had been any money for repairs, and the roof was in a very sorry state. But it had been her childhood home and memories of her mother came flooding back to her.

In the yard Nathaniel swung an axe with precision as he split logs for the fire. The little brother she had helped raise after their mother died was now as tall as any man around, with a wiry strength and more stamina than his older brother Ben. The gate latch clicked and he turned towards her, his face breaking immediately into a warm smile.

'Molly-Ann, is all well with 'ee? 'Tis a while since you've been out here.' He gave her such a hug he lifted her off her feet.

'Aye, Nat, all's well. I just wanted a breath of air and see the old place. Can't stop, I'm needed back to serve tonight.'

'Step in, have a rest and a drink of something. Don't know what we've got, but you're welcome to 'en.' He looked round the yard. 'Ben's about, but I dunno where.'

Molly-Ann went into the house, moved a pile of wire snares from the settle and sat down. 'How're you two getting by then? Have you picked up some work, or is it the poachin' still?'

'Well now, we been taken on by that Joshua, doin' a bit of this an' that. Dost know him? Big chap, said to be free with his cusses and his fists, but not much else.'

'I'd probably know 'en if I saw 'en, but can't call 'im to mind. If'n his business is on the shady side, you two better keep alert, be ready to run.'

'Aye, but he do pay well.'

'I'm just sayin'.'

'I hears you.' Nathaniel looked put out. 'He's been alright to us so far.'

Molly-Ann looked narrowly at her brother. 'You're nervous of him,' she said. 'Have he threatened 'ee?'

'No, Molly-Ann.' Nathaniel clamped his mouth shut; his sister knew that look, he'd say no more.

Ben came through the door. With a clatter of wood on stone, he flung the pig's empty swill bucket down, and a slight spatter of muck flew out onto the kitchen floor. His arms wide, he strode over to his sister and enveloped her in a bear hug.

'How's that swine Joe Grimwade treating you? It looks like you're getting fed and watered there, Molly-Ann. But I hopes they're not working 'ee too hard?'

'It's alright at the Boar. I'm even saving a bit, and Betty's seein' me right. She knows a good worker when she gets one.' She looked around the cheerless, filthy kitchen. 'You boys a'right? Got enough to eat? Living on rabbits?'

Ben laughed. 'Eat a lot of them, we do. But we got a few more pennies now, just have to watch we don't turn too much of them into cider.'

Nathaniel cocked an eye towards the door and lifted a hand in warning. Two heart beats later the door latch rattled loudly and a begrimed, tousled head looked in.

'Message from Master Joshua. Be at Catherine Hill . . .' he stopped in mid sentence, his eyes round, as he spotted Molly-Ann.

'Alright Billy, our sister'll say nothin', but have a care in future,' Ben said. 'Midnight is it?'

Billy nodded and fled.

'What you at, Ben?' The backs of Molly-Ann's hands felt prickly, as if a shiver had passed over them. She frowned.

'Just a bit of business. No need for you to know anything, that's the best way.' Ben's eyes looked as if they had a skim of ice; his voice was cold.

'I'll be on my way then, boys.' She pulled the blue shawl around her shoulders; the pleasure of the day had faded.


It was six weeks later; the early summer had come in uncommonly warm, and the heat from the kitchen fire made the Boar as hot as Beelzebub's place. Tendrils of hair clung to her damp forehead, she could feel her scalp crawl with sweat, and it was Wednesday again, market day. The public room was full of customers, mostly the rougher sort, and they all seemed to be calling for ale or cider fast as they could drink it. Molly-Ann took a deep breath and squeezed through the crowd, the weight of the tray of tankards almost too much for her.

And what was Joe the landlord doing to help? Nothing. Sitting on his fat arse on a stool talking to some man, their heads together, paying no mind to his other customers.

Molly-Ann scowled at the pair of them, Joe's back towards her. The stranger glanced up as if he felt the force of her glare. She paused and blinked. It felt as though her eyes and his were linked by an invisible thread. She couldn't drop his gaze. Surely she'd seen him about the town, though she couldn't put a name to him. But she liked what she saw; it felt as if a spark were passing between them, one that dazzled her and made her blind to all the rest of her surroundings.

There was a bellow from Joe. He rose from his seat blocking her view of the younger man. 'What are you doing, girl? That's dripping down my neck.'

Molly-Ann righted the tray; the slops must have gone over its rim. An ironic smile had lifted one corner of the other man's mouth and he looked away. Muttering an apology, she made her way back to the kitchen for another load.

On her return to the packed bar, she manoeuvred her way behind Joe and listened carefully to the conversation between the landlord and the tall, well-built stranger. Joe seemed to be negotiating a price, what for, she didn't know, but she heard Joe call him Master Joshua and wondered whether this was the same person her brothers had spoken of, back in the early spring. She'd made a point of remembering the name.

As the room cleared after the lunch hour, Molly-Ann began to tidy up, wiping over the tables, setting benches and stools back in place. She was surprised Joe hadn't made more fuss about the beer she'd spilt on him, not like him to forgive so easily. She rinsed her cloth in the bucket and bent to scrub harder at a stubborn stickiness on the table top. Without warning her arm was grabbed and Joe was hissing in her ear.

'You're going to pay for that girl. You deserve a thrashing for your clumsiness.'

He was dragging her out the back, into the kitchen as he

continued: 'Now Betty's out,' flecks of spittle sprayed her face, 'I'm going to teach you a lesson.' His fingers were digging into the flesh of her arm, while his other hand was fumbling with the buckle of his belt. Whatever it was he had in mind, Molly-Ann was not going to submit without a fight and, her blood up, she scratched his face as hard as she could with her free hand, aiming for his eyes but only drawing scarlet gashes on his cheek.

'Leave me be you devil,' she screamed. 'You've no right . . .'

Her arm was suddenly released and she staggered against the door post, grabbing the stone wall to steady herself. The landlord had been spun round and Molly-Ann gasped for breath, unable to speak for mingled fright and astonishment. The stranger stood in the doorway, flexing his fists.

'He giving you trouble?' He put his head on one side. 'You're Molly-Ann ain't you? I been looking out for you.'

That magnetic force trapped her eyes again.

'Business is business, Master Grimwade,' he said, 'but I hope you'll see your way to showing more respect to my friend here.'

Joe frowned at the younger man. 'What's it to do with you?'

'I've heard about Molly-Ann. I know her brothers. We don't want any harm coming her way.' He rubbed his fist with the other hand. 'You'd do well to back off, 'specially if you hope to profit from the business what we've been discussing.'

The landlord shrugged. 'She ain't worth it, and no better than she should be. She's no right to her airs and graces.' He sidled into the kitchen.

Molly-Ann followed Joshua as he left the tavern. 'Thank 'ee for stopping him. I was really a'feared.'

Joshua turned; his grey eyes now held a more calculating

look. 'Glad to be of service, my dear. It was good chance I came back.' He put his hat on. 'I'll be looking in again a'fore long. I hope I'll see 'ee then.'

Molly-Ann watched him stride away across Market Place, not sure if she had just lost her heart or won the attention of a knave, or perhaps both.


With that sudden changeability for which Somerset weather is notorious, and even though the almanac said it was indeed July, the following week saw rain day after day, and the evening customers called for a fire to offset the damp and the gloom. Molly-Ann looked up from the hearth after mending the blaze, to see Ben and Nathaniel coming into the public room. Wiping her hands on her apron, she went to greet them. They seemed to be unusually subdued and tired, and she wondered if all was well with their night-time ventures. The questions burned on her lips, but she knew better than to ask in public.

'Don't often see you in the Boar,' she said, instead. 'What can I get you? Cider?'

'Aye.' The lads sank onto seats in the darkest corner of the room; most other customers had sought the cheeriness of the fireside.

Setting down the brimming wooden tankards, Molly-Ann peered at each of her brothers in turn. 'You looks wore out. Had some work on?'

Nathaniel smiled wanly without meeting her eyes. She only had five years on him, but sometimes it felt to her as if it were decades, as if he was her child. He seemed almost fragile, vulnerable, despite his height and energy.

'I think you're living too near the edge, you two. What's

the trouble?' She pulled a stool over and sat between them, huddling them together like a mother hen with chicks.

'We've had a busy time,' Ben said. 'Not much chance for sleep.'

'No, and I'd guess you're allus looking over your shoulders, got yer ears tuned for footsteps.' Molly-Ann spoke in a whisper. 'You take care now boys, watch who you're dealing with.' She pulled them closer still. 'Is it that Joshua?' She barely spoke the name. 'He were here a week or two back. I reckon he's selling duty free brandy to Joe. I'm not sure what I makes of him.'

'That's the least of it, Molly-Ann,' Nathaniel muttered. 'It's good money we're getting, but I knows we're on the wrong side of the law.'

'Don't see how we can get out of it now,' Ben put in. 'We know too much of his ventures for him to let us go. I think we could do well by him, anyway.'

Molly-Ann glanced back across the room towards the fire. Orange flames with hearts of blue spurted from one of the logs, then died away. 'Can't you just go back to the night work at Roddenbury?'

Over by the fire, one of the other customers had turned a little; shrouded in a dark travelling cloak, he had been almost invisible to Molly-Ann. And who might you be, she wondered; not one of the parish constables or the magistrates – she knew them well enough by sight. Some informer perhaps? He was suspiciously reserved – stood out like a sore thumb, he did.

Nathaniel sighed loudly and shook his head. 'We've been up there a couple of times since spring. Allus runs across these folk chanting and whispering. I fear 'tis a witches' gathering – and that'll attract the magistrates. They've spoilt our chances of any rabbits or the odd deer for sure.'

Ben's eyes held a deal of anxiety as he looked at his sister. 'Do'ee know anything about these witches and warlocks, Molly-Ann? Is it the devil they're cavorting with? We saw a tall man in black that they seemed to bow down to. Terrified me, that did.'

There was a rustle from the direction of the fireside and Molly-Ann raised her hand. 'Best not guess, and best not talk in front of others. Hush now! I've heard no talk of witchcraft. You'd do well to stay clear though, if the magistrates start poking about the woods.'

A slight draught stirred the fire, as the tavern door closed behind the man in the all enveloping cloak.


A week later, the cloudless sky shone as if newly washed, and the droplets that still clung to leaves and twigs sparkled in the early sunlight. The Boar's door stood wide open to freshen the tavern and Molly-Ann breathed the chill air right down into her lungs, as if to wring the goodness out of it. Booths and stalls were being erected on the mud of the lower Market Place to her left, colourful awnings stretched over wooden frames, and goods of all sorts had been spread out on display by the early traders. Pedlars and chapmen had been drawn to the town from a wide area, hoping for a good demand from the better off townsfolk.

Molly-Ann leant her back against the tavern wall watching the lively scene without enthusiasm. The fair was held every year on the 22$^{nd}$ of July, the old religion's feast day of St Mary Magdalen. It was on this very day three years ago that her baby had been born, and had died. The little mite had had the cord around her neck, so Betty told her afterwards. Sarah was there as midwife, they'd done all they could to free the infant and chivvy her into life, but it was a little body as cold as marble that had been placed in Molly-Ann's arms when it was all over.

Maybe it had been for the best. Could she ever have loved a child born of that vile attack nine months before? She'd never know, she could only guess from her present feelings of loss. Had the baby lived, Rachel she'd named her, she would have been a constant reminder to the town of Molly-Ann's shame. Maybe it was as well, but every time the Mary Magdalen Fair came round she'd remember Rachel.

Her mind dwelling on the past, it was no shock to Molly-Ann when she spotted a face familiar from that time amongst the growing crowd. Working his way down the Market Place in her direction, lingering here and there at the stalls, stopping to acknowledge greetings from many of the older townsfolk, was the minister who had kindly, if unorthodoxly, baptised little Rachel, even though no breath had passed her lips. Molly-Ann was sorely tempted to duck back into the inn to avoid him; his well meant words would reinforce her already sad feelings. But it was too late. He'd raised a hand and was coming directly towards her.

She bobbed a curtsey. 'Mornin' Master Silcox, sir.'

'And a good day to you, my dear.'

She could see in his eyes that he remembered the date as well as she did. She hoped he wasn't going to break into a lengthy religious consolation for her troubles. She chided herself. He'd been thoughtful and generous to her three years ago; it would be discourteous to resist his good intentions now.

She smiled ruefully. 'I've not seen you in the town for . . .' she paused, thinking, 'a long time, sir. I hope you've not been unwell?'

'No, no!' His smile was warm, thoroughly genuine. 'I've

been away for much of the last year. My son and I have been in the Americas, ever since he returned from the war with the Dutch.'

Molly-Ann's eyes widened and she took a deep breath. 'Then I am truly glad to see you safely returned to Frome. What took you there, if I may be so bold?'

'We were seeking a suitable place for a religious colony we want to set up. Since the king's restoration, there seems to be no place here for those of us who dissent from the established church. We would be more comfortable living in one of the new colonial settlements, even if there are hardships and dangers to be faced there.'

'Your friends here will miss you, sir.' She looked into his face; the blue grey eyes looked tired, and the lines beside his mouth more deeply drawn than she recalled. 'I will miss your kindness very much.'

'My dear.' A new light had come into his eyes, as if he had been invigorated by a sudden thought. 'I shan't be departing for many months, maybe years, and that's if I go at all. John may accompany the colonists without me, we have not yet decided. I hope that you and I will have the opportunity for further talks in the coming months.' He looked down at his feet and Molly-Ann was surprised to see his cheeks had taken on a pinkish hue. 'I should welcome the chance to share with you the comfort of the word of God.'

She frowned slightly; she had no wish to be drawn into the austere world of the dissenters, with their severe clothes, morals and hairstyles. Master Silcox was smiling at her a little wryly, she thought.

'Anyway, I hope to remain in Frome for some time now. You may have heard, I'm starting a small day school, now that I've finally found premises.'

'I wish you every success, sir. The children will be fortunate in their teacher.'

The former vicar smiled and raised his tall black hat to Molly-Ann as he moved away towards the town bridge. Heaps of stone and stacks of wooden scaffolding poles obstructed the road; the works to widen the bridge had still not been completed. She turned back into the tavern. Master Silcox had reminded her that there were kind-hearted people about, and not only the villains that she usually encountered.

# CHAPTER 3

JOSHUA EMERGED FROM Pilly Vale, his footwear caked with mud, and looked back at the shady lane. The track beside the rushing mill leat was as busy as a beehive, stuffed with workshops, fulling mills, warehouses, and dyers' yards and drying towers. Clouds of smoke and steam billowed between the stone walls; the pounding of the hammers in the fulling mill was incessant. And as for the smell! The rotten cabbage stink of woad mingled with that of stale urine permeated the air. The traffic generated by this industry churned up the ever damp roadway, making it a sea of muck and filth. He scraped the sides of his shoes to clean them against one of the scaffolding planks that lay on the new bridge. His canvas spatterdashes had shielded his stockings from ankle to knee against the mire, and he was glad he'd thought to wear them. It might be summer, but the rain of the last week had left the lanes in a foul state, and the river was full and fast.

He looked up from his feet as a soberly dressed figure passed him; to judge from his black suit, steeple crowned hat and white neckbands, a minister of the puritan persuasion. Joshua gave the gentleman a cursory 'G'day to 'ee', and crossed the bridge into Market Place. Ahead, the Magdalen Day fair was thronged with folk buying and selling, or strolling in the sunshine, and others watching out for less legitimate opportunities to turn a penny.

The odour of stale beer hit him as he passed the open door

of the Boar. He bent his head a little to squint into the gloomy interior; he'd like to catch a glimpse of that Molly-Ann. He'd been too busy the last few weeks to pay an evening visit to the tavern to see her, but their meeting was an opportunity to be built upon. He promised himself that he'd find time to do so soon, but it was difficult when most of his "ventures" required his presence in the hours of darkness.

He smiled at his recollection of their previous encounter. She was an attractive young woman; had a real spark about her. He liked the way she'd been savaging the landlord's face before he'd stepped into their confrontation. Why had he done that, he wondered? It wasn't that he felt protective towards her exactly, perhaps more a sense of potential possession. The look she'd given him in the public room had certainly held some sort of promise; he needed to follow it up before it was lost in time. He'd always been stirred by that combination of blue eyes, fair skin and raven black hair.

Yes, he'd been busy every evening for weeks, organising clandestine deliveries of duty free apple brandy to various publicans, most but not all through the network of tunnels. He'd approached the likeliest landlords in the day, when they usually had time to talk, added a good half dozen to his list of eager customers. And of course that had meant extra work distilling greater quantities of the spirit up at the Catherine Hill premises. To expand production he'd had to recruit more men, buy in barrels and acquire more of the cider on which it was all based. It was lucky he could get by on so little sleep – but he certainly needed to find the time to follow up on the incident at the Boar. He took off his greasy brown felt hat and used it to fan his face: was the day growing hotter, or was it the recollection of that enticing girl?

He swore under his breath. He'd forgotten he was due

to send a further shipment of fleeces down towards the coast this very night. He'd have to rely on Ben and Nathaniel to go down, they'd managed it a few times on their own now, it shouldn't be a problem. If he could get it all set up this afternoon there might be time to get back into town before he needed to see the boys off on their way from Cowbridge Farm once darkness fell.

Joshua put his fingers to his lips. The piercing whistle summoned Billy, his messenger boy. Joshua put his head on one side as he looked at the urchin; as a small boy he himself had run errands to make a few pennies. A foundling, he had been raised on a baby farm at Lower Keyford, bringing his foster mother a small payment from the poor rate. It had been a harsh childhood; indeed he was lucky to have survived it by sheer determination and toughness. It had taught him both self-reliance and the value of striking the first blow, and striking it hard. He'd come a long way in his twenty-seven years and seen a lot of the world, especially during the time he was a soldier in the Netherlands and then serving in what they'd called the Maritime Regiment of Foot. He'd been back in his home town for the last year or so, during which time he'd set up both his wool smuggling network and the brandy distillery. He was proud of his hard work and initiative, and he knew he could go further still.

Billy ran off to Cole Hill with the message to Ben and Nathaniel as fast as his thin legs could go.


A heap of fleeces lay on the barn floor, creamy white, soft as clouds but redolent of their recent owners – that sharp yet slightly sweet, almost nauseous, smell of sheep. Joshua ran his fingers through the raw wool, appreciating the quality of the fibres: dense, silky smooth, fine as any to be found the length of England. He knew such wool from the Mendips found a ready market across the Channel; he'd been told it commanded a very good price. What did it matter to him if its export deprived the home industry of prized raw materials, or the king of his taxes? His colleagues in the trade made a fortune selling such goods to the continental weavers, and he was making a pretty penny transporting the fleeces over there for them.

He pulled himself up sharp. No time for day dreaming. The fleeces, brought to the barn a few at a time, now needed to be packed up ready for their journey and time was getting on. The sun was sinking and Ben and his brother would turn up at the farm within the hour.

He wrenched the strap tight on the first of the canvas packs. He'd wasted time, going back to the Boar. Molly-Ann hadn't been in the taproom or the public room, and Betty the landlady had said she'd let her have the evening off as it was quiet. She'd given him an old fashioned look when he asked where the girl had gone, muttered something about Molly-Ann visiting an old friend, before she turned away to serve another customer. Ah well, the girl wouldn't be far away he thought; just so long as it's a female old friend she's seeing.

The farm dog barked a warning outside in the yard; there was a rattle as it ran to the length of its chain. Joshua moved quickly to the side door of the barn and checked who was entering the yard. Ben had hushed the dog and Nathaniel was approaching the main door of the barn. Dusk was falling, the sky leaden with cloud.

'Come in the side,' Joshua called. 'Don't want the lantern light a-showin'.'

Together they packed up the fleeces, brought the mules from the stables, loaded the packs and prepared to set off as soon as the summer night was dark enough.

'Big investment here, boys. You guard the goods well, hear me?'

Ben grunted his assent.

'It's not just the excise men you got to look out for, there could be villains on the road might rob you.' Joshua unlocked an oak chest and lifted out something heavy.

Nathaniel raised his head to look at him; his eyes revealed his apprehension.

'I'm relying on you to see this load through safely. Me an' others got a lot of money tied up in this shipment. Here,' he handed each man a cudgel and a knife. 'Have these by you and don't be a'feared to use 'en.'

Ben nodded slowly, his expression thoughtful.

'I'll give you your wages now, eighteen pence each, show you the trust I've got in the pair of you. Stable the mules when you get back, I doubt I'll be here then.'

The laden pack animals set off towards the Maiden Bradley road, moving as near silently as Joshua would wish, their dark coats merging into the shadows of the roadside hedge. Moonrise was hours away and the night breeze gently rustled the leaves and grasses, masking any slight noise the mules made. Joshua turned back into the barn to sweep away all trace of the fleeces.

As he returned the birch broom to its place in the corner, the yard dog barked twice, then set up such a clamour it must have woken the nearby hamlet of Tytherington. Joshua paused, his hand on the latch of the side door: should he run, hide, or confront whoever was out there? He grabbed the short pole usually used to control the farm's bull, and with the lantern in his left hand, strode out of the barn.

His sudden appearance startled the intruders. The

mounted man at their head pulled up sharply as Joshua's lantern shone full in his face. The four men following him hung back in the shadows of the yard, but the dim light glinted on metal in their hands.

'And who might you be?' the rider challenged.

'What's that to you? Who be you, coming on private land and disturbin' our peace?'

'In the name of the king, identify yourself,' the horseman thundered back, shifting his horse from side to side as if to intimidate Joshua.

He swallowed hard. He'd not had trouble from the authorities out here at the farm before, he was just glad the goods were well on their way now.

'Joshua Whittock.'

'And what is your business here at midnight? I know you're not the landowner here. Seize him, men.'

Joshua's arms were held firmly, his pole and lantern taken from him.

'I'm here by rights. I rent this barn from farmer Seaman,' he shouted, struggling against the restraint.

His protest was met with evident indifference as the rider turned to his men: 'Search the buildings – start with the barn.'

Two of the dark clad men took his lantern into the barn. The horseman dismounted and followed, beckoning for Joshua to be brought in behind him. Joshua felt a wave of anger building up in his chest, but there was no point in fighting back when he was so far outnumbered. He let his arms go limp.

In the glow of the lantern the features of the rider became clearer; between the wide brimmed hat and the dark cloak he wore, Joshua recognised the face of James Baily, a local landowner and one of the magistrates of Frome. He wondered whether the authorities had got wind of his owling activities.

Thank God he'd had time to sweep the barn.

'Search the place,' Baily ordered. 'You know what we're after – tools, dies, scraps of metal, scales . . .' He stirred a heap of straw with his foot. 'Look everywhere. I mean to find the evidence.'

Joshua felt a chill on his skin. This was not a business he'd been involved in, but he could guess who Baily was after – counterfeiters. There'd been talk in the town of false coins being struck, and of genuine coins being clipped for their valuable metal, but this was a crime Joshua had never actually committed. His throat constricted. Counterfeiting was one of the most serious offences in the book, not one that he wanted to be mixed up in – they said the penalty was that for a traitor.


It had been a real test of wills. The magistrate, Baily, had been determined to make an arrest, didn't matter who, whether guilty or not. The man would lose face if he came away from the encounter empty handed, the parish constables he'd brought would spread the news all over town. Joshua had realised quickly enough that it wasn't the lack of evidence or his own ignorance of the crime that would save him, but an offer of information, the sacrifice of an alternative suspect to the law. His tale of night time activity and hammering noises in the outhouses behind Nicholas Stevens' cottage in West Woodlands had been delivered with apparent reluctance, and seemingly swallowed by Baily. He'd always despised Stevens. It was satisfying to drop him into Baily's hands.

The magistrate's look as he left the barn had given Joshua some concern, as had the man's threat, delivered with narrowed eyes: 'You're a marked man, Whittock. I'll be watching you, don't forget.'

After a few hours' sleep back at his attic room, Joshua pulled on a clean shirt, his newest breeches, and a fine woollen coat. The coat might be rather warm if the summer sun shone again today, but he needed to present a solid, respectable appearance if he was to implement the plan that had occurred to him overnight. As he left the room he took a wide brimmed hat from the hook, and crammed it on his head. He clattered down the winding wooden stair, fastening a sheath knife to his belt as he went, then checked on his horse as he passed through the yard. He'd done no more than unsaddle the mare when he got home in the early hours, but Billy had done his chores this morning and the bay was fed and groomed to his satisfaction.

Catherine Hill was busy with folk, some sauntering slowly as they gazed at the goods on sale, others walking as briskly as possible on the steeply sloping cobbled roadway, intent on their own purpose. To break his fast he bought two cinnamon cakes for a halfpenny from a child with a basketful on her arm; they were still warm from the oven and he licked the last crumbs from his fingers. The sky was heavy with cloud, but so far no rain fell.

His dreams last night had been full of Molly-Ann. It might have been a sign, it might just have been his growing impatience, but that dream had inspired him to action and he meant to track her down today; he couldn't concentrate on much else while his head was taken up with that girl.

In his mind he'd worked out a list of those innkeepers he needed to see this morning – at the top of that list was Joe Grimwade. And now he had an additional task on his mind: to glean any information he could on James Baily. Frome's taverns were a likely source of news on the magistrate, but there were a lot of them for him to get around and the sooner he started the better.

Joshua stood back as two customers left the Boar, then stepped into the gloom of the entrance passage. He turned into the public room where a few men were taking an early lunch of bread, cheese and ale at tables by the window. At the back of the room Joe was arranging tankards on the shelves. Joshua approached and the landlord looked at him warily.

'Well Master Grimwade, did you sample the goods I sent?' Joshua wasn't going to acknowledge their recent exchange over Molly-Ann; as he'd said before, business was business. 'You'll not find better.'

'It's good enough.'

'How many shall I put you down for, reg'lar like?'

Joe glanced across the room, then back to Joshua. 'Send me a couple on Friday night, after we're shut. I'll open the side gate.'

Joshua nodded. 'Good day to you then, Master Grimwade. Until Friday.'

Over the landlord's shoulder he'd spotted Molly-Ann pass down the entrance passage in the direction of the tap room. In half a dozen strides he was at the doorway of the smaller bar, and was gratified by the spontaneous smile that lit up the young woman's face as he ducked under the lintel and entered the room.

He nodded towards her. 'Mistress. I hope I find you well?'

She looked down briefly, but almost immediately her eyes held his again. 'I thank 'ee, yes.' Her cheeks had gone quite pink. She seemed surprisingly coy for a tavern maid, he thought; perhaps he should press home his apparent success. 'I wondered if I might see you come Sunday – do you have the af'ernoon free? We could take a walk along the river meadows, if you like?'

Joshua felt an unaccustomed flutter in his chest as she

nodded her assent.

The scrape of leather on stone interrupted his thoughts and he turned as Betty Grimwade passed along the corridor, her footsteps brisk and businesslike.

He smiled down at Molly-Ann and put his hat on. 'Sunday, then.'

The next four taverns he visited, the Anchor, the Crown and Thistle, the Black Boy and the Bell, had yielded payments for deliveries of apple brandy but no useful information on the magistrate, and Joshua was becoming frustrated. It seemed to him that the best defence against Baily's vindictiveness was to arm himself with incriminating information on the man. If he was involved in some form of corruption, if he'd committed any crime in the past, if there were any iniquities he was concealing, Joshua could use them against him should he himself come under further suspicion.

He turned into Apple Lane and under the stone archway of the Angel's courtyard. A small figure was sweeping the straw and muck of the yard into a pile; the boy looked up at Joshua's approach, his dark eyes large and wary in his thin face, until he grinned at sight of his new patron.

'Billy! Just the lad! Would you know a gentleman by the name of James Baily?'

'Aye, Master Joshua. Ee's 'ere now. I saw 'en through the windeye of the snug. I know it's 'im 'cos I heard landlord greet 'en by name as 'ee give me his horse to stable.' The lad looked up to the sky as fat drops of rain started to spatter his shoulders.

'The snug, eh? Thanks Billy.' Joshua gave him a halfpenny and pushed open the inn door. Purchasing a tankard of ale, he carried it down the stone flagged passage and quietly entered the little room, then pulled the brim of his hat well down over his face. He settled himself in a corner as inconspicuously as possible and brought out his clay pipe and tobacco.

Two men sat on either side of the table in the window, the light full on them, apparently oblivious of his presence. Raindrops were chasing one another down the small panes, but already the sun had broken through; it was but a passing shower. He knew both men by sight: the magistrate in dark green breeches gathered just below the knee and a matching thigh length coat with a fashionable number of buttons down the front, and Dr Joseph Glanvill, newly installed vicar of St John's, in a black coat, vest and breeches, with white clerical bands at his neck. His attire might be sober, but Joshua recognised that the fabric and tailoring were of the finest quality. Short stemmed wine glasses stood on the table before them, together with an almost empty flask of red wine.

Joshua pulled his hat even lower and slouched in the seat puffing at his pipe, his ears strained to catch their conversation. The men appeared to be discussing finance; he heard a few figures mentioned, the words 'loan', 'interest' and 'returns'. What, he wondered, might be the subject of their discussion? The vicar sighed and stretched an arm out for the wine; there was a chink as the flask made contact with the rim of his glass, then a second as Baily's glass was topped up.

'I really don't think I'm in a position to assist you, Mr Baily,' Glanvill said. 'I'm about to purchase property in Bath. I'm not sure how much capital I shall need for that. No, I think you'll have to look elsewhere for funds. A shame, I can see this is an exciting project and could offer a huge return to an investor.'

Baily's gruff voice was a distinct contrast to the vicar's clipped London accent. 'So be it. The gentlemen of the area don't have the capital. You were my remaining hope.'

'Have you approached the manufacturers? I understand that the real wealth of Frome lies in their hands, the cloth trade having been so prosperous of late.'

'I'm damned if I'll go to them for finance, saving your presence.' Baily's shoulders slumped. 'Tradesmen, jumped up artisans. They may have money but they're not gentlemen. And they're dissenters. I'm surprised you should suggest them, sir.'

The vicar chuckled and rubbed his thumb and fingers. 'Needs must. If you want investors they'll be the ones to go to.'

Joshua frowned. Whatever was Baily involved with that he needed so much money? Was he perhaps in debt? It seemed unlikely considering the extent of his landholding. And they'd spoken of a project with high returns. He wondered what was planned.

The vicar placed his empty glass back on the table. 'I'll bid you good day sir, and wish you luck with the scheme. Of course, finance is but one hurdle. You'll still have to persuade the landowners to sell to you; it could be a contentious matter, there may be a lot of opposition.' Glanvill rose and walked unsteadily across the room, glancing at Joshua as he went.

Dealing with opposition was something that Joshua knew about. He pursed his lips. Threats and blackmail would be an unsatisfactory way to gain a hold over the magistrate, especially if he could find no grounds for them, but providing a much needed service to him might be a way to gain his favour instead.

He cleared his throat and crossed the room. Baily looked up; his curling long dark hair contrasted with a direct and powerful stare.

'What the devil . . . who d'you think you are, disturbing

a gentleman?' He frowned. 'I know you. You're the fellow who was at West Woodlands last night . . .' His glance moved down to the knife on Joshua's belt.

'I'd like to make you a business offer, sir.' Joshua touched the brim of his hat. 'If you should ever require someone to deal with . . . opposition . . . I'm yer man, none handier.'

Baily's laugh was almost explosive. 'If this scheme goes ahead I may be in need of a persuasive operator. What's your name again?'

'Josh Whittock, sir. At yer command.'

# CHAPTER 4

EYES THE COLOUR of cornflowers: more mauve in them than sky blue. He put his head on one side; perhaps periwinkles were a closer shade? The minister Gideon Silcox liked to pin down, to classify, to identify, the important things in his life and Molly-Ann's eyes were of the very greatest importance to him. They had been brimming with sorrow this Magdalen Day morning, even while her lips smiled. She was a brave young woman. She put on a cheerful face although her heart was bleeding, as he felt sure it was, for that poor little baby she'd lost. His own chest felt crushed with sympathy.

And despite the lowly life she led, she seemed to have an innate goodness, dignity and self-possession that he admired. Admired from a distance though, as how could he, a man of the cloth, possibly make an offer to a woman in her position? Life, he knew, had not been kind to her. The death of her mother had been a blow to all her children and the family's fortunes had declined sharply; her brothers had done nothing so far to recover them, and she had a hard time of it at the Boar. He wished he could lift her out of that degradation, give her some comfort. He could almost feel the weight of her in his arms, her warm soft skin, as he imagined himself lifting her to a new life. She was his last thought at night before sleep took him and, now that he was back in Frome, hers was the face he invariably hoped to see as he walked about the streets. Most of his congregation would be scandalised if they knew of his urgent desire for her; they'd strive to throw him out as sure as sure. There might be no impediment in law to him, a widower in his fifties, seeking to marry Molly-Ann, a single woman of full age, but the congregation, society, his own family, would be appalled. Could he find the courage to bring down such opprobrium on himself?

And would she accept him, anyway? A man old enough to be her father! He might offer her social respectability, loving support and financial security, but he had to admit that neither his person nor his personality could promise her much excitement. Perhaps she'd have to remain in his dreams, not in his arms.

The minister sighed deeply and glanced up. He realised he'd been standing for several minutes at the side of the town bridge, looking over the stone parapet onto the fast flowing waters of the River Frome. Behind him were the everyday noises of carts, horses and pedestrians; in front the sunlight sparkled on the churning, muddy water of a river in spate. Flashy they called it here; its level rose rapidly with rain, picking up soil from the fields that drained into its basin, and falling back to a gentle flow again in a very few days as the torrent moved north to the Avon at Freshford. The new bridge was a great improvement on the old medieval structure – and that too had served to keep the town's feet dry, better than the ancient ford that had carried traffic out of town in the past, towards Bath.

Gideon Silcox squared his shoulders. He had God's work before him and what was he doing but giving way to lustful thoughts and river gazing. He turned towards Pilly Vale as a sturdily built man tipped his hat to him in passing. Not someone he'd seen at chapel, but there was ever hope.

He knocked at the door of the first cottage. After a pause

he was bidden to enter. An expression of surprise greeted him; it seemed the woman, surrounded by a brood of children, had never received a visit from a clergyman before. The whine of three spinning wheels gradually faded as their motion slowed and the eyes of the woman and her two eldest daughters grew rounder in apprehension. A third girl of perhaps six years was holding onto the smocks of two toddlers to keep them away from the cooking fire, the little ones' lower parts entirely naked.

Gideon introduced himself to the dumbstruck family and continued: 'I am offering places for children of five to eight years at my day school, where they can learn to read, write, and hear the word of God. Children of these tender years suffer by being set to work too early. I beseech you madam, to allow your young ones to attend.'

'School? You wants them to stop working and do book learning? And I suppose I'd have to pay for it?'

'Only a penny a day each child.'

The woman's roar echoed off the stone walls. 'Where'd I find the money for that? And what good 'ud it do 'em? Nay, Master, it's not for the likes of us, we needs them to spin as soon as they can sit still. My man's up aloft there a'weavin' and we dursn't run short of yarn for 'im, or there'd be hell to pay.'

Greasy fingers were smearing something on his white stockings, and Gideon felt the time was right to leave.

'Thank you for your attention, and should you change your mind . . .'

'Aye, I'll let 'ee know. Gi'e 'ee good day.'

He pushed the door shut behind him and braced himself for the dirt and disappointment of the next cottage.

'You've a visitor, sir.' Old Sarah smiled knowingly as she swung the soot-blackened cauldron on its chain over the fire and stirred the logs into life, later that morning. 'He's waiting for you up in your chamber. I've prepared bacon and bean stew for you both. I'd some leeks in the garden and I found a couple of handfuls of mushrooms to go in it, too.'

Gideon's rent paid for their frugal meals and it was good to know that Sarah ate well enough now – and with her foraged ingredients her meals were delicious. He put his foot on the first step; he was tired after his long morning talking to the labourers at Pilly Vale. Caution was advisable in ascending and descending, the stairs to his room were more like a ladder, very steep indeed with narrow treads. At his age, especially, he didn't want to risk any broken bones. It was no wonder that Sarah had been willing to relinquish her attic and confine her life to the ground floor of the Keyford cottage, where she had a narrow bed in a curtained alcove, and everything in easy reach. His visitor must, he thought, be family or a close friend; she would not have sent a stranger or even a member of the congregation up here to wait for him.

'John!' Gideon felt a surge of pleasure. 'What a delight! It's been too long. I haven't seen you for weeks.' He shook his son by the hand, the formal gesture accompanied by the warmest smiles imaginable.

'I hope you've been well, father?' His son's face was equally radiant and the younger man took the liberty of patting his father on the shoulder. 'Your landlady suggested I wait up here for you once she recognised who I was. She didn't know how long you'd be and, I assume, didn't want me under her feet.' John's eyes held a question. 'It rather looked as though she was busy cooking, or pickling or something. There've been some strange smells coming up from below. I felt she didn't want me seeing too much.'

Gideon gestured to the single chair where his son had already laid his voluminous dark blue cloak. 'Take a seat, John. She's a clever old soul. Always cooking something up, mostly stuff from the hedgerows. She knows a lot of old country remedies, keeps them in her head as she can't read, and helps doctor the poor when need be.'

'Country remedies are all very well, but I hope the more ignorant in society do not misconstrue her actions and intentions.'

'She's tidied all her potions away now, she's certainly cautious of strangers seeing her preparations,' Gideon said. 'You may have noticed that great dresser stacked with jars of dried herbs and spices; she has every conceivable ingredient at hand. I'll reassure her that you'll not speak of it. You'll find her stew is excellent.' He seated himself on the neatly made bed. 'Now, tell me what you've been doing and where. Oh and how is your leg? Has that wound given you any trouble?'

'Not in the least, ten months on and I've been granted a full recovery save for the scars. I have been more fortunate than many, thanks be to God.'

John picked up the small book he'd laid down at his father's arrival, and tapped it gently with his finger. 'I've been spreading God's word, and visiting our brethren between Bristol and the south coast, telling the congregations about the lands we saw in the Americas last year, encouraging them to think of joining our colony in the north, in New France.'

Gideon nodded.

'Many took to the idea enthusiastically, especially in the rural areas where the landowners are more oppressive to dissenters. In the towns, where we are in greater numbers with more support for each other there is, I suppose, less incentive.'

'Understandable. And were they mostly the poorer labourers, or did you find skilled people willing to go?'

'Many craftsmen: smiths, cobblers, carpenters, a baker. People we'd need, but the majority are labourers I'd say.'

'And all committed to the chapel? It would be best to have only people of our own persuasion, avoid conflict as far as possible.'

'I've been wondering about that.' The younger man looked troubled. 'If we refuse people who have different views on worship, or indeed have no faith at all, are we as intolerant as the society we plan to leave? Is that the welcoming sort of community we think God wants, or are we becoming repressive in our own way?'

Gideon scratched his head. 'You make a good point. We need to seek the Lord's guidance. I will raise this at a future meeting.'

John stood and looked out of the small window in the gable end. 'I passed through Frome a couple of weeks back, travelling between Bath and Warminster, but you were from home at the time. I put up at the Crown and Thistle, but went over to the Boar for the evening as I'd never been in there before.'

Gideon felt his heart rate increase; he looked up at his son. Could his connection to Molly-Ann have been revealed?

'I overheard some talk of meetings in the woods at Roddenbury. I thought you should know. The local people were anxious that the magistrates might take an interest in affairs there. I think *they* were concerned for their poaching activities, but the authorities may suspect that dissenters' meetings are being held.'

Gideon nodded, his pulse rate was steadying. 'As you surmise, our friend Dr Humfry was here on a few occasions in the spring and early summer, and the congregation met clandestinely with him to hear the Word. Since the act was passed, our people have lacked the comfort of his teachings here in town. Roddenbury is the nearest safe place for the congregation to reach on foot – but maybe not so safe after all, if people are talking.'

'And how is Dr Humfry?'

'Very busy, I believe, now that he's moved to London, and sorely missed in Frome for his erudition and persuasive preaching.'

'But his successor at St John's, Dr Glanvill, I hear he's well respected.'

'A man of zeal and brilliance they say, and most interested in the works of the devil, especially witchcraft.' Gideon pursed his lips. 'I understand he is writing a book on the subject. But he too is about to leave the town, he's appointed rector at Bath, which is of course more prestigious if one is concerned about such matters.'

Sarah's voice came through the stair hatch, summoning them to their meal. They descended to find places laid and a steaming pot on the table ready to be served, together with a basket of oat and barley griddlecakes. Gideon gave thanks for the food and poured cups of ale, while Sarah ladled out the bacon, vegetables and beans.

'Will you be stopping in Frome, Master John?' she asked. 'It would be good company for your father here, if so be you did.'

'Nay, mistress, my work takes me to Rode tonight and Trowbridge tomorrow, and once I'm done there I'll head back to my own little home at Wanstrow. I have made good friends there and we are working to build up the congregation in the place.'

Gideon turned to the old woman. 'I don't have such a need of company do I, Sarah? There's the congregation to minister to, always someone wants something of me.'

'Aye, but I mean family to give 'ee loving kindness and fellowship.' She paused. 'I'm sure you still miss your wife.'

Gideon laid down his knife. 'Well, yes, that's true. But it's the lot of most of us to lose a beloved wife or husband; we have to accustom ourselves to the loss and take up our work again.' The pain was as sharp after seven years as it had been at the first moment he lost his dear Celia.

John's sympathetic look was welcome. He was a loving son, a source of satisfaction to his father as he was taking such an active role in pastoral care. Gideon's pressing concern was the decision over who was to accompany the pioneers to the new colony: if John went they might never meet again in this life; if they both went he'd lose all hope of Molly-Ann; if he alone went he'd be parted forever from both of them. He put the concern to one side.

'Will you be here on Sunday, John?' Gideon asked. 'You'd be warmly welcomed at chapel. Come and bid farewell to the old meeting room, we're about to transfer to a new room in Master Smith's own house in Rook Lane. It's much bigger and lighter than the one he's provided for us up to now.' He drained his cup.

'You're fortunate in your sponsor.'

'Yes, the wealthy manufacturers of Frome are a godsend, not only to us but the Friends and the Baptists have their wealthy patrons as well. It was a sad day for the country when the new king chose to restore the Church of England. He'll return to the ways of his father in religion, quite possibly.' He shook his head. 'All the death and destruction the country underwent, and what benefit have we gained? The Church is again looking towards Rome in many ways; we dissenters are being increasingly harried, and self-interest is the watchword for many of the new clergy.'

John nodded sadly. 'But at least the new king has agreed to rule *in* parliament, not to rule without it and against the interests of the people. So far, at any rate.' Both men sighed.

Sarah cleared the plates and put an earthenware jug on the table; its olive green glaze identified it as the local Wanstrow ware, a gift from John. 'Barley, honey and crab apple. I hope you'll find it a refreshing drink on this warm day, masters.'

'Perhaps we'll take our drinks out in the garden?' Gideon rose from the table. 'I have a few matters to discuss with you, John.'

His son looked hesitant.

'I realise you need to be on your way to Rode soon. This won't take long.'

They settled themselves on the garden seat – a rough plank balanced on two piles of bricks, and Gideon brought a letter out from his coat pocket.

'I have had news that Doctor Humfry will be here next Tuesday.' He had dropped his voice and his son had to lean closer to hear. 'I will inform the meeting on Sunday that he will lead a service at Roddenbury on Tuesday night – I don't want word getting about any sooner for risk of informers. Are you able to join us?'

John shook his head. 'By then I will be over at Devizes. The congregation there have asked me to speak about the opportunities for us in the Americas. I regret I cannot change the date.' He took a sip from his cup. 'I'm sorry to miss the doctor's address. Do tell me afterwards what he has to say.'

His father nodded. 'I fear he may bring news of further actions the king and his government plan for our discomfort. I am concerned every Sunday that the magistrates may become aware of the numbers attending our service and enforce the new limits.'

The two men watched as a group of swifts soared and swooped across the sky, their calls shrill in the afternoon peace.

'I thank God that Dr Humfry came through the last pestilence unscathed,' Gideon said. 'He continued to minister to the sick throughout. Not many would have had the courage to remain in London last year, not if they had the means to leave.' He slapped his knees. 'Now, about the school. Master Smith has been very generous in advancing funds, and we have cleared the debris and fixed the roof of that hall I told you I have leased. I believe it should now be watertight.'

John nodded his approval.

'We have limewashed the walls and even installed an iron stove for heating in the winter; that was our chief expense.' Forms and a table, and shelves, were still needed, but Gideon was reluctant to ask too much of their benefactor. 'The payments the children bring will not cover these costs. I must remember to make an appeal to the congregation on Sunday.'

'How many pupils do you hope to take?'

'I am finding it hard to attract any, to tell you truly. I am confident though that word will spread once we have the first few. If as many as twenty come I may need to recruit assistance.' He sighed. 'And then if I should join your venture to the colonies, I will have to find someone to take it over from me. Problems seem to be never ending.'

John smiled and patted his shoulder. 'God will provide, as you always tell me. Now, I must be off, but I will be here for the service on Sunday and say farewell to the old meeting room.'

'Excellent! And after, we might take a stroll in the river

meadows if the weather is fine. The wildflowers are beautiful at present.'

Calm had settled on the tiny cottage. John had set off for Rode and Sarah had retired to her curtained bed in the alcove while the sun was still well above the horizon. Gideon Silcox pulled a small table to the attic window to catch the last of the light and to conserve his candles. He looked forward to an hour's reading before bed, but first he had a letter to write.

Twenty minutes later, he signed his name with a flourish at the conclusion of a proposal to the authorities, such as they were, in Newfoundland. He intended to charter a ship, he told the governor, to give passage to up to eighty settlers, men, women and children, with fowls, sheep and cattle, with the aim of creating a God-fearing settlement in their colony. God willing, they would arrive in springtime, ready for the planting season. He requested the governor's consent and asked for his guidance in choosing a location for the village, specifying that it should have wood and sweet water, proximity to the coast, and land suitable for both arable and stock. After his discussion with John about the inclusion of members of other denominations, he decided to gloss over that point, and to focus instead on the useful practical skills that would be introduced by his flock.

He laid down his pen and wiped his fingers on an inky rag. He felt directed by God to organise the departure of members of his congregation and many more from other Wiltshire and Somerset villages, and was happy for those who were travelling to new lands with their families, confident of a bright future with freedom to worship in their own way. For himself, however, such an undertaking would be at great personal cost if he had to forsake all hope of Molly-Ann.

As he gazed out of the tiny window, watching the Keyford folk moving up and down the narrow street, many in pairs or family groups, it seemed very hard that he should be denied happiness in his old age. Marriage with the girl was his dearest wish. As the dusk crept along the street, gradually hiding the muddy track, the odd heaps of refuse, the swinging sign of the Crown Inn almost opposite, he considered the chief obstacles to their union.

John, now in his mid-twenties, was surely mature enough to acknowledge that his father should be free to marry again, and seek contentment in his declining years. He would find such a conversation painful, no doubt; a slight on his mother perhaps; but he was a very rational young man. Gideon decided he should try to talk with him as soon as possible.

His congregation was altogether more hidebound. They would know of Molly-Ann's past and indeed her present situation. He could see in his mind's eye the heads nodding together, the tongues wagging, the steely cold look in the eyes. They held strict principles, and their own minister was expected to be supremely above scandal. Forgiveness might have its place in their tenets, but it would probably not extend to him if he were to voluntarily invite such censure. His only course would be to tender his resignation and to leave.

To leave . . . What if he were to travel to Newfoundland with the settlers, taking Molly-Ann as his wife? They could marry and perhaps find a place where neither of them was known, and start a new life together with John nearby. He would do all in his power to make her happy and secure, if only she would consent.

His enthusiasm spilling over into haste and uncharacteristically terse writing, he placed a blank sheet of paper in front of him and drew up a letter of resignation. He would not send it until he had spoken at length with John, but the draft was a token of his determination.

# CHAPTER 5

B EN'S HEART SWELLED fit to burst with pride at the trust Joshua had placed in him and Nat to transport this valuable cargo. As they set off from West Woodlands he raised his head and consciously tuned all his senses to be on the alert for danger. He was determined to prove his worth to Joshua: this was a man with the power to help him get on in life.

The road down which the train of pack animals trotted was bordered by rich meadows that were watered by the young River Frome, but were lost to sight now in the summer night. Ben breathed in the scent of the new mown hay. The evocative smell seemed strangely enhanced, as if the day's warmth had developed its fragrance but kept it imprisoned, until the darkness released it. The heavens had mostly clouded up. Stars still shone to the east but the rest of the sky was smothered now, the half moon a diffused brightness high above them. A waning moon, though: not a good omen.

The surface of the track became paler as they reached the chalk lands south of Maiden Bradley and now it was easier to see the way ahead. Over the months, his confidence in the mules' night vision had grown: he would put his trust in them to follow the road while all he needed to do was keep them going at a good pace. Behind him Nat hummed one of his favourite hymns, despite the warnings he had given him. He himself kept silence, his ears attentive for the beat of hooves ahead or behind. As they cautiously crossed the high road to

London, the church clock at Mere, still a mile or two distant, chimed two. Ben felt his spirits lift, they were almost there without mishap and had made good time.

It wasn't until he was within touching distance of the massive gates that he realised the inn yard of the Cock was closed, the gates firmly bolted. On previous nights they had stood wide open to receive the train of pack animals, allowing them to get off the street and out of sight with all speed. Ben glanced back and could just make out Nathaniel's shrug in the near darkness.

'We got ter get these under cover fast,' Ben hissed. 'I'll try round the back.' Passing the leading reins to his brother, he slipped around the wall of the inn and, to his relief, found an unshuttered side window with a glow of candlelight behind it. He tapped the glass gently and a few heartbeats later the casement was opened and a head looked out.

'Who's there?'

'Josh's men from Frome. Can'st let us in the yard?'

'I'll come out to you, wait there.'

Ben couldn't identify the man to whom he spoke; the feeble light behind him threw his features into deepest shadow. The candlelight faded and moments later a figure emerged from the rear of the building, one hand cupped around the flame to shield it. The light now fell on the fellow whose lower face was concealed by a kerchief, but still Ben did not know him for sure, although his stance and build seemed familiar. Was it the man, Matt, who had previously received them here at the Cock, or had the brothers walked into a trap? The mules were becoming restless, stamping and snorting; Ben was anxious that, denied their rest and fodder, they might set up a braying that would awaken the town. He would have to put his trust in the man.

'The inn's not safe,' he hissed through his scarf. 'We can't take the delivery. Prevention officers were in town this af'ernoon.'

Ben saw the alarm in the fellow's eyes.

'You've got to press on. Make for Motcombe, just this side of Shaftesbury, Chapel Farm, on the causeway. Ask for Henry Toogood, say Matt sent you.'

'Can you come too, guide us there? I don't know the road.'

Matt looked away and swore under his breath. 'I'll send a lad with you, I'd be missed here.'

Ben could feel the man's anxiety, it was infectious.

'I could send someone with lights towards Gillingham, as a decoy. That might help if they've set patrols.'

Ben nodded.

'You press straight on.' Matt pointed to the road out of the town square. 'Boy'll catch you up soon if I chivvy him out. Beasts might create, but let's hope they keeps quiet.'

Ben could feel a knot of fear twisting his gut, but what was to be done? He couldn't abandon Joshua's goods; he had to try to save them from falling into the hands of the excise men – if that happened it wasn't just the loss of the investment, they'd all be for the gallows.


A couple of hours later they were on their way home, riding north from Motcombe at last. Ben shivered. His shirt was rank, soaked with the cold sweat of fear, and now that the brothers were relieved of the responsibility of the contraband and the hot flush of excitement was cooling, the linen had grown chill against his back. The sky was a leaden grey: daybreak had been a dismal affair of an imperceptibly lightening sky, no glimpse of the sun or a colourful dawn to lift the spirits. They'd parted from their guide back near Mere and were making for home as fast as the weary mules could take them. The poor animals had had a very long journey, but at least they were now unburdened, other than those ridden by the brothers.

Ben slowed to a walk as they climbed the slope some way past Maiden Bradley. He turned to look at Nathaniel. His brother had been trembling as they rode into Motcombe at first light, found Henry Toogood, and handed over the incriminating fleeces for the remainder of the journey to the coast. Joshua owed them for saving his valuable cargo, he reckoned. They'd salvaged his investment from what could have been a disaster. Once he learned what they'd done, he ought to reward them handsomely. Ben wondered if he would, and whether Nathaniel would think it had been worth it. The lad's face had been as pale as a moth; he hadn't said a word but his eyes were terrified.

It was a relief to be on their way home, but ever since they'd passed Stourton, Ben had thought a couple of times that he'd heard distant hoof beats behind them. He waved Nathaniel and the mules ahead of him at a bend in the road, and hung back to watch the track behind and below him, the grey light strengthening moment by moment. Sure enough, his fears were confirmed as a pair of horsemen emerged from the cover of a hedgerow some five hundred paces behind, then swiftly turned back; perhaps they had seen him.

Ben kicked his heels into the flanks of his mount to catch up with his brother. 'Riders behind. We'll take cover in the woods like before, try and lose them.'

Nathaniel looked terrified again. 'They'll nab us for sure, Ben. What'll we do?'

'We're armed. If they spots us we'll fight our way out, but

with luck we'll give 'en the slip.'

The mules, sensing their nearness to home, picked up the pace and within fifteen minutes had reached the county boundary and the stand of trees. Ben and Nathaniel guided them off the road and into the woodland beside the stream, seeking the shelter of the dense leaves. Ben signalled to his brother to follow him in dismounting and, grasping the cudgels Joshua had provided, crept back towards the roadside. Taking cover behind a stout trunk, he glanced down at the ground: the mules' hoofs had left a clear trail into Little Bradley Woods. He tried to steady his breathing; in the silence each gasp seemed as loud as a pheasant's alarm cry.

He glanced across at Nathaniel, who sheltered behind an oak with a screen of hawthorn around its base. 'Take a look,' he hissed. 'Are they coming?'

Nathaniel peered gingerly between the hawthorn leaves, then pulled back, looked over to his brother and nodded. Ben raised his cudgel and indicated Nathaniel should do the same. The first officer appeared on the pathway. He had dismounted and was looking intently at the prints in the mud. Ben brought the heavy club down with all his force and the man crumpled to the ground, his head a mass of blood and bone. Twigs snapped as his companion turned and started to run back to their horses. Nathaniel shook his head. 'I won't . . . I can't. Not in cold blood!'

Ben raced after the officer, tugging the knife from its sheath at his belt. The man tripped and pitched forward. Ben was upon him, forcing him down on the ground, the body beneath him writhing powerfully in desperation to escape. Ben yanked the man's head back by the hair and drew the blade across his throat. Fingers scrabbled in the leaf mould, then stilled.

'God, Ben. What've you done? They'll be after us for this.'

Nathaniel's whole body was quaking. 'Did you have to kill them?'

Ben wiped the knife in the dewy grass. His hands were shaking so much he could barely make them obey him. He took a few deep breaths. 'I'd sooner not have. But it was them or us, Nat. Now, we got to hide they bodies. I think I knows the place.'

He caught the rein of one of the mules and positioned the animal close to the first corpse. 'Help me get him up.' Together they heaved the lifeless bodies onto the backs of two of the mules and Ben took the reins. 'You go back to Cowbridge with all the others and stable them, then make your way home. I can use the forest track back from here to meet you at Cole Hill. I just pray none of Lord Weymouth's gamekeepers are in this part of the woods this mornin'.'

In the shadow of the Angel's archway, Joshua shook the hand of a gentleman in a fine green coat. Ben and his brother hung back in the roadway until the older man had walked away.

'Thank the Lord we found you, Master Joshua!' Ben said, as he and Nathaniel touched their hat brims. 'We've spent all morning trying to track 'ee down. It weren't plain sailing last night, if you catch my drift.' Ben knew better than to blurt out his news by now: you never knew who might be a-listening in.

Joshua scowled at them. 'We'll go in the Swan, find a private corner to talk there. Come on, up Apple Alley. I don't need all the town seeing us together.'

The three settled themselves in an alcove at the back of the public room. The landlady's giant curly-haired dogs sprawled on the flagstones before them and formed a living barrier to anyone who approached their table. Nathaniel gulped his ale.

'We been looking all over town for 'ee since noon, Joshua. We've not slept since God knows when, but we have to tell 'ee how we fared last night.' Ben scratched his head. 'We sorted out some problems.' He paused. 'But I fear other matters may be harder to resolve.'

'Don't talk in riddles, man. Start at the beginning, and it's the truth I want to hear – don't you go giving me any lies.' Joshua leaned forward. 'And keep your voice low.'

Ben glanced at Nathaniel. Anxiety contended with exhaustion in his brother's features; the lad looked worn to a frazzle. 'All was fine till we reached Mere. They'd had an alarm. The prevention officers were in the town.'

Joshua swore.

'Inn was closed to us. That fellow Matt that works there, he told us to go on to Motcombe, to the next post. I didn't know whether to trust him or not, but we had little choice.'

'Aye. He's a handy fellow.'

'We reached Motcombe alright, Chapel Farm, but the mules were flagging and we were too, 'specially with the fear of the excise men, and not knowing the ground.'

'You did well. I'll see you right.'

'Aye, but. Now we come to the harder matters.' Ben took a swig of ale. He feared his further news would not please Joshua one bit. 'They tracked us coming home. From Stourton. Two riding officers.'

Joshua was staring at Ben, his eyes riveted on his face. 'Did they stop you? Did they follow you to the farm? What happened?'

'They caught us up,' Ben dropped Joshua's gaze. 'I had to silence them.'

'You killed them? Where? Did anyone see you?'

'No. It were in the woods by county bridge. I've disposed of them, there's no trace. Their horses ran loose. No one can pin it on us.'

'I hope you're right. And the bodies?'

'I flung 'em down a well. No reason for anyone to discover them, no one else will use it.'

Nathaniel shivered. His voice was barely a whisper. 'They'll haunt our place. We'll never be free of them. And you've poisoned that well. My God, it'll stink and show everyone what we've done.' The lad was trembling, his face drawn and his hands clutched the stool he sat on.

'Not you Nat. I was the one that did for 'em.'

'But they'll hang me just for being there.'

'Not if no one finds out. I'm goin' to sink a new well up by the springs, and fill in the old with the spoil. No one need know anything, so long as you keeps yer mouth shut.' He looked meaningfully at his brother.

'I understand, Ben. But that's it for me. I'm quitting this game. I'm having no hand in it anymore.' Nathaniel sat back in his seat, his expression one of determination.

'That's as maybe,' Joshua snarled. 'But you knows a lot about my business young Nat. I won't take kindly to any loose talk. I'm minded to stop your mouth up for good an' all.'

'Now Josh, that's not needful,' Ben's tone was conciliatory. 'Nat here can hold a secret better than any man, he knows the penalty – and I don't mean what the courts would do to him.'

'Aye, it's what I'd do he'd have to fear.'

Nathaniel wrung his hands together. In an instant Joshua took hold of his wrist. Ben put his own hand on Joshua's and looked directly into his cold grey eyes.

'I'll vouch for him, Josh. He won't blab.'

Joshua released his grip. The fingers had left deep

impressions on Nathaniel's flesh that darkened as the blood flowed back. He nodded. 'That'll be your neck if so be there's a squeak out of you, Nathaniel. Don't you forget it.'

The three looked up as Helen the landlady appeared at their table. 'More ale me lovers? Or have 'ee done? We've some hot meat pies if you wants one.'

Nathaniel handed her his tankard, shaking his head. 'I'm going. I'll see you later Ben.' He crammed his hat on as he made his way to the door.

The savoury smell of the pies had followed the woman from the kitchen. It was more than either Ben or Joshua could do to decline one. The rich gravy ran down his chin as Ben bit into the crisp butter pastry. He'd forgotten his last meal, he was ravenous and a beef and ale pie was exactly what he needed. The two men ate in silence. All too soon the last crumbs had been swallowed and Joshua fixed Ben with a stern eye.

'I'll hold you responsible for yer brother's silence. He seemed a risk right from the start. I don't want him turning traitor, gossiping, or talking to the magistrates.'

'He'll not. Family's everything to him, he'll stand by me.'

Joshua grunted. 'Talking of family, I was speaking with your sister this very morning.'

Ben looked up. He recalled the threats Josh had made regarding the girl in the past. A slight smile twisted Joshua's lips, but the man's face was inscrutable.

'Tell me,' Joshua went on, glancing over his shoulder at the other drinkers, 'does she have any admirers at present? Is she spoken for?'

Ben felt a tumult of confusion in his head; his thoughts seemed to be twisting together. He didn't want his sister getting mixed up with this nasty piece of work, did he? Howsomever, Joshua was a man of enterprise, probably growing wealthy too, with all his schemes. It would do no harm to his own standing with the man if so be he was romantically involved with Molly-Ann. Any case, there wouldn't be much he could do to prevent an entanglement he decided. Joshua'd always get what he wanted and, to be honest, he himself had never had much influence over Molly-Ann.

'Not as I knows of. Why, be 'ee keen to get to know her?'

'Aye. Pretty girl. She's certainly caught my eye.' Joshua leaned back and his wooden chair creaked a little. His smile had grown broader and his eyes had lost their focus.

'You could do a lot worse, Josh. She's a fine girl, hard working, knows her own mind.'

Joshua's fierce eyes were suddenly more intent on his own. 'And it might mean more work, and more important work for you too, Ben. There's a new venture coming up and you could be very useful to me – especially as you've just shown your own mettle in a tight spot.'


After he'd parted from Joshua, Ben led the mules he'd had since last night out of the pack horse ground on Behind Town, and onto the roadway. He'd had to ride one bareback with just the leading rein, and tow the other, but at least it was quicker than walking. After he'd returned them to Cowbridge Farm he planned to get back home for a bit of sleep. God knew where Nathaniel had got to. It was indeed time for the brothers to go their separate ways. Nat always had been a touch religious, he thought: too much of a conscience there. Let him go back to poaching or find employment with someone else, Ben had had enough of him. The lad was holding him back.

Ben took the Keyford road past Gore Hedge, but his path was blocked just beyond the Crown tavern. A cart was half over, one wheel askew: the axle must have broken. Household stuff had spilled across the narrow road; children were crying, and a dog running loose in and out of people's legs. Ben swore, he was dead tired and wanted nothing but his bed.

'Begging yer pardon, sir . . .' a raggedly dressed man, his face hollow cheeked, his arms emaciated, had hold of the mule's head collar, '. . . we're in sore need of a place to stay – I can fix this wheel good enough for a short way – but we need a roof tonight and can't travel far.'

Ben scowled at him. 'Well I've no place for 'ee. Where'm you from?'

'Stoke St Michael. There's nothing there for us. We heard there's work in Frome, but we can't find any lodgings.'

Ben kicked his mule on; a gap had opened up through the crowd of people. 'You could ask one of they ministers.' He nodded in the direction of Gideon Silcox, who was just emerging from Sarah's cottage. 'They'm allus keen to do good works.'

The mules kept up a good pace after their rest in the town and soon covered the two miles home to Cowbridge farm. As soon as he'd stabled them, Ben set off through the fields and soon reached Cole Hill, noting with disquiet the presence of a single magpie in the yard. At last he was able to kick off his boots and fall into bed exhausted. The work on the well could keep till tomorrow, he'd decided.

# CHAPTER 6

THE OLD KETTLE sang as the water came to the boil, and Sarah lifted it carefully, a cloth around the handle, to fill a small pot. Steam rose from the infusion of meadowsweet leaves and she inhaled the fragrance, careful to waste none of the goodness. The early Sunday morning sunshine turned the vapour golden.

'Five minutes and that'll be ready for you, sir. I'll put a spoon of honey in to sweeten it.'

'Bless you, Sarah,' Gideon Silcox said, taking a seat by the table. 'Your medicine is as good as that of any physician.'

'Your headaches do concern me, sir. They seem to strike you very frequently, and so hard. Are you worrying over something, or working at your books too much?' She strained the infusion into a cup and stirred in the honey.

'No more than usual. But I had little sleep last night, sitting up with old Mistress Morgan. I fear she'll pass away in the next few days, poor soul.'

'Aye, she's taken my maudlin daisy daily for her chest, but she told me she just needs something to soothe her, she's ready for her end.'

'She seems to have given up the fight,' Gideon agreed. 'I spoke at length with her, as far as she could for her cough. Will you be called to her laying out?'

'Who else, I'd like to know?'

'And then you've to affirm she was buried in woollen, I

understand?'

'Aye.' She pictured in her mind the great book in which the churchwarden would record her attestation. She shook her head. What good was it to those who'd passed on, to be shrouded in wool? It wouldn't bring *them* any warmth. She snorted. 'Waste of good cloth. I'd sooner have it on my back when I'm alive.'

Gideon smiled. 'Wear a woollen cloak now and we'll use it as a shroud for you in due course. You'll have the benefit of it then.' He sipped the infusion of meadowsweet. 'And anyway, it gives more work to the weavers, for which we must be thankful.'

Sarah nodded. It was good to have such a kindly man as her lodger.

'I want to pay a visit to that family from Stoke St Michael before this morning's meeting,' Gideon said. 'I'd like to be sure they are as settled as maybe; it's a poor place we found for them in Hunger Lane, just a cellar, damp and dark. I hope they can find better soon but there's precious little available and nothing they can afford, so far. The town's growing fast and nowhere to put the poorer people.'

'Will they come to meeting, sir?'

'I've tried to persuade them. They may do, if only out of a sense of obligation. And as you know, we're bursting at the seams in the old place, it'll be good to move to the new room Master Smith's offered us, allow us to welcome in more folk.' He took a sip. 'Though I know we are running a risk by doing so. Five is the most the Act allows to meet for worship, other than in a church, and we exceed that many times over.' He drained the cup. 'Right, I shall go ahead to prepare for the service. John hopes to be there in time, he's riding over from Wanstrow; at least he has a fine morning for it.'

The minister's brow looked less drawn now, and Sarah made a note to collect more of the fragrant herb for future use.

Gideon Silcox had only left the cottage a few minutes when there was a knock at the door and Molly-Ann peeked in, her hair shining from a good brushing, her dress the best she owned – Sarah recognised it as having formerly belonged to Betty Grimwade, the girl's mistress, but she had taken it in at the waist and augmented it with ribbons at the neckline.

'Sarah, I'm glad I've caught you, I need to ask a favour.'

'Well, you've caught me just as I'm about to set off for meeting. What is it you want young Molly-Ann? Can we talk as I walk to Rook Lane?'

'It's private. I won't take a moment of your time.' She looked down at her hands. 'I heard the girls talk of a flower that belongs to the fairies – cuckoo flower they named it – they . . . they said the roots can be used for a love potion. I wondered if you knew aught of this, of how to prepare it?'

'Oh, Molly-Ann! I thought you a sensible girl, not one that believes in fairies and love potions!' Sarah turned away to tie the ribbons of her tall black hat. 'I don't hold with these superstitions, there's nothing in them, and if there were, it would be the work of the devil.'

Molly-Ann's shoulders had slumped.

'What do you want to go and get mixed up with that nonsense for? You leave well alone, that's my advice.'

'But Sarah, I'm desperate!'

'I've no time now, my girl. Service will start shortly. Don't delay me with this silly carry on.'

Sarah shooed Molly-Ann out of the kitchen before her, turning to lock the door as she stood on the step. 'Get along with you. Unless he's some lord, or blind as a bat, you've no need of magic or special draughts to attract the man. Just turn your smile on him and he'll be eating out of your hand.'

'D'you really think so? He's walking me out this af'ernoon. I do hope it'll be the start of something for me.'

'Well good luck to you, but I don't want to hear more of your wicked thoughts, especially on the Sabbath.' Sarah smiled and turned downhill towards the cottage where the meeting was to take place. 'Come and tell me all about him tomorrow.'

She took her seat on the wooden bench in good time; she knew what a crush there would be in ten minutes as the last ones tried to squeeze their way in. The popularity of the Congregationalist meeting had increased rapidly over the last twelve months and it was as well they were about to transfer to this new place. She looked forward to hearing more about it from Master Silcox. The minister was punctilious in entering the room on the stroke of eleven, together with his son John, but the same could not be said of some members of his flock who continued to drift in, or to make an apologetic entry, all eyes upon them. Indeed, the first hymn was over before the last of the people entered. The latecomers had to remain standing as all the forms were now filled to capacity, with children put to sit on the stone floor to make space. Sarah didn't like to see them down on the dusty flags; they couldn't follow the service from there, and were tempted into chattering and fidgeting. A baby cried and was quickly soothed by its mother. Master Silcox soon had the adults' undivided attention at least, as he opened the subject of the new meeting place. It was, he told them, to be in a commodious, light chamber in Master Robert Smith's property – Rook Lane House – on the corner where Rook Lane met Behind Town. The clothier had generously offered the use of a fine chamber – his own parlour indeed - at no cost to the congregation. Sarah was eager to see the new room and, she hoped, perhaps something of the other parts of the house and its furnishings. She felt sure it would be a warm and comfortable home, without ostentation or display, reflecting Master Smith's reputation as a self-effacing, though very tenacious and prosperous man of business. The chapel was indeed lucky to have such a wealthy benefactor.

The service progressed with the usual hymns and prayers, and towards the conclusion of the meeting the minister stood to read the notices. Sarah focused her attention. She sometimes found that despite her best efforts her mind wandered off on a tangent these days. To her pleasure she learned that Dr Humfry was to preside at a special meeting on Tuesday evening "at the usual location" as Master Silcox put it in an effort, as she realised, to keep the prohibited services secret from the authorities. Sarah and the other regular attendees knew the place – Roddenbury Hillfort – to be within the area proscribed by the Five Mile Act, inside which it was a crime for Dr Humfry, as the former puritan incumbent of that parish, to hold a religious service. His old congregation held him in such high esteem however, that they were willing to break the new law if it meant they could hear his teaching once again. The legislation had only been in effect a year or so, and to date no attempt had been made to enforce it in Frome; perhaps the authorities realised the number of dissenters they would be contending with, or even felt some degree of sympathy with them, Master Silcox had said. Sarah certainly felt nothing but excitement at the prospect of Dr Humfry's coming visit and his sustaining words.

The monks of old, how they must have suffered, John Silcox mused, a couple of hours after the service had ended.

They were surrounded by temptation day and night, and in the company of other repressed men, many of them cultured, articulate and caring. At least he was out in society where the majority of the people around him evinced the more usual pattern of desire for a member of the opposite sex. Like that pair he had just noticed, slipping through the riverside bushes on the other side of Rodden Meadow. John lifted his hat and ran his fingers through his short, fair hair. His interest in men, he repeatedly told himself, was wrong, unnatural, against God's word. But still it was the male figure that had excited his interest, not the raven haired young woman walking beside him.

His father was coming towards him now, from the end of Pilly Vale where he had stopped to pay a call at one of the larger cottages beside the fulling mill. John rose from the tree stump on which he had been waiting, and raised his hat to the older man.

'I'm sorry to have delayed you John; that took longer than I had envisioned. At least I should have a few pupils to start the class, however. The mill foreman is willing to send his three along, and will encourage others he thinks may benefit.' Gideon groaned softly. 'Of course, they do seem to be the most boisterous and self-willed children I have yet encountered. I shall have my work cut out.'

'Too easy a road wouldn't suit you, father.' John said, and smiled wryly, thinking of his own path through life.

'Let's follow the meadow down to Wallbridge and from there we could take the track up to the new church at Rodden if that would interest you?' His father pointed upstream through a dense stand of willows. 'I'm still finding my way about Frome, seeing where the folk travel from in order to attend chapel. It's a long step for many.'

Gideon strode ahead, humming the tune of this morning's closing hymn. His son glanced back at the young couple, sitting decorously now on a tree trunk facing the sparkling river. There seemed something familiar about the set of the man's shoulders. He drew a deep breath. How did *Joshua* come to be here in Frome of all places? But was it indeed him? Perhaps he was mistaken. He looked again, but the man's face was hidden. He quickened his pace to catch Gideon.

Could he go through with his intended confession; what would his father say, he wondered, if he dared to speak about his private feelings and desires? He'd be horrified probably; perhaps incredulous that such emotions could exist. Yet Gideon had never enquired whether his son wished for a wife and children. John sliced off a head of cow parsley with his stick. Might the dear old chap have some inkling of how matters stood with his son? He wondered whether he could find the courage to speak today. Indeed, should he speak, or hold his peace? The unexpected sighting of Joshua and his own immediate response made his mind up: it was not a fleeting emotion that he had experienced a year ago. He closed his eyes, overwhelmed by the misery of hiding his true nature from the person he loved most in the whole world, his father, for all the years ahead. No, he would speak out.

The sun was beating down now from a cloudless sky, and sweat ran down his spine and soaked the linen at his waistband. Ahead, Gideon marched on, his speed that of a young man, then he stopped abruptly and motioned towards the river. Peering between the green spears and yellow flags of iris, John was delighted to see two mallards with five ducklings, a few beads of water glittering on the fluffy backs. Father and son smiled at one another without comment and resumed their walk, this time shoulder to shoulder.

'I wanted to broach with you a very personal matter,' Gideon said, his eyes on the further horizon.

John stepped back a pace; had his father become a mind reader?

'I find it easier to talk, to express my feelings, out of doors,' Gideon continued. 'I hope you have no objection?'

John felt his guilt rise up in his chest and fairly choke him. 'I'm sure it's better here in the meadows, father, in the midst of nature and surrounded by pure, fresh air.'

His father shot him a narrow glance. 'Just so.'

John sighed. Were the years of easy relations, open discussion, personal confidences between them about to come to an end? He feared they were.

'This is, as you surmise, a very delicate matter, John. I don't really know where to begin. I want to clear my conscience, to do away with all pretence, to discuss the future openly with you.'

'Your conscience, father? It's not as if *you're* the guilty party.'

'Oh, but I am, my son. How could I even have thought it? And the impact on our congregation will be shattering. No, I've decided to resign and start afresh elsewhere, perhaps in the Americas with you and the colonists, if you can forgive me and accept my grave error.' John had never before seen his father's expression so full of pain and pleading.

'*Your* error?' He put his hand firmly on Gideon's shoulder and held his eyes. 'You are in no fault whatsoever. It is I who am to blame. I must seek *your* forgiveness.'

Gideon's eyes were simply puzzled now. 'What are you talking about?'

John guided his father to a patch of buttercups where they could sit.

'My unnatural feelings for men and one man in particular.' John put his head in his hands. 'I have endeavoured to repress this attraction. I've tried and tried to master it.'

Gideon blinked several times. His silence lasted a full minute. 'Is this why you drive yourself to work so hard, constantly moving from place to place?' he asked gently. 'Are you trying to out run your own self?'

John watched as a woodlouse - a chuggy-pig he'd called it as a boy - struggled to climb the height of a fallen twig; at the top it could go no further and scrambled back down again, its segments flexing as it turned.

'Yes, I suppose. I'd like to escape the feelings, but they're ever with me. I've no interest in women in that way. But I have in the past had the most salacious thoughts imaginable about a certain man, and now, to my astonishment, I fear that my path may again have crossed with his.'

Gideon was looking across the river. A blackbird's song came from a hawthorn tree above them. 'This was not at all what I wanted to speak with you about,' he said, 'but as you have opened the matter, I will of course hear your thoughts and try to help you towards what is right for you. Do you wish to tell me more about this individual, or perhaps you prefer not to identify him by name?'

'It was during my time at sea, what, a year ago now. In the battle off Lowestoft I took a musket ball in the leg as you know, and lost a lot of blood. I'd fallen, couldn't escape as the enemy boarded our ship.' He rubbed his hand across his face. 'A great burly Dutchman, his clothes covered in blood, stood over me, his sword poised. I knew it was my last moment, but strangely I couldn't pray, I just thought of you and mother. Then the fellow grunted and his mouth spewed blood in a torrent. He toppled beside me, a hatchet buried deep in his back. An English marine bent over him and wrenched the weapon free, then struck him again, this time to the back of the neck. The savagery in his eyes! I'll never forget them. They were as hard as the steel of that axe blade, while his face was aglow with passion - passion for violence and slaughter.' John shivered. 'That was my first encounter with this man. I owed him my life for sure, but he said after that it was his duty; his sole purpose was to kill the enemy and save our men for more fighting. I idolised him, he stirred such emotions in me. I haven't stopped thinking about him.'

'Did you see him again in the wars?'

'I was put ashore with the other wounded, but when the ship was decommissioned at Portsmouth and we were paid off I had the chance to thank him again over a drink. He said a few things about impressed landsmen being worse than useless on a fighting ship – he was probably right. '

Gideon shook his head. 'I'm sure your ministry brought comfort to dozens of unfortunates, even if you were never a success as a seaman.'

'Maybe. I couldn't express my feelings for him there in that tavern. But that image of him, afire with fury, with bloodlust, sheer savagery, that will never leave me, dreadful as it is to a rational man.'

'But rationality is only a portion of our mind. The irrational: desire, excitement, violence – that is perhaps the more potent element, and one that does not always submit to control by the will. I begin to see why you would be attracted to such a man.'

'A full year ago, and I have thought of him every day since. And now I think I have seen him here in Frome. What are the chances of that?'

'Has he recognised you?'

'No, no. To see someone in a different context . . .' John shook his head. 'He certainly felt no great bond with me at the time. In fact, I probably have no place at all in his memory.'

Gideon steepled his fingers. 'I feared I'd never see you again when you were pressed into the navy at Lyme. Your first letter home was a comfort, but I knew how hard a time you would face aboard ship when you had no experience of the sea.'

'At least it didn't last too long. I came away with my life, even if it took some time for my leg to heal. But the impact of my discovery about my true nature – that will remain with me forever.'

'Might I take a little time to absorb and consider your revelations, before we debate them further? I have to say, I am very anxious about what this will mean for you.'

'Of course, father. I just want to be able to talk with you about it at some point, and candidly.' John pulled one of the golden flowers to shreds. 'But tell me now what is on *your* mind. It's rare for you to have personal concerns that trouble you so.'

'We touched upon it, but lightly, when you ate with me and Sarah last week.' He paused and drew a breath. 'I miss your mother, John, both as a beloved individual, and as a wife. I am minded to marry again, but it may mean parting from the congregation, as I fear they would be opposed to the individual concerned. I wanted to discuss with you both the intention, and the object of my affections. Of course, I would do all in my power to prevent any deterioration in our own cordial relations one with another.'

'Who is this woman? Is she a member of the chapel?'

'No. And therein lies the difficulty. She is not considered a gentlewoman at all. I'll be honest: she is a tavern maid. She is unmarried, but I am aware she is not chaste.'

'My God.' John could feel the blood drain from his face. He was as shocked at his own blasphemy as he was at his father's news. 'This is not . . . not at all like you.'

'I know. But despite hours of prayer and self-recrimination, I can't change my feelings.'

'Well then.' John smiled. 'At least you will have sympathy for my position, also.'

The swish of boots and long skirts brushing the buttercup stalks interrupted the Silcoxes' conversation. They looked up simultaneously as the young couple made their way past them; the periwinkle blue eyes of Molly-Ann moving from John to his father before a smile radiated from them. Her heavily built companion touched his hat to them as he passed, but no smile was forthcoming. John watched the broad back, the powerful arms, and swinging gait of the fellow then closed his eyes as he tried to think of a freezing mountain stream instead.

When he looked again at his father, Gideon's face was blanched and his eyes full of an intense sadness. John chastised himself. He should have known that his father would be devastated by his own awful admission.


By the end of the afternoon, clouds were towering ahead of him, stacked tier upon tier on the western horizon. The higher levels were a brilliant white, as pure and shining as the wings of angels; the lower clouds a significantly darker shade, grey and even purple where the mass was densest. John kicked his horse into a trot. He was surprised how calmly his father had received his shocking news; as a man of strict religious principles Gideon might have been expected to forcefully condemn such sinful inclinations. That he had not done so reminded John of the breadth of his father's vision: he would always listen to all sides before reaching a fair judgement. A salutary lesson, he reminded himself, when considering Gideon's own revelations. The weather was coming towards him; it would be a race to get back to Wanstrow before the storm broke.

He emerged onto Marston Ridge as the first lightning flickered along the skyline ahead. The land fell away to left and right, fields of wheat and barley to the north, pastures to the south sweeping down to the hamlet of Marston Bigot. The early evening light was strange; as the clouds thickened, the air seemed to take on a coppery hue. Distant thunder murmured.

To the left of the highway stood a massive oak, its boughs reaching out at all angles, some dead, others crowned with dense foliage. As he watched, a figure seemed to detach itself from the tree trunk many feet above the ground and swung crazily, its legs jerking and thrashing. John reined in his horse, at first unable to comprehend what he saw. The movement of the figure stilled, even as John's breathing quickened. He kicked the mare closer, then stood in the stirrups, drew out his knife, and hacked at the taut rope.

He had cut through just two or three strands when with a snap the remaining fibres parted and the man's body fell to the ground, striking John's leg in its descent. He scrambled to dismount and with shaking hands loosened the noose around the man's neck; as he did so a great gasp shook the recumbent body and the chest began to rise and fall as life returned.

John had barely had time to form a prayer for help, but his thanks to God for the man's restoration were fulsome. The face was losing its congestion, the eyes starting to focus and return to a more normal appearance. He rummaged in his saddlebag and found a small flask of brandy which he held to the man's lips.

'Praise be to God that I was at hand,' he said, shaking his

head. 'What can have ailed you, my friend, that death was the refuge you sought? And by your own hand . . .' John pressed his lips together firmly; this was not the moment to chastise the poor man. 'When your body recovers we shall speak further, and I am sure that together we will find a better answer to your woes.' He raised the man's head and shoulders – he was only a youngster, John noted, probably not yet eighteen and lightly built. To judge from his stained shirt, threadbare breeches and torn stockings he might have been living rough for a while.

'What's your name?' he asked gently. 'Can I help you back to your home?'

The younger man coughed and put one hand to his throat. John winced.

'Nathaniel. I'm not going back.'

'Then I shall help you elsewhere – perhaps to my father's home in Frome?'

The younger man shook his head. 'Not Frome,' he croaked.

'Will you come to Wanstrow then? We can attend to your ills there.'

'Why didn't 'ee leave me be?' He moved his head from side to side. 'Death would have been the best answer.' A fit of retching seized him until he lay back exhausted.

John, Nathaniel and the horse were all soaked and chilled by the time they reached Wanstrow that evening. The storm had swept over Selwood, thrashing the trees, deluging the woodlands and turning the roadway to a channel of mud. As they came into the ancient little settlement the sun was setting and its last rays sparkled on the wet roof of the church.

Leaving the horse in her stall with a promise to return very shortly with hay, water and a brush, John helped his guest into the cottage. The young man was shivering helplessly and John quickly lit the tinder and sticks that lay ready on the hearth, then picked up a blanket and wrapped it around Nathaniel's shoulders.

'A hot drink and food and you'll feel better, I'm sure,' he said. Nathaniel's expression was not encouraging.

A dish of fried eggs, some bread from a kindly neighbour, and a cup of mulled cider did bring some colour back to Nathaniel's face, but his eyes were still desolate, John thought, as though there was nothing at all to live for. Three candles brought a warm glow to the little room, the light reflecting from the highly polished oak of the table between them. Nathaniel looked up at him and sighed.

'You'd have done better to leave me to die. Better for me: better for the world. I've been party to murders, to crimes. I've nothing to my name. No skills to sell. The constables will be after me – they'll finish the job I started.'

John felt his chest tighten. Was he harbouring a criminal under his roof? Was the man truly a dangerous murderer? He seemed as meek as a kitten; it was hard to credit his assertion.

'You say you were a party to murder. Was it your intention to kill? Was it you who struck the blow? Perhaps it was in self defence?'

'I didn't do it myself. I'd not have used force. But I *was* there and we *were* a'breakin' the law. I'm as guilty as he who pulled the knife. The law will have me – it was two of their own what died. They'll do all they can to pin it on us – I can't bear the guilt or the fear of capture. I just want to end it all.'

John studied the backs of his hands as he thought of the responsibility he owed towards both justice and to this desperate man shaking at his fireside. The silence lengthened as he considered what on earth he was to do.

'Look, Nathaniel – may I address you so?'

The younger man nodded.

'I think you need to tell me the whole story from the beginning. Tell me the honest truth, it's the only way I can help you.'

'But Reverend . . .'

'I'm not a minister, just a lay preacher, a servant of the chapel. I hold no official position. I wouldn't want you to be misled.' John looked into the youngster's blue eyes.

Had he not had Gideon as his father, a father to whom, in the past at least, he had been able to unburden himself, would he too feel such an oppressive sense of guilt that he would end his own life? The scales of sympathy were coming down in Nathaniel's favour, for John at least.

'I'll do all I can to support you, but I can't perjure myself if I were ever called as a witness. I can't say I'll keep whatever you tell me secret, but I'll do all I can to advise and help you.'

Nathaniel nodded absently. John wasn't sure whether or not he understood. The lad pushed his empty plate aside. 'My brother and I were owlers.'

John's lack of comprehension must have shown in his face.

'Smugglers: running contraband out of the country to foreign parts. We were taking shipments of Mendip wool down to the coast. But the excise men were onto us and tailed us homewards. It were last Wednesday, around daybreak. We tried to give 'en the slip, but they nailed us. I refused to stab 'en in cold blood, but it finished with the two of 'en dead.

'I've told Ben I'll have no further truck with the smuggling, but those men will be sought and whether or not the magistrates come for us, I know their deaths are on my conscience, and I can't live with it. My brother's dug hisself in deeper with they villains. I wanted him to pull out like I did, but if so be he did, I know they'd take revenge on our family.

I'd be even more burdened then.'

One of the candles had started to gutter. John trimmed it, absentmindedly.

'They may have a hold over you through threats against your family, but you could  clear your name and save the rest of your family by turning king's evidence.'

'I couldn't do that to my brother, never. However bad he's turned, I couldn't.  And my sister'd never forgive me.' Nathaniel's hands twisted nervously together. 'And that thug, he'd be after me, he's threatened before now. He's the one we worked for.'

'I think you should lie low until we know whether or not you're a hunted man. If it comes to it, you might be able to flee the country, but if you're not accused you could pick up a new life here in Somerset, away from this villain, and your brother's influence.' John tipped the last of the mulled cider into their cups. 'Meantime, you can bide here. It's known that travelling preachers and others tarry here from time to time. If you don't mind a truckle bed, you're welcome to stop with me.'


The next morning, Monday, the cooing of a wood pigeon woke John early. From the roof ridge above his attic bedroom, it called 'You fools you!' over and over again as the sun burned through the dawn mist. The world looked and sounded just the same as every day that had gone before, he thought, yet he himself was a new creature, radically different. Had he not bared his soul to his father, made confession of his guilt, and acknowledged his grievous fault? But at the very same time, he recalled, his past had risen up before him and his body had responded immediately. If he was to be reborn, he must learn to govern his instinctive reaction to Joshua's presence; a lesson that would take some learning. He thanked God that he was not drawn to this young man, Nathaniel. He would do all in his power to help the lad get his feet back onto the straight and narrow road, as an instance of the good works the Lord required. He examined his conscience as he climbed down the ladder to the kitchen. There was not an ounce of attraction towards Nat in his body: the sensuous muscles of the man in Rodden Meadow however, were another matter. Reform, so easy to promise, would be hard to achieve.

'I've set aside a couple of days this week to cut my hay.' John put down his breakfast mug of ale. 'Would you be willing to give me a hand, Nathaniel? Then I'll be done in half the time.'

'Willingly! I owe you a great debt and a little scything will start the repayment. I already find my mind more composed than it were last evening.'

'Good.' John pushed the loaf of bread towards his guest. 'Eat your fill. We've a hard morning ahead.' He thought of the three acres that went with his cottage. 'I pray the weather will be kind, to give me a good store of winter feed.' He bent to pull on his work boots. 'While we work we can think about your future.'

Nathaniel looked up sharply.

'May I suggest that you secure for yourself some employment and a home well away from this brother who seems to be such a baleful influence. Indeed, you may wish to consider emigrating to one of the new colonies that are being formed – a hard life, but potentially great rewards in a society that values liberty.'

'It is a thought, Master Silcox, but I'd sooner bide here in Somerset if I bain't a wanted man.'

John pursed his lips. 'I shall make discreet enquiries about that in the town.' He filled an earthenware flagon with ale, and wrapped the remains of the loaf and a hunk of cheese in a clean cloth. 'I could ask who among the clothiers is in need of workers. We may find you some honest employment in one of the mills, then lodgings close to – does that appeal to you? Or would you perhaps like to serve as an assistant in my father's school? He needs a kind and careful person to help him.'

'I'm not fit for that. I've no book learning, nor experience with childer. Nay, that's not for me. A chance at a mill would be much the better. I've worked the fields and woods to now, but I can see industry would be a more promising future.' He stood and nodded to John. 'I'd not have thought of myself as having a future of any sort over the last few days. While I was living a vagabond's life in the woods I lost all hope and belief in myself. But your words and actions have restored me, and I'm grateful to 'ee for all you've done, sir. I'll allus be in your debt.'

# CHAPTER 7

I T WAS BARELY five weeks past midsummer. There was no noticeable change yet in the daylight hours, and indeed the sun was still gilding the weathercock atop St John's church as Sarah left her cottage the following Tuesday evening on her way to the illicit meeting. It was good to get out in the fresh air after performing her duties on behalf of Mistress Jane Morgan, and she wondered fleetingly who would be responsible for laying *her* out once her days were ended. No point in worrying, she decided: she certainly wouldn't know anything about it. The weather had turned cooler and drizzly during the day, but the evening sky was bright as the clouds cleared, and she had pulled a thin cloak over her shoulders before leaving home, in anticipation of a late night return.

The houses along Keyford and down to the little ford over the Adderwell Brook were all in shadow now; the sun had dipped below the horizon but the sky was yet golden. She took the field path down through scrubby pastures where a few ponies grazed among the ragwort, crossed the river by a narrow plank bridge, then trudged up the further slope to pick up Feltham Lane as it headed out towards East Woodlands, a couple of miles southeast of town.

Over the years Sarah had mapped out in her mind the precise locations of various perennial plants that grew in hedges and on the roadside verges. It was her habit to gather supplies of her medicinal herbs and foraged foods systematically as they came into flower or fruit, as the new leaves appeared, or as the plant died down and she could dig up some roots. Now, although dusk was falling, she knew where to find clumps of wild raspberries at the side of the lane, and if she was lucky and no one had got there before her, she could spend a while gathering some of the fruit. Sure enough, the plants were bearing their crimson berries well hidden by the heart shaped foliage. She lined a cloth bag with a quantity of the leaves – they too, once dried and made into an infusion, would provide considerable relief to women in childbirth – then picked a good handful of the fruit, finding them by touch as much as by sight. She fastened the bag to her belt by its drawstring, then set off to tramp the last half mile through East Woodlands to Roddenbury, the colours of day fading to a bluish grey as night descended around her.

The steep path up from the lane that led to Longleat was rutted and muddy; she lifted the hem of her black skirts to avoid the mire, but her feet were already feeling damp from the moist ground. Figures were climbing the hillside ahead of her, following the twisting path up between the ditches and banks of the ancient earthworks. Her eyes had grown accustomed to the dim twilight of the lane, but under the scattered woodland trees great wells of darkness lurked, and she stayed on the open ground as far as she could. The people were congregating in a wide depression at the top of the hill, probably twenty or more, the majority women but a few men also. All wore the sombre clothing traditional in the chapel, together with hats and enveloping cloaks like Sarah's own.

A lantern was lit at the centre of the gathering and the warm light fell on the familiar face of Gideon Silcox. Sarah's pulse calmed a little after the effort of climbing the hill; her anxiety as to whether she would be able to find the meeting eased. The minister moved aside and the lantern light fell instead on the sharp features of Dr Humfry. Sarah thought he was looking thinner than ever; he must have been under great strain over the last year, doubtless working too hard in London in the interests of his followers during the time of the pestilence. He stepped up onto a tree stump where all could see him clearly. 'Let us pray,' he began. The congregation bowed their heads and he delivered an opening prayer in a low but clear voice, then bid them sing a hymn together.

Sarah had shuffled a little to her right to get a clearer view of the well loved Calvinist preacher, but there was a sharp scratch on her ankle and she found that her foot was trapped; she must have blundered into a patch of blackberries. She bent down to pull her skirts away and free her foot, but was knocked sideways into the brambles as someone collided with her. There were screams, the lantern went out, and suddenly the woods were full of running feet as dark shapes careered past her heading pell-mell downhill. The brambles' thorns had caught in her hands as well as her woollen skirts, and she moaned in pain.

A hand clamped onto her shoulder, pressing her down and there was heavy breathing just above her. A high-pitched voice close to her ear cried: 'I 'ave one sir, over 'ere.'

'Hold tight then,' a gruff voice replied. 'Looks like the rest have got away.' Sarah was hauled to her feet, both arms held from behind. The brambles still wrapped about her ankles entangled their vicious stems yet tighter about her legs.

'Sirs, let me go, my skin is being torn by these thorns . . . I beg you, let me free myself.'

The man behind her snarled: 'Serves 'ee right. Bowing down to the devil in the night time, you deserve a scourging.'

A lantern bobbed closer and the deeper voice spoke. 'Damn

it, just the one taken? There were twenty others. What's the matter with you men? Couldn't you have snared a few more?'

Others were gathering behind the speaker, mumbling excuses. She could see the light reflecting on three or four pale faces, teeth and eyes glinting against the blackness of night. Her knees felt weak; where had all her friends gone? Had they indeed managed to get away from these murderers or thieves or whatever they were? She did hope so, for their sakes. At least these men in their big boots were trampling down the brambles. She lifted one of her own feet and managed to extricate it from the clinging stems, then the other. Her arms were still pinioned though, and her hands were growing numb. She trembled uncontrollably, whatever was to become of her?

The reek hit her first as she was pushed into what folks called the blind house. Damp, mould, darkness she could cope with, but the smell of putrefaction, of some small creature rotting away and befouling the air, made her throat close up and her stomach heave. And behind it lay the tang of stale urine, and probably worse. Sarah resolved to stay on her feet until daybreak; she dared not sit on the floor of the lock up, her clothes and skin would be sure to come into contact with something loathsome if she did. The stout oak door had been shoved shut behind her, the bolts slid into place, the men's voices had died away; she was alone in the dark.

The only aperture in the tiny cell, apart from the door, was a window far above her head, too small for an adult to climb through, even if they could reach it from inside. Neither moon nor sun would shine through it as it faced north, but at least the moonlight tonight was bright enough that the glow was reflected down into her prison, and she would be able to judge when dawn finally broke.

She rubbed her chafed wrists. The bonds had broken her skin, but at least they'd been removed now, and she could work some life back into her hands. She felt for the cloth bag of raspberries; they would probably be crushed, but there might be some fit to nibble. Then she remembered: one of the men had snatched it from her, perhaps thinking it contained money. Who the villains were that had seized her, she had no idea. At first she'd feared they meant to rob or kill her, but it was soon evident that they were supposedly acting in the name of the law, although on what grounds they'd not said. It was, she thought, probably a good sign that she was on her own in the blind house, it suggested that no one else had been captured but her. She reflected back on the minister's warnings about secrecy; he had said that the reason they met at Roddenbury and at night was to avoid observation; that the congregation was to tell no one of their gathering or the identity of the speaker. She stamped her feet; the summer night had been mild, but in this stone box the air was very chill. It was clearly imperative that she reveal nothing to the authorities about the purpose of the gathering, who was there, who their leader was or what had been said or done. She assumed they had fallen foul of the new law, but she would not incriminate others or, she hoped, herself, if she could avoid it. She made her mind up to be patient; she would use the time in prayer for others. But what she would give for a hot cup of peppermint tea!

Birdsong was the first indication that daybreak was near. First one then dozens of shrill calls reverberated around the churchyard. She could just picture the little things hunting for food, warming their bodies ready for the day, sitting on the twigs and boughs of the copper beech, singing their hearts out. At last, the opening in the roof paled a little: dawn was coming.

A scuffling above her head attracted her attention. A low voice called her name. She replied, and a moment later a small package dropped from the unglazed hole in the roof. Luckily she caught it as it fell and, unwrapping it, found bread and cheese. She called her thanks and a voice responded: 'Be of good cheer. We are all praying for you, Sarah.'

By mid-morning the town was thronged for market day and Sarah was hurried through Anchor Barton's narrow alleys and down to the top of Market Place, the parish constables each gripping one of her arms, her hands again bound behind her. People she recognised stopped and stared; she was well known in the town and she felt like curling up like a hedgehog to hide from the shame. They turned into Hill Lane and almost immediately up the step into an imposing three storey property on the left. Sarah's eyes took a while to adjust to the gloom of the interior; the dark wood panelling seemed to render the entrance hall as dark as the pit after the summer sunshine outside, and she bumped against an awkwardly placed table. The constables' hands kept her from falling and propelled her into a parlour whose stone mullioned windows overlooked a garden. An oak table had been positioned before the window and two gentlemen sat behind it, their backs to the light. On the table lay her cloth bag, stained with patches of raspberry juice, and various papers and books. The younger man wore a rich green coat and had a full head of curling dark hair: she recognised him as the justice of the peace, James Baily. The other man, his hair greying at the temples, continued his animated discussion with the magistrate, and took no notice of her arrival in the room: she knew him to be the new vicar of St John's, Dr Glanvill. At a sign from Baily the constables released their grip and stood aside. Sarah looked about the room; the only other person present was an unsavoury looking fellow who stood with his back to the door, presumably to guard against her escape. She didn't know him and had no wish to make his acquaintance. Her gaze travelled up to the beautifully adorned ceiling: it was as though an artist had created a garden of rosebuds and trelliswork up there.

'Your name?' Baily had fixed her with a piercing glare.

'Sarah Dymock, sir.' Bringing her attention back to the present, she reminded herself that she had decided to give no information to these men, and would deny all knowledge of the night's events.

'What were you doing at Roddenbury last night, Mistress Dymock?'

Sarah shook her head.

'It would be best for you to tell us all. We'll have it out of you one way or another, so I advise you to speak now. What were you doing there?'

She pressed her lips together and looked out at the garden though what flowers bloomed there she could not afterwards have said.

'Who was there with you in the crowd?' His voice was becoming more strident.

Sarah breathed hard.

'Who was the man at the centre?'

There was no sound in the room. She could see he was losing his temper, but his next question came out as gently as a turtledove.

'And what was the purpose of these leaves and fruits in this bag, taken from you by the constable?'

Sarah couldn't help her look of surprise – what was their

interest in her wild raspberries? But again she held her tongue.

The vicar spoke next:       'Examine her for marks of the devil. If any are found she should be swum three times in the river.'

Sarah's heart seemed to stop. She stared at the two men in disbelief: witchcraft? Was that what they suspected?

'Begging yer pardon, sir.' One of the constables had stepped forward. 'There's more evidence. We found crumbs in the lockup this morn. She'd conjured bread from the air, or magicked the birds to bring it to her. Her certainly had none when she were put in there.'

Glanvill nodded at the magistrate then turned back to her. 'What do you say to all of this, mistress?' he barked.

Sarah lifted her chin and stared at the vicar as fiercely as she could, even though her heart was now racing with apprehension.

'Mute, eh?' Baily nodded to Dr Glanvill. 'You may have her searched.'

Glanvill's eyes lit up.

'If you find the devil's mark on her, or if she doesn't sink when thrown in the river, I will remand her to Ilchester gaol to await the next Taunton assizes.' Baily shrugged and turned to the constables: 'Dr Glanvill has expressed concern at the growth of witchcraft hereabouts. He wants access to this creature for his researches until such time as she's examined, so I place her in his custody for the time being.' He motioned with his hand. 'Take her away.'


His father's urgent summons had brought John back to Frome from Devizes that same Wednesday, but it was past noon when he reached the cottage on Keyford, to find the tiny place in uproar. Members of the chapel were coming and going, seeking or recounting news of the previous night's events. Sarah's normally tidy home was a shambles, chairs and stools askew, the fire out, and Gideon was trying to act the host in her absence, although his mind was elsewhere.

His father clasped John with evident relief when he saw him, and steered him to a chair beside the cold hearth. 'Let me tell you what's happened,' he whispered, as he passed his hand through his greying hair leaving tufts standing upright. 'Our meeting with Dr Humfry up at Roddenbury was broken up by the authorities. Whether they had spies out or we were betrayed, I don't know. Fortunately they were poorly organised, it was pitch dark, and our people knew the ground. We all scattered and fled by myriad paths, but no one was sure who had been taken, apart from Sarah. This morning we've been able to confirm that she's the only person they seized. I'm terribly worried for her, she's an old woman, she shouldn't be persecuted like this.'

'And our friend Dr Humfry – has he been able to leave the area?'

'Aye, a reliable man escorted him to Rode in the early hours. He'll be able to travel safely to Bath then London from there.'

'And what of Sarah?'

'She was held in the blind house cell overnight. I took some victuals to her this morning early. Since then, she's been hauled before the magistrate.'

'Do you fear she will reveal Dr Humfry's presence?'

'Who knows what any of us would say under pressure.' Gideon rubbed his eyes; a night without sleep had left them red and puffy. 'I think she'll do her utmost to keep the secret, but I dread to think what they may do to her if she resists.'

'We need to speak with whoever is holding her now, whether the justice of the peace, or the constables. She's quite frail; she can't be subjected to such treatment.'

'I know,' Gideon replied. 'I keep thinking she is bearing all this for the congregation, it isn't fair on her at all. And I ran from the scene myself, like a coward, without stopping to aid her. I shall go and offer myself in her place; she's not the one they're after.'

John studied his father's face. 'That's very principled. I applaud your decision, but have a care. *You* will be accused of involvement yourself.'

'I am aware of that. But Sarah's release is far more important. Let us go and confront this so called gentleman immediately.'

'No, wait, he'll be dining right now. Leave it an hour; our embassy may be better received then.'

Gideon nodded his assent, then took his son by the arm, steering him out of the back door and past the earth privy, then down to the rhubarb patch at the end of Sarah's garden. He turned and looked at John directly. 'I've had sleepless nights since Sunday, thinking about your dilemma. I want to take this opportunity to talk with you now. Who knows what may happen once we go down to try to rescue Sarah. This may be our only chance to talk privately.'

He pulled his son down to sit on the plank bench.

'John, this revelation of yours has not altogether surprised me. In a way, I suppose I was aware that your leanings have not been in the same direction as those of most young men. I observed over the years that you were not greatly drawn towards women. Perhaps I hoped that your upbringing, your reading of the good book, had brought you to a sense that lust, dalliance, the hot behaviour of most youths, was immoral and unsuited to a serious-minded son of a minister. I believe I counted our family fortunate in that.' Gideon smiled wryly then rubbed his hands over his cheeks. 'Maybe I should have enquired further at the time into your personal inclinations, but this was not a subject that either of us would have been comfortable discussing in the past.'

John shook his head. 'I wouldn't have had any wish to discuss it then. Indeed I didn't know at that time just what I did feel, or that it was so different from most men's inclinations. I just knew I had no wish to replicate the behaviour of the young men I saw in town, trying to seduce the girls, paying low women, or even simply flirting with the better sort.'

'What you choose *not* to do with the female of our species is entirely up to you. The Bible would encourage us to marry and raise families, but clearly that isn't for everyone. Scholars, hermits, some of our own church leaders choose not to follow that path. But you have suggested to me that you are drawn to a more active involvement with other men. Do I understand that correctly?'

'Indeed, I acknowledge that I have sensed a strong attraction to certain men. I emphasise, however, that I have not pursued this by word or deed.'

'That is a relief to me, John. Such actions, as you are well aware, would be entirely contrary to God's word and I pray fervently that you will always have the strength to resist such a course. Notwithstanding the actions of the nobility in this regard, for common men such as us, the law also sets its face very firmly against congress between two persons of the same gender. The ultimate penalty would be demanded.'

'I am aware of that, father. I would not risk it, nor the opprobrium it would bring down on our family and the chapel. No, I am resigned to a celibate existence, and that I should endeavour to hide my feelings for any unfortunate man who should become the object of my desire.'

'Difficult as it will be for you, I think that is the wisest course, my son. And it would be worse than hypocrisy for you to seek to disguise your nature by feigning an attraction and perhaps a marriage with a young woman whom you could never truly love. That would be a hideous thing to do.'

'I'm glad you think that, I was afraid you might feel the opposite and try to push me towards such a travesty.'

'So be it. I will pray that you receive God's guidance. Now let us go and speak with this magistrate.'

Time seemed to be drawn out like a thread of wool on a spinning wheel, growing thinner and longer as the outside world ran on, while inside nothing moved in the dark panelled hallway of James Baily's Hill Lane mansion. As John fidgeted, the carved back of his chair chafed his spine; a seat designed expressly for the discomfort of visitors, he felt. His father was bending forwards, his head in his hands, either in prayer, meditation, or perhaps to avoid contact with the vindictive chair. He felt sure that Baily was in the house and was deliberately keeping them waiting; a brief conversation, muffled by the stone walls, had reached his ears some while back, but it could have been merely the servants talking.

Just as he had hit on a suitable topic for profitable contemplation – the schedule of tools and materials to be taken to the colony – a door into the hall opened and the magistrate emerged, his face revealing his irritation.

'Damn me, I'd forgotten you were waiting. What can I do for you?'

The Silcoxes rose, hats in hand, and introduced themselves.

'It is in connection with a woman you are holding in confinement, sir. An elderly member of my congregation,'

Gideon said.

'Sarah Dymock? What of her?'

'We come to plead for her release on the grounds of common humanity. She is frail, and rough treatment could be the undoing of her.'

John nodded in silent corroboration.

'I offer to take her place in custody,' Gideon said.

Baily looked startled. 'You, sir? But what involvement do you, a puritan minister if I am not mistaken, have in matters of the dark arts?'

'The dark arts!' Gideon was clearly struggling to master his shock. 'Sir, this is a devout, God fearing, respectable woman. I can vouch for her honesty. Indeed, as I lodge at her home, I am privy to all her good works and respectable way of life.'

'So just what was she doing on Roddenbury Hill, chanting and bowing down to a tall man dressed in black on Tuesday night?'

Gideon drew himself up to his full height. 'We were holding a religious meeting, listening to the word of God, not the devil!'

John glanced at his father: had he been provoked into saying more than he should, or was he deliberately making a statement of his commitment? The magistrate's eyes reflected the consideration he was giving to the minister's declaration.

'And would it have been your intention to keep this meeting from the attention of the authorities in order to hide the identity of your preacher, by any chance? And would your preacher have been a known Calvinist and seditious rabble rouser by the name of Humfry?' Baily turned away before Gideon could respond. 'I thought Glanvill's tale of witchcraft too far-fetched. Treason is the real threat, not old women with bags of leaves.' He swung back to the Silcoxes. 'Give me a full and honest statement of the event, who was there and your involvement, and I'll release the old woman. You will be investigated, however, and may face some very serious charges.'

# CHAPTER 8

'I CAN UNDERSTAND your annoyance, sir.' James Baily smiled ruefully at his friend the Reverend Dr Joseph Glanvill, as the smell of coffee permeated the air of the vicarage parlour. 'But to be quite candid, in this day and age, we in the law do not give the same credence to tales of witchcraft and devil worship as was the case a generation ago.' He stilled the expected interruption with a gesture of his hand. 'I have lately received instructions from London: charges of witchcraft are discouraged. This case against the woman Sarah Dymock would be dismissed at the assizes, there's no argument about it. I'm afraid the Church will have to acknowledge that the political climate has shifted and it too must move into the modern era.'

'Modern era be damned!' Joseph Glanvill rose to his feet so rapidly he overturned the oak chair on which he had been sitting. It crashed onto the highly polished floorboards. 'I hoped to glean valuable details for my studies from that old woman. Another day or two and I could have broken her – I'm sure she has had knowledge of all kinds of devilry, charms, familiars . . . I would have extracted far more from her. But you couldn't resist the pressure of that puritan, Silcox. I'm astonished at you, sir.' He righted his chair and resumed his seat.

James Baily sipped from his cup. His friend had done well to introduce the pleasures of coffee drinking to Frome, but in other matters he was living in the Dark Ages. 'It was an open and shut case, my dear sir. The minister confessed that the purpose of the gathering was not witchcraft but illegal preaching, thereby implicating himself but exonerating the old woman from charges of devil worship. I will investigate the offence he has admitted in my own time, the culprits won't be going anywhere after the bail bonds I have taken, but these medieval charges you would have me lay are preposterous. I now regret my initial enthusiasm for the prosecution of the old woman. I'd have been the laughing stock of Taunton had it come before the court.'

Dr Glanvill's expression was not that of a mollified man. 'I find this so frustrating. My treatise - I shall subtitle it *The Full and Plain Evidence Concerning Witches and Apparitions* – would have been enhanced by her confessions, detailed examples of such devilry are crucial.'

'Yes, and so titillating! Fear not, I am sure your work will find a ready audience without Mistress Dymock's additions. They would probably have been fictitious anyway, made up just to appease your demands, to stop you torturing her.'

'Torturing her? My friend, I would have been torturing the devil, saving her soul in the process.'

Baily snorted. 'I doubt the value of any confession given under torture. But at least the incident has revealed the activities of these dissenters: bringing that fellow Dr Humfry back to Frome to preach, indeed. We shall put a stop to that at any rate.' He drained his cup. 'Thank you for that delicious beverage. I regret I must leave you, I have an appointment with one of the manufacturers who, as you previously suggested, may be interested in investing in my building project.'

'Ah, and who might that be?'

'Walter Singer. Resides out at Egford, on the way to Mells.

Do you know him? At least he's not one of these dissenters, even if his wealth comes from the wool trade. I must be on my way. Could you call for my horse?'

The views west always struck a chord with James Baily whenever he rode out of town towards Mells or Buckland Denham. The rich pastureland rolling away below him; the darkness of Selwood bordering the horizon to his left; the pattern of enclosed arable and meadowland spreading away to the right and round behind him to the distant chalk scarp above Westbury: it was a magnificent rural vista. He thanked God for returning it to its rightful rulers, the king and the nobility. His father had fought in the king's cause, had been heavily fined by parliament, and lost most of his wealth; the family had been relieved that the new king had seen fit to restore most of their lands to them. But although he might be rich in terms of his landholding, he was embarrassingly short of ready money, and it was this predicament that had driven him to exercise his imagination in seeking ways to augment his fortune. After his family's losses in the wars, he had a deeply held aversion to selling off any of his estates; he would prefer to fill his coffers through new commercial projects, however much the aristocracy might despise such methods. And of course, his personal pleasures had been a drain on his resources over the years. He kicked his horse on in a futile effort to distance himself from that thought. Gambling, women, drink, all had proved a bottomless chasm swallowing up his modest income.

He watched as smoke rose from the limekilns in Vallis Vale below him. He had devised a scheme that would bring him financial advantage from the new challenges that faced the industrialising town: its increasing need for wage labourers, the rising population, the demand for housing, and the availability of building materials. If he could attract an investor and acquire suitable land, he was certain that big profits could be made by someone with his acumen and drive.

The magistrate returned to his Hill Lane residence in time for the midday dinner and delighted with the outcome of his visit to the wool merchant, Singer. The fellow had said he was honoured by his visit, and thrilled at the invitation to invest in the development project. Baily had already calculated exactly how much he would need from him, and the lowest rate of return he would offer, and Singer had not demurred at either. The merchant said he was only too pleased to invest in such tangible assets, he'd been anxious about the safety of the coin he was amassing in his treasure chests and was looking for a suitable investment. What splendid timing! The magistrate had to admit he was a little taken aback by the wealth that seemed to be being generated by manufacturing; it might be an area for him to investigate in the future. He flung himself into one of the cushioned chairs his wife had introduced into their parlour and called for a glass of wine. His next step would be the acquisition of land, and it might not be so easy to lay his hands on the most suitable site, one that was close to the town centre, on reasonably level ground, and at an attractive price.

Over the following week, James Baily rode about the town, a notebook and black lead pencil in his saddlebag, reviewing the location, aspect and ownership of the surrounding land. Some, as at Wallbridge and Rodden, was clearly liable to flooding whenever the river rose. Other areas were still held as open fields under the old agricultural system: tiny strips worked by families who had held them for centuries. And being Frome, some areas were steeply sloping and would present problems or at least incur additional costs for a builder. There was however one particular district to which he kept returning. It lay to the west of the town, alongside the old track to Vallis. The southern portion was relatively level, accessible, and above any risk of flooding. To the north and west there was pastureland or rough ground given over to the growing of teasels and woad for the woollen industry, but the exact site he had in mind was at present laid out as enclosed fields divided by tracks and hedges into neat rectangles. And it was, he knew, all held by a single landowner, the lord of the manor of St Catherine's Richard Yerbury, a man said to be living in very reduced circumstances in spite of his title.

Back in the comfort of his study, he pondered his next step. The loan he had negotiated with Singer would be sufficient for the outright purchase of the land, but was ownership actually necessary? If he could persuade Yerbury to lease the property to him, he could then use Singer's finance to purchase materials and engage craftsmen and masons to construct dwellings. Given the demand for housing in the town, it would be no trouble to find tenants for these and he would then have a steady income from the rents they paid him, his only outgoings being the interest to Singer and the ground rent to Yerbury. He rubbed his hands together. Granted he would never actually own the land or houses, after the term of the lease each would revert to the freeholder, but that would be long after his demise.

Baily sharpened a fresh quill with his penknife, dipped it and jotted a few figures on a crisp sheet of paper. Costs could be kept to a minimum by building the houses as terraces with uniform width frontages and to a consistent height; materials could be sourced locally – forest marble, timber, lime for mortar and plaster; craftsmen and a supervisor for the works could be brought in from Trowbridge or Westbury if none suitable were available in Frome. He tapped his teeth with the quill, sat back and sighed contentedly. This was a very promising scheme. The question arose as to why no one else had thought of such an undertaking. He raised his eyes to the window of his study. Through the misting of raindrops he saw Joshua Whittock striding purposefully down the street, the shoulders of his coat dark with rain. Perhaps others had had a similar notion. A number of houses had indeed been built recently along the north east side of the road toward Vallis. He didn't like the idea of competition for the scheme, nor would he want any opposition to his plan from the local gentry. An intimidating presence such as Joshua's would be useful in ensuring the smooth running of the venture, as he himself had suggested. He'd used the man a couple of times already, securing the custody of felons, obtaining information, reminding some of his associates of his authority. Whittock was proving to be an astute fellow – Baily found this surprising in a man of such lowly birth. If he demonstrated loyalty to the magistrate, Baily would entrust more controversial work to the man, in spite of his uncouth manners and speech.

The rain had stopped the following morning as Baily and Joshua rode out of Badcox together.

'See these new cottages?' Baily waved his riding crop towards the recently built two storey terrace overlooking the track to Vallis. 'My aim is to build scores of these simple dwellings, some facing onto that path running down to St Catherine's manor house,' he pointed to his right, 'Long Row they call it, and many more on this pasture behind, with a grid of streets to make efficient use of the space. As many as I can finance.'

Joshua was nodding. 'A brave scheme, sir. A big investment.'

'Aye, and big returns, I trust.'

They turned their horses' heads and trotted along the rutted track of Long Row, muddy water splashing under the hoofs. To their right, the roofscape of Frome muddled its way behind Badcox and down to Catherine Hill; to their left the enclosed fields billowed away to the open country, the ridge and furrow of medieval plough land still evident beneath the sheep-bitten turf. A hundred paces northwest, a hedgerow marked the furthest boundary of the field of New Close, and a similar distance to the east another indicated the start of neighbouring Mill Close.

'Both these enclosures would be ideal for building; reasonably flat, well away from flooding; easy access to places of employment at Spring Gardens and Welsh Mill.' Baily could barely restrain his enthusiasm.

They were approaching a large property, clearly the residence of a gentleman, but a house whose origins were lost beneath the accretion of centuries of extensions and adaptations.

'St Catherine's Manor,' Baily said. 'Home of the lord of the manor, or one of his homes at any rate. He's rarely here I'm told. The Yerburys own the land we've been looking at. He's the man I need to persuade.' He paused. 'One way or another.'

A thin skein of smoke rose from the house's tall chimneys. Baily stood in his stirrups to look over the crumbling garden wall. The wooden shutters behind the windows of one of the ground floor rooms had been drawn back: it appeared Yerbury might be in residence. 'No time like the present,' he muttered, then turning to Joshua, 'No need for you to open your mouth. Just scowl and look threatening. Here, tether the horses.'

Baily dismounted and handed his reins to Joshua, marched up to the front door and hammered on the peeling paintwork. The door was opened a hand's width by a frowsty-looking woman, her apron stained with brown patches, her shawl threadbare.

'I have business with Master Yerbury. Is he at home?'

There was no response from the servant.

'Can he see me immediately?' Baily's voice had risen.

'I shall ask the master,' she finally muttered, and started to push the door closed. Joshua put his hand out and forced it wide open, smiling at the woman, a hard glint in his eye as he did so.

'Tell him it would be to his advantage and that I will take up very little of his time,' Baily called after her as she hurried off.

The small coal fire that burned in an iron grate gave more smoke than heat to the drab parlour into which the two men were shown. The master of the house, stooped and dishevelled in appearance, shook their hands and inquired their business, peering at them short-sightedly. 'You'd better not be seeking payment of any debts. I've not incurred any for many years, I just live in a very small way.'

'Indeed, no sir. I come to put a business proposition to you, which may well bring you financial returns,' Baily said.

Richard Yerbury looked warily at Joshua. 'Financial returns, eh? I trust this isn't some deceit or stratagem you're trying on me?'

Baily saw Joshua glance behind him at the partly open door, then slam it shut. A muffled shriek came from the hallway.

'Let me lay my proposal before you, sir.' Baily's voice was now sickly sweet. 'I understand you own the pastures, New Close and Mill Close?' He glanced up, interrogatively.

'Yes, the enclosures were bought as part of the manor by my ancestor, John Yerbury, in the third year of the reign of the present king's grandfather.'

James Baily straightened his shoulders. His family's antecedents were as proud as those of Yerbury, he felt sure. 'Quite. I imagine some farmer rents them from you as a sheep run?'

'Aye. The ground's not fit for arable. Stony, poor soil, though it drains well. What of it?'

'I'd be interested in leasing the land from you. I want to develop it with houses. There'd be no outlay for you, but you'd receive the ground rent – a significantly bigger return than you presently take, I'm sure.'

'Houses? But that would alter the place hugely! What view would I have from my windows?' He gestured towards the grimy panes. 'My fields all built over? Folk going to and fro, past my door? I think not, sir!'

Baily fought down his instinctive response, and twisted his features into a kindly smile. 'My dear sir, think of the income you would receive without any risk or effort on your own part. It could be as much as' - he paused, calculating rapidly - 'ten guineas a year.'

'But the noise, the dirt, the disruption!'

'Perhaps you could remove to one of your other properties while the work is undertaken? And once the dwellings are completed and occupied, you would see an increase in that ground rent I mentioned.'

'Well I don't know. Come, sit down.'

He led the way to a heavy oak table, swept a pile of papers

aside and took a seat, pointing his visitors to two others. Joshua held his hat in his hands, scowling determinedly at Yerbury from beneath his brows. Baily's pulse was beating faster: it looked as though his proposals might be well received. Yerbury's eyes now held a spark, he seemed to be engaging with the project; Baily could almost hear the rusty cogs turning in the old man's brain.

'Set out your terms precisely, Master Baily.' Yerbury's forehead was creased as he concentrated. 'What do you want and what do you offer me?'

'Give me leases to build on those two fields. A year's lease for a parcel of land at a time, each parcel will be divided into a number of plots. It will take some years to complete all the dwellings, best to do it a block at a time.'

Yerbury's 'Yes . . .' was long drawn out.

Baily began to realise that the old man had a sharp mind beneath his unprepossessing exterior.

'If a plot isn't built on in the year, you'd need the lease extended. I'd be willing to do that for a fee. A guinea I think.'

Baily looked up sharply.

'And three shillings for the year's ground rent per plot.'

Baily slammed his fist on the table. 'Two shillings is my offer.'

The two locked eyes. Yerbury smiled. 'Half a crown,' he growled.

'Don't forget, I'm taking all the risks on this investment, all the work of organising it. You're getting guaranteed rents for no labour at all.'

Yerbury laughed. 'And once the dwellings are completed, we'll renegotiate the leases. I'd suggest 99 years or three lives, whichever is the shorter, in the traditional way, and as the last life falls in, the property reverts to me – or my heirs – both land

and buildings.'

'I must insist on certain guarantees, Master Yerbury. Firstly, that you give me the absolute right to take all the land on lease, with no other developer pre-empting me?'

Yerbury nodded.

'And secondly, that you guarantee to grant me the new lease on each completed dwelling, to sub-let or occupy each as I see fit, with no restriction on tenant or rent?'

'Yes, I'll leave all that in your hands, subject to agreement on the ground rent that comes to me in each case. I can tell you that I will be looking for a significant return there.'

Baily blinked. It looked as though he had secured his plan, but he took his hat off to Yerbury: the old fellow had surprised him.

Their host had opened the parlour door. 'Woman, wine for our guests,' he quavered then returned to his seat. 'Gentlemen, a toast to a good day's business.'


Baily sat down in his study and indicated a seat to Joshua. A stack of papers on his desk was topped by a handbill from the magistrates at Warminster, regarding the disappearance and suspected murder of two of His Majesty's excise officers, just over the Wiltshire border. He moved the pile aside.

It was one thing to drink in the snug of the Angel with the vicar, but Baily didn't want to be seen enjoying a convivial glass in public with Joshua. And he needed privacy while he set out what he required of this man in the coming months – who knew what ears were flapping in a tavern, as Joshua himself had recently demonstrated. He had caught the sound of female voices coming from the parlour as he entered his home; his wife was doubtless entertaining her friends over the new tea table.

It seemed her extravagant tastes for such fashionable things as porcelain tea dishes and silver kettles and teapots would never be satisfied. His household finances seemed to be entirely beyond his control; he badly needed this development scheme to go well.

The maidservant brought pewter tankards of strong beer to the two men. Joshua clearly appreciated its quality as he licked his lips after the first draught. 'A smoky flavour, sir. Not one I've tasted hereabouts a'fore now.'

'It's a Welsh brew. I have a taste for it and have it delivered specially from Bristol from time to time. It keeps well. They supply it in glass bottles.'

'Must be the devil to transport safely!'

Baily laughed. 'Now, I want to engage you for some tasks in connection with this building work. Are you willing, if we can agree terms?'

Joshua nodded slowly. 'How would you propose to pay me for my time, sir? I too have many business enterprises underway and would have to engage other men to supervise those, if I am to work for you.'

'Naturally.'

A burst of feminine laughter came from a nearby room and Baily scowled briefly.

'I could offer you a percentage of the profits of the scheme?'

Joshua pursed his lips and frowned. 'If you've no objection, sir, I think I'd prefer to be paid an hourly rate. It would better reflect the varying time I'd put in, not to mention that it'll be a long while till you see any returns, with the best luck in the world.'

'Very well.' He shrugged. 'Let me have a note of your time at the end of each month.' He rose and opened the casement window; its diamond panes flashed as they caught the sunlight. 'It's clearing up nicely, should be a fine afternoon.' He observed a young woman hurrying down Hill Lane, her dark curls tousled by the breeze, and smiled to himself. He resumed his seat as Joshua drained his tankard.

'Your immediate task is to find out for me who built those new cottages along Vallis Way. They've only been there a year or two. The developer may have ideas about extending further. Ask the people living there what leases they have and with whom. I want to know who I've got to keep an eye on.'

Joshua looked up, his expression alert.

'And find out who the mason was that worked on them, and if his work is well respected; he may have contacts among other reliable craftsmen. I have to admit I know little about these practicalities; we must judge these people by their previous work and reputation, and ensure their future commitment. Financial rewards will have their place: punishment for failings might also be implied.'

A smile passed across Joshua's face.

# CHAPTER 9

THE BREEZE HAD tugged her cap loose, the ribbons were no longer holding it on her head and her hair was flying everywhere, but Molly-Ann's hands were full and there was nothing she could do to tie it back in place. She would just have to put up with being a source of amusement to the passers-by in Hill Lane, and laugh it off. In one hand she carried a freshly baked cake wrapped in a linen cloth, rich with butter, lemon and currants; in the other hand a basket packed with fruit, vegetables, and even a small pot of honey. Betty Grimwade had loaded the basket generously and encouraged her friends to donate items as well, and now it was Molly-Ann's job to deliver the gift. The older inhabitants of the town knew Sarah well, and loved her for her kindness and practical help in their times of trouble. Hearing about her mistreatment at the hands of the magistrate, they had rallied round to show their support. Molly-Ann fitted the last item – a punnet of raspberries from a widow at Conigar – into the basket, tied the ribbons of her cap with a double bow, and set off up the hill towards Keyford.

In Sarah's cottage she found the elderly woman wrapped in a shawl sitting beside the hearth, where a split log was burning slowly and giving out a pleasant smoky apple smell. The afternoon sunlight picked out the lively orange and yellow of a pot of marigolds on her window ledge.

'I'm glad to see you, my dear.' Sarah's smile crinkled the

corners of her eyes as she admired the basket of provisions.

'What can I do for you?' Molly-Ann asked. 'Do you need any firing brought in, or any errands run?'

'Could you just make me an infusion with some sage leaves?' she pointed to a jar on the dresser shelf. 'It's perfect for anxiety and upset such as I've had. I couldn't ask the minister to make it for me, kind as he's been!'

'Yes, all the town knows what he did to save you from those wicked men, throwing himself on their mercy in your place.' Molly-Ann swung the ancient kettle towards her, on its chain above the fire. 'He's been talked about as a real hero, offerin' himself up when he could've got away with it, not that I understand what it is they say he's done so wrong.' She poured hot water carefully over the dried leaves and set it to stand.

'We don't believe it was wrong: listening to a righteous man explaining the word of God. But them in charge has changed all the laws and seems it's against the king to gather and praise God in our way.' Sarah closed her eyes. 'I can't talk about it anymore. It's all made me feel my age. I just want to sleep.'

Molly-Ann picked up the wrinkled hand and gently soothed it, before straining the infusion and handing her a steaming cup. 'And where's the minister now? They've freed him on bail, haven't they?'

Sarah opened her eyes. 'Yes, thanks be to God. He's gone to speak with the warden of the Blue House. He hopes they might be able to offer me a room there in the almshouse. It would be easier than keeping on in this place, even with the minister here on hand. I'm not up to cooking and cleaning and foraging anymore. It's time to step aside.'

'I'll miss your fresh herbs and things, but I can understand.

I hope you gets a place.'

She unloaded the basket. 'Master Silcox is a very good man,' she said reflectively. 'He supported me in my despair, whether I was a member of your chapel or no. He always tries to make things right, rather than judge people. And he doesn't care what it costs him – look how he's given himself up in your stead. He's a man in a thousand.'

Sarah nodded and sipped her drink. 'It is a shame he's so lonely in his life. He needs a good woman to make him whole again.'

Molly-Ann watched thoughtfully as the smoke curled from the apple logs. Much as I admire him, she thought, I'm not the right woman for him. I'm not the right sort at all. He deserves a truly religious woman, someone on his own level. He'd despise my common ways. And I do love him, but as I would a father. No, I'd want a man with more red blood in him, someone to excite me, someone I'd desire, rather than admire.

She walked the long way back to the Boar as the afternoon ended, through the flax fields on Locks Lane, down to Wallbridge and, skirting the muddy patches, along the path through Rodden Meadow into Pilly Vale. She wanted time and space to think, to remember her afternoon with Joshua here in the very same meadow, a week ago. She wondered why it had been so long without a further meeting. Had she said or done the wrong thing? Maybe he thought her too foolish, or too serious. Perhaps she had upset him in some way. Surely not; he'd spoken of nothing more than town gossip, the relative merits of the taverns, acquaintances they had in common. Perhaps she'd appeared lukewarm, maybe she should have been more forthright? She swiped the stick she'd picked up against a cow parsley seed head; the brown seeds scattered to the winds.

She'd not learned a lot about him from their conversation, he kept both his past and present rather secretive. Apart from his lodgings, his horse, and the fact that he was in business on his own account and had little free time, she hadn't been able to extract much from him. The hints dropped by her brothers had warned her not to press Joshua on his business enterprises, and she found it very difficult to judge his financial worth, or his social position.

Her physical response to him had, however, been much clearer to her, and she had striven to conceal this from him during their walk by the river. It had seemed as if her skin tingled when he took her hand to help her over a fallen branch. She had found herself drawn to walk or to sit very close beside him, even while her brain was telling her that it was not the wisest thing to do.

The noise and smells of Pilly Vale enveloped her. The mill leat was running a strangely blue colour, presumably tinted by the scourings of one of the dyers' vats. She turned across the town bridge and jumped as she almost collided with the object of her recent thoughts. Joshua looked as startled as she felt, but instantly his grey eyes took on a fierce warmth as he raised his hat and nodded to her.

'Good day to 'ee mistress. I'd been thinking of you, and here you be, like magic.'

Molly-Ann felt her throat tighten, horribly aware that she might say something that she'd immediately regret. 'I've just been thinking of you too, and the lovely afternoon we spent by the riverside.' She hesitated. Might he think she was pressing for another meeting?

'I hoped very much to see you,' he said. 'I thought we might visit Nunney Fair together – it's next Saturday. Would you be happy to ride on my horse if I lead her?'

Molly-Ann's pulse was throbbing in her ears – the fair, and in Joshua's company, and to go by horseback! Throwing discretion to the winds, she smiled broadly. 'I'd love to go, thank 'ee!'

The notes of drum and flute reached them on the breeze as soon as they left the highway at the hamlet of Ridgeway, to descend the last mile into Nunney. Molly-Ann turned to Joshua who trudged alongside the horse, his hand grasping the reins by the bit. 'Will there be dancing? I do love to watch, or maybe even join in – or would you rather not?'

Joshua's expression was not encouraging. 'You can if you want, but I'm no dancer. I'll watch, but I'm not joining in. I'm more interested in the fights. They say there'll be singlestick and wrestling too. That's more to my taste.'

'Will you enter the contest?' Her forehead was creased with worry.

'Not today. I've got other plans.' His smile had something of the cat about it. His eyes held hers and she felt all the hairs on her arm stand on end. To be here, alongside Joshua, was what she wanted but at the same time she felt as though she was walking over a deep pool, on ice that creaked and groaned beneath her feet.

The lane led them down into the village where they found the narrow streets lined with stalls and booths selling trinkets, cloth, pottery, cakes and pies. Crowds had been attracted from Frome and the surrounding villages as well as Nunney itself, and it was difficult to do other than move in the direction of the general flow. Joshua turned into the yard of the George Inn to order stabling for the horse, and Molly-Ann was relieved to be out of the press of people for a few moments. Across the river from the church stood the castle, its four round towers roofless, one wall almost completely destroyed; the damage of twenty years ago fresh in the minds of local people, even though weeds and moss had begun to camouflage the work of parliament's army. In the meadows down Donkey Lane, an area had been marked out for the public entertainment. Here, a country dance was concluding and the umpires in charge of the wrestling matches were assembling.

Joshua took her arm and steered Molly-Ann into a gap in the front row of spectators. She could feel the warmth of his skin through the light fabric of her sleeve, and instinctively leaned a little towards him. She had not attended one of these contests before, only glimpsed such bouts from a distance in town, and was not sure what it entailed, or indeed, whether it would be to her taste, but Joshua seemed intensely interested and she would not try to dissuade him. She could feel her cheeks burning as the fighters stripped to their drawers and each then buckled on a heavy leather belt.

The blows the two contestants landed on each others' heads and chests jarred Molly-Ann's nerves as if she was being pummelled herself. The raucous shouts and whistles of the men and women around her made her ears ring, and when one of the wrestlers kicked his opponent's legs from under him, then beat his head repeatedly as he lay trapped on the ground, she closed her eyes and hid her face against Joshua's coat, trying to control her sobs. Joshua had been swinging his fists, twisting and turning as if mirroring the fight, but slowed his actions as she burrowed her head into his side, finally stopping still and putting his arms around her.

'You're shaking, Molly-Ann. Don't 'ee enjoy seeing a good fight like this?'

There seemed to be genuine surprise in his tone. Molly-

Ann wiped her hand over her eyes before looking up at him. 'Why do they do it, Josh? It fair sickens me to see the pain and the blood. Is it for the money?'

'It's a good purse.' He stroked the tendrils of hair off her face. 'But mostly it's pride in their own strength, in beating the other fellow. And it feels so good to feel your fist strike his flesh.' Joshua's own colour was up, his breath still coming fast; she could even smell the rank scent of violence he exuded. He grunted and a change came over his expression; the grey eyes looking down at her seemed to have lost their sharpness. 'I shouldn't have brought 'ee here, Molly-Ann. It's not the place for you.'

Molly-Ann ceased to hear the crowd's noise, concentrating on Joshua's words.

'I'm sorry,' he said gruffly, 'we'll go back to the food stalls.'

A pasty of mutton and turnips soon restored Molly-Ann's equilibrium, and strolling along the lines of booths she observed the number of envious or admiring glances cast towards them by other young people. Joshua was liberal with his coins she noticed, buying her the ribbons and handkerchiefs she took a fancy to, as well as a couple of butter fairings to nibble as they went along.

The afternoon grew hot, the sky cloudless and the air still. The trees along the brook offered inviting shade, and Joshua held her hand as they crossed a half-dozen stepping stones and found a dry place to sit. She didn't take her hand back as they listened to the water tumbling over the pebbles and down toward the village mill, and gradually their fingers intertwined.

Monday morning: the day for scouring the Boar's kitchen floor and the back yard. Molly-Ann threw a bucket of water sluicing across the flagstones outside and followed it up with a thorough scrubbing with her broom. Her sleeves rolled up, and her skirts tucked out of harm's way behind her coarse wrapper, she was working up a fine sweat. Betty Grimwade nodded her approval.

'Looks like you're taking yer spite out on those flags, girl! Is something eating at you?'

Molly-Ann paused and leant against the back wall for a moment. 'Nay, I'm just a bit angered at myself. Can't make my mind up.'

'Not like you, Molly-Ann. You normally sees yer way clear to what's what.'

'Not this time, mistress. It's that Joshua. I'd like to trust 'en, but I have a warnin' feeling too. Yet I'm sorely tempted.'

Betty pursed her lips. 'A badger don't change his stripes. What he *is* now, he'll allus be. It's your choice, but it's clear how close *he* comes to the wrong side of the law.' She squinted up at the sky. 'Another fine day. I wouldn't mind a month of sunshine.'

Molly-Ann resumed her scouring.

'You be careful, girl. He's got a vicious streak if he's riled.'

As if on cue, a man stepped through the side gate onto the wet paving.

'Nat!' Molly-Ann called. 'Mind yer feet, you nearly got them soaked!'

Her brother gave her a lop-sided grin. 'Sorry. Have my boots spoiled your clean yard? Thought I'd look in as I haven't seen 'ee in weeks.'

'See if you can talk sense into yer sister, Nathaniel.' Betty turned back to the kitchen. 'You knows him well enough, so 'tis said.'

'Know who?' He raised his eyebrows.

Molly-Ann took his hand and led him to a bench against the wall, out of the sun.

'Josh Whittock.'

Nathaniel's face froze. 'Don't you get mixed up with he, Molly-Ann, for pity's sake. I regret I ever heard his name, let alone worked for him. He's got our Ben in thrall, lad acts like that man's God A'mighty. Don't 'ee have anything at all to do with him, please.' He looked into his sister's face. 'Oh God, it's too late isn't it?'

'I do love 'en so, Nat,' Molly-Ann whispered. 'He's been a real gentleman so far, been treating me more delicate than any man afore.'

Her mind was back on the road home from Nunney, riding in front of Joshua, his arm securely around her, as dusk fell and the moon rose over Cley Hill; she'd felt like all the flowers in the roadside verges were singing for her. Folk said what a hard man he was, but they'd not seen the Joshua she knew now.

'Molly-Ann! He's the wickedest man I've come across. He's led our Ben astray and I don't want you to go same way. Please, for my sake as well as yours, think again.' He shook her arm. 'Please?'

'I shall think about 'en.' She knew that was no lie. 'But I'm four and twenty years old now. I need to find a husband, and one with some wealth and standing would please me well. You look to your own affairs, brother, and keep out of mine.'

'Listen, you talk to that minister, Master Silcox. He's allus been a kind friend to 'ee. Hark to his advice if you won't heed me.'

'Sir! Master Silcox, sir!' Molly-Ann pushed against the heavy oak door to the schoolroom beside the churchyard, and peered into the quiet room late the following day. The north facing windows were glazed with thick greenish glass, formed into little diamond shaped panes and set in a lead work frame. A shiver passed through her as she stepped over the threshold. The smell of unwashed children's bodies lingered on the air.

A head with two bright eyes popped up from behind the master's desk. 'Billy!' Molly-Ann's surprise was clear in her voice. 'Are you here to study? Where is everyone? Where's Master Silcox?'

'They've all finished and gone home, mistress. I stay on to sweep floor, empty rubbish, sharpen 'is pens. 'Ee lets me listen to class for free and pick up what I can.'

'And where can I find him now? Has he gone home?'

'Nay, he'll be back in two shakes to lock up.'

As Billy spoke, the door opened fully to admit the minister, a bunch of carrots in one hand and a bundle of candles in the other. 'Pupils paying in kind, as you see, Molly-Ann. Eh, we all have to eat, I suppose.' He smiled at Billy. 'All done lad? You be off now, then.'

'Forgive me for intruding, sir,' Molly-Ann said, 'but I came to ask your advice. Might I speak with you please?'

Billy pulled the door shut behind himself as he left.

Gideon Silcox indicated the form on which the children would normally be seated. 'I'm afraid it's not very comfortable, but please join me. I am always at your service, my dear.'

Molly-Ann looked up at him as she took a seat. His expression as ever was one of kindly attention, but there seemed to be more sadness in his eyes than she usually saw, and the skin below them certainly appeared more puffy than normal.

'Sir, I shouldn't be worrying you with my concerns when you may have greater troubles of your own. Please forget I was here.'

She started to rise from the bench but Gideon put out a hand to stay her. 'Don't go. A talk with you may do much to clear my own mind.'

Molly-Ann frowned.

'Please tell me first how I can help you,' he said.

'It was my brother Nat said to speak with you, sir.'

Gideon nodded.

'He don't like the man I'm keeping company with – Joshua Whittock. Nat worked for 'en, then they fell out, but my other brother Ben's still employed. I think Nat's got a grudge against Josh. I just want to be with him, maybe marry him if he asks me. I've not known him long, but already he's everything to me.'

She looked down at her hands, her cheeks on fire, and didn't notice the deep breath Gideon drew and held, his eyes closed for several seconds.

'Would this be the man I saw you walking with, by the river a couple of weeks past?' he asked gently.

'Oh yes, we saw you and your son, that's right.' Molly-Ann smiled up at him. 'You were sitting in the buttercups.'

Gideon nodded, but his eyes seemed to have lost their life. 'I'm afraid I know nothing about the man. I can't advise you . . . I can't . . .'

To Molly-Ann's concern he bent forward and buried his face in his hands; a succession of shocks seemed to shake his back. 'Master Silcox, please, what ails you?' Molly-Ann rested her hand gently on his shoulder; she could feel him trembling through the cloth of his coat. 'Don't distress yourself, sir. Tell me what it is, as I would tell you.'

His tear-smeared face turned to her. 'Would that I dared, my dear. No, this is something I must keep to myself. Nothing can be done to remedy it now, and to speak of it would cause harm to others.' He drew a great breath and sat upright. 'I wish you every happiness with your young man, Molly-Ann. I hope you will ever think of me as a loving friend.'

'Sir, I think of you as dear to me as a kind father, and I would do anything in my power to ease this sadness of yours.' She held out her hand to him; he took it in both of his.

'I know you would, my dear, but I fear it's not in your power any longer.'

Molly-Ann's feet took her back outside into the sunlight, but her mind was struggling to make out what the minister had been trying to say. What problem had caused him such distress? Her eyes dazzled by the late afternoon sun, she crossed in front of the Bell tavern and headed down through Anchor Barton towards the Boar and her evening's work, pre-occupied with her anxiety over Gideon.

# CHAPTER 10

GIDEON SANK INTO the chair behind the master's desk and covered his face with his hands. His eyes stung and he closed them yet he could still see hers, shining as she had declared: 'He's everything to me'. It was like seeing the bright sun blazing from a sky the colour of periwinkles, the same shade as her eyes. It dazzled him and at the same time scorched all his hopes.

It was over. He must no longer hope for marriage with Molly-Ann. She had torn his future up as casually as a wanton child might destroy a beautiful butterfly. No room for doubt, he'd heard the words from her very lips, he would never be able to believe himself mistaken, or ill informed. It felt as though his stomach was tying itself into a knot; he rubbed his belly to ease the pain then rested his arms on the desk, his head on top of them, his eyes shut. He pictured the couple as he had seen them in the meadow, the man's face stern, his eyes flinty-grey; Molly-Ann's smiling and alive, darting here and there. Her cheeks, usually so pale, had carried a slight blush as she walked along beside him. Certainly he looked a healthy, well-built fellow, probably capable of a hard day's work. Hopefully he'd be able to provide for Molly-Ann; he appeared to be well dressed and solvent, but there was a coarseness about him that Gideon had not liked. He had the feeling that there wasn't much heart beneath that stout chest, and that what there was would be more concerned with his own needs.

Might he change her mind through argument and reason, he wondered? If it were a practical matter maybe he could, but in the realm of affection, desire, love? No words of his were likely to move Molly-Ann. He hadn't the skill to do it; he had seen in her face how smitten she was.

Gideon rubbed his cheeks; his fingers came away wet. The light in the schoolroom was greener, dimmer, now. An hour or two must have passed since Molly-Ann left. His throat felt choked, and he coughed. She had gone. Doubtless he would see her from time to time, but she could no longer be allowed to feature in his fondest daydreams.

He took a deep breath. He should pray for her future happiness, for the success of her new relationship, for a blessed outcome for her . . . He smashed his fist on the desk with a mighty blow.


Ten days had passed since Gideon had learned of the destruction of his dearest hopes. He had stuck to his routine, not knowing what else to do: the schoolroom everyday from 7am to noon; attending to his chapel duties of visiting the sick, the aged, and those in need most afternoons; and conducting the meetings on Sunday morning and afternoon. He knew that the days passed, that summer was running to its end – unlikely as that was, given the gloriously hot sunny weather that everyone remarked upon – but it seemed to him that he existed in a void. Life had lost its colour, its noise, even its smell. It was as though he was inside a great jar formed from the thick greenish glass of the schoolroom panes; in here, sound was muffled, light was dimmed, and he was cut off from any meaningful contact with the rest of humanity. He delivered the children's lessons automatically, watching over them as carefully as ever, his brain responding to their answers, but he could not find it in himself to engage with them, or indeed with the members of the congregation, as he had done in the past. In the evenings he sank into his chair with relief at the peace and quiet of his attic room, but found himself reading and re-reading the same Bible passage without absorbing any of its meaning. And when he laid his head on the pillow, it was with the certainty that however tired his body was, sleep would be impossible while thoughts of what might have been, and of the comparative desolation that lay ahead, chased through his mind all the night long.

Tonight, the bellman's call of 'Two in the morning and a dry, clear night' stirred him from his rumpled sheets. One thing was settled now. He opened the drawer in which he stored his personal papers and took up the letter of resignation he had drafted, tore it in half slowly, then ripped it again and again with increasing ferocity, finally taking the shreds downstairs to scatter them on the smouldering fire. He leant his hand on the oak beam above the hearth. The wood was rough to the touch; deeply indented with marks of the adze as well as natural cracks between its fibres. The fragments of paper flared into life, the brief flames yellow, rushing up then dying almost as soon as they ignited. Charred remnants glowed scarlet at their edges, a little smoke rose then they crumbled to black flakes.

Later that day, as he made preparations for their frugal noontide meal setting out bread, cheese, onion relish, and apples on the table, he glanced at Sarah, sitting in her favourite chair beside the fire, her eyes closed. Even in his self-absorption, he had been aware of the change that had come over her, the suddenly increased frailty, a loss of confidence, and her need of physical care. His enquiries at the Blue House had met with a positive response and he hoped to be able to complete the arrangements for her admission to the almshouse within the week. He sighed and passed his hand over his face. Sarah's move would leave him without a home, unless he could arrange to take over the lease of the cottage. He really didn't feel able to summon up the energy to deal with the matter at present.

A rapping at the cottage door caused him to look up and cry 'Enter!' while Sarah stirred and woke from her doze.

'Father!' John came in, removing his hat and clasping Gideon's hand. 'How do I find you? I imagine you've been anxious about these legal charges – have you had any further news?' His son looked steadily at him, frowned and shook his head. 'Forgive me for saying so, but ... you are looking not at all well. You've lost weight since I was here last and your face is very ... drawn.'

Gideon turned away and gestured with his hand. 'I've been rather preoccupied, and not only with these accusations.' He sat heavily on a stool and put his head in his hands. 'My thoughts revert continually to the disclosures you made to me in Rodden Meadow.' His shoulders slumped. 'I have prayed and prayed for God's counsel, beseeched Him to guide you. I hope my efforts will not be in vain.'

John looked rueful. 'I am sorry to have caused you such anguish, especially at a time when you have so many other concerns. Tell me,' he glanced towards Sarah, 'have you been able to approach the young woman of whom you spoke to me?'

His father shook his head. 'No. My hopes for the future .. . they're all dashed.' He looked up to find Sarah's sympathetic eyes upon him, but she said nothing.

John put his hand on Gideon's shoulder and turned to the

elderly woman. 'How long has he been like this? Is there a tonic you might suggest to raise his spirits, to fortify him a little?'

'He's been agitated for the past week, or more. I've been poorly myself so I've not noticed how badly, I'm ashamed to say.' She made to rise from her chair.

'No, just tell me what to do,' John said.

Sarah pointed to a small sealed bottle on her dresser. 'St John's wort. Check the label. A few drops of that tincture in water each day. It'll take two, three weeks to have full effect, but for anxiety and melancholy there's nothing better.'

Gideon looked down at the drops of crimson tincture swirling like spots of blood in the cup of water his son had poured from the kettle, and drained the liquid.

A further knock echoed through the cottage. John pulled the door open to find a stocky man on the step, holding a folded and sealed paper out towards him.

'Master Silcox?'

'Yes. Or do you seek my father, Gideon Silcox?'

'Aye, the minister, that's the one. Here, from the magistrate. Official summons.' It was Ben who thrust the document into John's hand, touched his hat, and turned back into the busy Keyford street.

'What's that?' Gideon took the paper, broke the seal and scanned the writing. 'I've been expecting this. I'm to return for further questioning by that magistrate Baily, tomorrow. He gives no hint of what he'll ask. How can I prepare a defence if I know nothing of their case?'

'Does he give the charges?'

'No. I assume it will be that I attended the meeting, and that Dr Humfry was preaching within the proscribed area.'

'But can they prove it was Dr Humfry who spoke?

If they've no proof of that, surely there's no case for you to answer?'

'Thank you for accompanying me. I appreciate your support.' Gideon patted his son's arm the following morning.

'Two heads may be better than one,' John replied. 'We must attend carefully, try to ascertain the exact charges and what evidence they have against you.'

On arriving at the magistrate's house they were immediately escorted by two parish constables into the parlour, where James Baily sat at the oak table, his back to the window. He laid down the document he had been reading and fixed Gideon with a cold stare. There was no offer of a seat on this occasion. Behind him, Gideon heard the door open and close and boots crossed the back of the room; he did not turn around.

'I have surveyed the statements given by yourself and others present at the scene on the evening of 29th July at Roddenbury,' the magistrate said. 'You are hereby charged with conspiracy to organise an illegal religious meeting in contravention of the Five Mile Act; with attending the said meeting; and with obstructing the king's justice by assisting in the escape of the banned preacher. I shall commit you for trial at the next Taunton assizes. In the meantime your bail terms continue.'

Gideon swayed slightly until his son held his arm in a firm grip. The charges were more serious than they had anticipated. The Lord only knew what evidence they had against him other than his own brief statement. Surely none of the congregation had incriminated him in Dr Humfry's escape? His statement had given no more than the bald facts of his presence that night, he had named no others, certainly not the preacher. How did they hope to prove that it was Dr Humfry who had actually preached?

He turned to leave Baily's presence, but stopped as he recognised the man who had entered the room behind them. Joshua Whittock stared back at him, the man's eyes boring into his own. There was no doubt the fellow knew who he was, and now he too knew a great deal about Whittock. Gideon's hands and feet felt cold, and again he was grateful for John's hand supporting and guiding him. As he moved towards the door, Gideon felt a rush of blood suffuse his face. This man upon whom Molly-Ann was determined to throw herself away, had the effrontery to smile superciliously at him. Gideon glanced at his son, intending to make some remark to hasten their departure, but the words were lost when he saw John's expression. For some unaccountable reason his son's face appeared bloodless, even his lips were grey; the hand on his own sleeve was shaking; the eyes seemed fearful of what they saw, yet unable to break the contact. Now it was Gideon's turn to guide John's footsteps, and together they stumbled through the shadowy hall and out into the harsh sunlight.

'That's the devil who stole my pearl from me,' Gideon managed to mutter to his son, his vocal chords seeming unwilling to obey him. He could feel a wetness on his cheeks. 'I'm sorry, dust in my eye.' He pulled a creased handkerchief from his pocket. '*That* was Joshua Whittock.'

John seemed at a loss for words. He looked up the street as if momentarily lost, then up at the sky, and down at the cobbles. He shook himself like a dog coming out of the river. They had reached the corner of Hill Lane and Market Place before John came to an abrupt halt. 'So when we saw the fellow in Rodden Meadow, the young woman with *him* . . .

was that the same young woman of whom you spoke to me?'

'Yes.' Gideon almost stamped his foot in exasperation. 'And she is a priceless jewel of whom he is utterly unworthy. It mortifies me to know she hopes to be his wife.'

'I'm sorry,' John murmured. 'Can't her friends dissuade her? Put the facts to her?'

'It's not a case of logic, seemingly.' Gideon couldn't avoid a bitter tone creeping into his voice.

'Look, father, we've both had some shocks this day. Let me take you back to your lodgings now. I'll pick up a little something to strengthen us and we'll work together on your defence to the charges.'

Thirty minutes later, in the kitchen at the Keyford cottage, Gideon held up the small glass to the light; the amber liquid was as clear as clear. 'I wouldn't normally touch strong liquor, John. It's contrary to my teachings to the congregation. I am now a downright hypocrite.'

'Regard it as medicine,' John said. 'It is, if it does you good.' He tipped a little more apple brandy into his own glass. 'The landlord did give me a quizzical look when I asked for a gill of it to take away. He recognised me from the time I stayed at The Crown and Thistle a few weeks back, he knows me to be connected to the chapel.'

'Well it's served a turn. I feel much restored. But before we settle to this matter of the accusations, there's something I had quite forgotten: I have to speak with the warden at the Blue House again, about Sarah's removal there. I promised to pay him the surety he required and must do so today. If you walk with me we can discuss a few points as we go.'

Their task completed, the Silcoxes were shown out of the almshouse by the warden. The late afternoon sun sparkled on the fast flowing river below them and a woodpigeon called from the willow trees.

'It'll be good to see Sarah settled, and she'll soon know all the old women in there, if she doesn't already,' Gideon said.

John nodded as he placed his tall hat on his head. 'At least that's one loose end fastened. We must resolve the question of a roof over *your* head speedily as well. But can you afford the cottage on your own? I was thinking . . . I might leave Wanstrow and could share the place with you, if that met with your approval?'

Gideon smiled for the first time in many days. 'A splendid idea. We'll be company for each other.'

Their conversation had taken place in the front yard of the almshouses, beside the river parapet. As Gideon turned away from the quiet corner, he saw Molly-Ann leaving the Boar next door, a basket on her arm.

'Gi'ee good day, sirs.' She bobbed a little curtsey, and both men raised their hats.

Gideon felt that he had lost the power of speech. His heart was thumping in his chest, there were a thousand things he wanted to say to Molly-Ann but his brain seemed incapable of framing a single sentence. It was as much as he could do to introduce her to his son. She too seemed conscious of the awkwardness of their meeting, but responded cordially to John's remarks about the weather, Sarah's health, and the arrangements at the almshouses.

Behind Molly-Ann the lower Market Place was as busy as usual. People hurried past or sauntered along enjoying the sunshine; there were carts and wagons entering and leaving the town, and a line of pack animals was being led towards Pilly Vale by a scrawny youth. A bay mare trotted past and Gideon's gaze moved up to the rider's face. Joshua Whittock stared down at him, his brows creased. The horse continued on its way, its pace unchecked, but Gideon felt a queasiness in his belly. Molly-Ann was clearly unaware of Joshua's brief presence; she smiled sweetly and took her leave of the Silcoxes.

Gideon glanced at his son. John's features seemed to have frozen, his smile quite gone, his eyes strangely wistful as he looked up Market Place, following the direction of the horse and rider. 'Yes,' Gideon said, 'there he goes. Joshua Whittock: the origin of my troubles.'

The pull up the hill past St John's church seemed more tiring than usual to Gideon and once they reached the flat where Behind Town crossed Rook Lane and the road to Keyford led off up the next rise, he felt in need of a rest. Father and son sat on a low wall at the side of Gore Hedge, a triangular piece of ground between the converging tracks, from where they could watch the passing travellers.

'I'd suggest you base your defence on the identity of the preacher at Roddenbury,' John said. 'If the prosecution cannot prove that it was a proscribed minister, their case falls right away.'

'If it were I who had preached, they would indeed have no case as you say, since my old parish of Wanstrow is more than five miles distant, but Dr Humfry was speaking within the five mile limit of his former living of Frome, so he *was* breaking the law and I *was* abetting the offence.' Gideon shook his head slowly; there was, he felt, no denying his guilt in the eyes of the law, even if it was God's will that he had been pursuing.

'Yes, yes, but if we keep silent over the identity of the preacher, if none of the group names him, how can the charge be proven?' John's eyes shone with the ferocity of his determination.

'Much as I love our people, I doubt we can rely on their discretion in this,' Gideon said. 'One or more is sure to let slip the information, probably inadvertently.'

John shrugged. 'I shall make it my business to visit them all today and explain the need for silence. I'll not ask them to lie, of course, but to plead ignorance.'

'But John, they *do* know who he was. By saying they don't know, they would be perjuring themselves.' Gideon mopped his brow; it was very warm here in the full sun. 'I don't see how I can deny these charges.'

'Apart from Sarah, no one was taken, no one identified. The magistrate won't know who to summon as witnesses other than her.' John's tone was thoughtful. 'And Sarah will certainly refuse to speak.'

Gideon held his hands up. 'As you wish. But I don't want anyone else incriminated in any way, John. I'll accept my punishment rather than involve the others.'

'I understand, father, but we must still make a fight of it.'

The shadows were longer, the streets quieter now as the two men turned towards Keyford. Gideon looked back as hoofs pounded the hard ground behind him. A bay horse was bearing down upon them. He had just time to shove his son onto the grassy verge when he was knocked to the ground by a heavy blow to his shoulder. Dust clouded the air as the horse swerved away and skidded to a halt its trampling hooves still only an arm's length from Gideon's head as he lay recovering his wits.

John shouted at the rider, but Gideon couldn't make sense of what he was saying. His son's words were cut short as a vicious kick from the horseman landed on his chest.

'You two can keep away from Molly-Ann in future,' Joshua's voice bellowed above them. 'I see'd her visiting your schoolroom before, and now yer talkin' with her in the street.' He circled his horse; the hoofs again struck the road close to Gideon. 'If I find you coming between us, I'll deal with you proper.' He pulled the horse round and galloped away.

John rubbed his chest and offered his father his hand to help him rise from the roadway. Gideon steadied himself against the fingerpost that pointed out the roads to Nunney and to Keyford.

'Has he injured you, father? Are you hurt?'John's eyes were still on the horse and rider, even as he held his father's arm. When he turned back there was more sadness than anger in his expression.

'My shoulder is a bit bruised, a graze or two,' Gideon replied, and rubbed the injured place. He took a deep breath to recover himself. 'Master Whittock seems as possessive towards her as she is infatuated with him.'

A month had passed, and now the London newspapers were full of lurid accounts of the destruction caused in the capital by a devastating fire. Indeed the scale of the conflagration was only slowly becoming apparent as city dwellers spread into the countryside seeking refuge with friends and relations, and bringing tales of entire parishes left as piles of smouldering rubble and ashes. Gideon wondered how Dr Humfry had fared during those terrifying days and nights when the sky must have been filled with clouds of dense smoke, and roaring flames had devoured homes, businesses and livelihoods. He dared not enter into correspondence with his friend at this time, lest his communications be intercepted and used as evidence against him. His prayers, at least, were secure.

He had surrendered to his bail at Taunton assizes, John accompanying him on the journey and into the grim courtroom. The grand jury had found there was a case to answer, it had been marked as a true bill, and Gideon now studied the twelve men of the petty jury who were to hear the full evidence. All were complete strangers to him, drawn from the western side of the county; there was no point in challenging any and seeking substitutes, he had no clue as to their compassion, intelligence or religious leanings, all looked equally dour. He stood in the dock and the charges, as laid by Baily the magistrate, were read out. Asked how he pleaded, he declared in the strongest voice he could find: 'Not guilty.' To have entered a plea of guilty would have meant the judge proceeding to sentence him immediately; as John had advised, he had to contest the case as well as he could.

As justice of the peace, and having been present at Roddenbury, James Baily had provided an account of the event, including Gideon's own statement, which the judge read out to the court. Gideon could see John making entries in his pocketbook; notes would doubtless be passed to him shortly, he guessed. The judge peered into the well of the court. 'I believe there is a man here who was present on the night? Joshua Whittock is called as witness.'

Gideon felt the floor sway, and grasped the rail of the dock; he noticed his son turn quickly to catch sight of the fellow. The man who was becoming his bane shouldered his way through the press of people. As Joshua took the oath his eyes met Gideon's; there was a coolness, a steadiness in them as though he believed his prey was cornered.

Joshua claimed to have been at the back of the crowd on Roddenbury – Gideon could not have said whether he was or not – and he corroborated Baily's account. At last Gideon was invited to question the witness, and John's notes were handed to him. He glanced over the scribbled questions. John's notes were clear, and the crucial questions had been subject to an emphatic underscoring.

He lifted his head and stared at Joshua. 'You claim to have identified the preacher at Roddenbury. Please tell the court again who you believe it was.'

'Why, Dr Humfry.'

'And who is he?'

'Used to be vicar of Frome, 'tis said.'

'Please describe the man.'

The smile faded from Joshua's face; his forehead creased. 'Middling height; in his forties perhaps; average build. He wore a wide brimmed hat.'

'Please describe his face.'

'Hidden by the hat brim. But I know it was he.'

Gideon pulled himself to his full height. 'I knew Dr Humfry well when he lived in Frome. He is tall and spare, not at all as you describe him.'

Gideon fiddled with John's notes. 'Please tell the court what the speaker said at the meeting.'

'He spoke about God, and the fight between good and evil, and . . . and . . .' Joshua hesitated.

'You seem to be entirely unaware of what was said, and by whom. There is no evidence that Dr Humfry was even there.' He turned to the judge. 'Your Honour, I suggest this witness was not present and his evidence is wholly unfounded. His claims are fabricated.'

The judge pursed his lips. 'Why would he lie to the court? What motive has he?'

'Your Honour, he and I have had a profound personal disagreement. Indeed, he assaulted and threatened me in the public highway not a month ago. It may be that he sees this case as a means to clear me out of his way.'

The judge frowned at Joshua. 'Perjury is an extremely

serious offence. I shall detain you for further questioning, Whittock.' He glanced across at the jury. 'Gentlemen, you can discuss your verdict immediately. It seems to me the prosecution is based on dubious evidence. I shall expect your decision to be one of "Not guilty".'

Ten minutes later John guided his father out of the courtroom, his arm around his shoulder, smiles and applause from well wishers all about them following Gideon's acquittal. Gideon's knees were on the point of collapse after the tension of the morning and it was with relief that he sank onto the settle in a nearby tavern and considered the choice of pasties offered to him by a serving maid.

'A victory today,' John said, 'but Baily may make Frome an uncomfortable place for us in the future.'

Gideon sighed. 'Yes, that Joshua won't let it rest either, he'll take this as a personal affront especially if it makes him look weak in Baily's eyes. And I fear we may have to do without further visits from Dr Humfry.'

# CHAPTER 11

THE CLACK OF the yard gate set off a panicked squawking and a fluttering of feathers among the last remaining chickens at Cole Hill. Nathaniel shoved the gate shut behind him and crossed the filth spattered cobbles toward the house. He frowned at the state of the place. Since he was last here two months before, filthy straw had been blown into piles by the wind; slurry had run into the yard from the field to form a pool; and the smell of ammonia from the pigsty suggested that the poor creature within had not seen clean bedding for many, many weeks.

Before he reached the kitchen door he heard a rhythmic sound from behind the building, interspersed with occasional grunts and mutterings. He followed the paved path around the house and into what had once been a productive vegetable garden, now sadly overgrown with brambles and nettles. Beyond, Ben was engaged in shovelling earth and rubble from a sled into the mouth of the old well. A track of flattened grass and mud showed where the sled had been dragged many times from a newly dug hole some fifty paces up the slope.

'Good morrow, brother.'

Ben raised his head sharply and swore. 'What the devil do 'ee want here? I hoped I'd seen the last of you.' He leant on his shovel and scowled at Nathaniel.

'I've come to collect my belongings. I've got a room to call my own now, somewhere to put my few things as well as rest my head.'

Ben curled his lip. 'Moving up in the world are you? Cole Hill too starved and poor for 'ee?' He pointed up the slope. 'I've dug us a new well, there by the springs. It's sweet water.'

'It's not the house; it's the associations and you that I'm minded to avoid, Ben.' He nodded to the old well, now filled almost to the brim with clods of earth, turf and chunks of rock, the windlass dismantled. 'You'll have this on your conscience for eternity, brother. I've seen no sign of justice coming for 'ee, and I won't be the one a-telling of your foul deeds, but you'd be wise to seek the Lord's forgiveness for what you've done. Throw yourself on His mercy before 'tis too late.'

Ben pushed his felt cap to the back of his head and stared at Nathaniel. 'Have 'ee turned to religion? You've never held with all that Bible bashing afore.' His eyebrows met above his deep set eyes. 'Who's got at you? And who've you been blabbing to about your sins?' Ben threw down the shovel and came towards his brother, striking one fist into the other palm. 'If any whisper of this gets out, I'll know exactly who to look for and I'll not be the only one who knows. Aught happens to me, Josh will be after 'ee – he'll know who's talked, and he's got a sure way of dealing with any that cross him, let me tell you.'

'It won't be me that informs on you, but I shan't be surprised if your crime comes back to haunt 'ee, one way or another.' Nathaniel had planted his feet in the wet grass and was jutting his chin belligerently. 'I accept I'm guilty, and while I rejoice to say I've been shown the light of God, it don't mean I'd choose to surrender myself to the law.'

Ben tore the cap off, rolled it up and swiped it violently against his own leg. He pointed his finger at the younger man.

'Don't you bring none of that religious talk here. I don't want to know. Can't see what good it's going to do you, neither. They'll want 'ee to give up drink and cussin' and poachin' an' all our old ways.' He turned back to his work. 'And what you living off now? You say you've got a place to stay. What? In town?'

'Aye. I've found work as one of they wire drawers,' Nathaniel said, 'and now I've got the means to pay for lodgings. It ain't much, but 'tis better than living in a house that reeks of murder, of evil, and the sufferings of others.'

Ben took a step back, the colour coming fast into his cheeks. 'That's no way to speak to your own flesh and blood! Take yer things and go. And never come back here again, brother or not!' He turned his back and reached for the shovel.

'Before I do,' Nathaniel had raised his voice, 'there's one thing I must tell you. Our Molly-Ann, she's keeping company with that Joshua Whittock. You know as well as I do that he's a man brimful of wickedness. If you care at all about the girl, I'd ask you to talk to her and get her to understand: no good can come of it. I'd wager she'll suffer for her ungodly passion. He's got a heart of stone; he'll take what he wants and cast her off.'

'She's a grown woman. She can choose her path for herself.'

'Aye but.'

'It's none of our business,' Ben said. 'In his way, he's fond on her.'

Nathaniel rolled his eyes and walked to the house, where he collected together his few items of clothing, a second pair of well worn boots, a comb, and, from beneath a wobbly table leg, his mother's New Testament. Wrapping all in an old blanket, he left Cole Hill. He hoped never again to set eyes on the place, yet at the same time he mourned the loss of the home of his earliest memories.

Sitting in the Sheppards' workshop at Rack Close next day, Nathaniel pulled the worn leather glove from his right hand and sucked the ball of his thumb. The blood in his mouth tasted of iron and he spat it out then pressed a rag to the wound; it certainly wasn't the first injury he'd received during his work for Master Sheppard. The gloves seemed to be of little or no use in protecting the wearer and he flung them to the dirt floor muttering, then picked one up and examined it closely. The weak point was the seam where the thumb piece was stitched to the palm. It was as easy as anything for one of the wires to penetrate that join and impale his flesh. All that was needed was a second layer of strong leather over that crack to seal the seam; if he could pick up a suitable scrap he would see what could be done.

The bleeding had stopped and he pulled the gloves back on, they would have to serve for the present. He laid his work back on his knee and reached down to the basket for more wires. The other workers had finished for the day and gone home having completed their hours. He missed their company but at least it gave him a chance to concentrate on getting the wires correctly spaced first time. The job was tedious and had proved to be very wearing, his fingers were sore from drawing the wires through the leather backing of the card boards and his back ached from bending over the close work. The second stage, fastening the spiked leather strips onto the faces of the paddle shaped boards, provided some variety in his duties, but was tricky and it had taken him several days to master the skill. He threw the finished board into the basket as the light from the shed doorway was suddenly blocked out. He looked up to find his employer in front of him, his frown directed at the half filled basket of carding paddles.

'Is that all ee've done today?' The elderly man shook his head. 'You're still a deal slower than most of the men. If you don't improve . . .'

Nathaniel pointed to the cuts on his hands. 'I've a plan to make the gloves stronger, sir. If it works we'd be able to work a lot faster. Will you let me try, perhaps with an off cut from the leather we use on the boards?'

John Sheppard looked doubtful but nodded. 'I've an order come in from Yorkshire for a gross of these card boards. The carrier leaves tomorrow at day break. I'll expect you to work on tonight to make up the last two dozen. If you think your new glove will help, you'd best do something about it, but no time for that now. Look sharp, and check the quantity when you've done.'

It was close to midnight before Nathaniel had completed the order, working by the light of a horn lantern in the dusty shed and adding his paddle shaped boards to the basketfuls standing ready. His eyes were watering with the strain and his fingers felt too stiff ever to bend again, but he'd eventually reached the total of one hundred and forty-four – he counted them all twice to be sure – and was at last able to snuff the candle and stagger away from Master Sheppard's yard and head home.

Home: he knew he was fortunate to have an attic room to himself, but that was just about all he did have. A straw mattress on the floor, a tiny hearth, a broken seated chair, and a plank on bricks for a shelf and table. The rain came through one corner of the roof; one pane was missing from the tiny window, replaced by rags stuffed in against the draught; and the door latch was held together by cord. It was a start though. He could be independent of Ben and of Joshua Whittock, put all that behind him. John Silcox had vouched for him to the landlord of the decrepit house in Anchor Barton, and to Master Sheppard. He was lucky to have such a well respected friend and would do his best to justify the faith placed in him. But for now he could do nothing more than collapse onto the rustling straw and hope the fleas would not be too active tonight.

Sunbeams were trying to penetrate the grimy glass and cobwebs of the casement window when Nathaniel woke with a start. He flung the blanket aside and pushed his feet into his boots; having lain down in his clothes, the only other item of apparel he needed was his hat. He clattered down the stairs, rinsed his face and hands under the yard pump and unlatched the gate into the cobbled lane. He paused as a group of small children chased past, the sound of their wooden pattens echoing from the stone walls, then they veered left into the grounds of the new school hall, their voices fading as they turned the corner.

Master Sheppard was in Rack Close before him, leaning on his stick as he hobbled around, checking on the activities of his workers. The elderly man, dressed in a dusty blue coat and breeches, followed him into the workshop which Nathaniel had left only seven hours earlier, and poked his stick at the empty baskets.

'You got them finished then. I was here at dawn to send them off, counted them and checked your work.' Master Sheppard nodded to himself, his face serious. 'Good enough. And what are we to do about your idea for the gloves, eh?'

Nathaniel scratched his ear. 'I don't have any skill with

a needle, sir. It's a job for a glove maker, or perhaps a cobbler. With your agreement I could show him what's wanted, get a sample made up?'

'Aye. Have it done properly, I don't believe in cutting corners. See to it now lad. The sooner we have better gloves, the sooner we can complete the next order.'

A few hours later, Nathaniel trudged up Catherine Hill heading back to Rack Close, the finished sample in his hand. He'd eaten nothing all morning, the sun was beating on his back and he could feel the sweat prickling his shoulders. He swept his hat off to wipe his brow and push the damp hair back from his forehead; as he did so, his eyes met those of a familiar but unwelcome figure. Joshua Whittock was leaning one shoulder against the gate to his yard, clay pipe in hand.

Should he say something? Warn the brute off Molly-Ann? Nathaniel scowled at the bigger man but held his tongue. As he turned the corner at the Sun tavern he glanced back; Joshua was watching him still, and spat derisively in his direction. Nathaniel's stomach clenched. How could his sister see any merit in the fellow? He should have given the man a piece of his mind. He shook his head; was he always going to be so chicken-hearted he wondered, or would his new faith in the Lord give him the courage to do what he knew he should, in spite of the danger to himself?

Master Sheppard studied the sample of the reinforced glove on Nathaniel's return to Rack Close. 'You can order a dozen in two sizes for the wire drawers,' he said. 'And I'm going to speak to my son John about you, young man. You might not have the practical skill for this work, but you have a head on your shoulders.' He drew sixpence from his pouch and handed it to Nathaniel. 'A little bonus for 'ee. Now, my son John is building up his own interests in the woollen trade, he doesn't want to take on my maltings business, my eldest will have that. No, John reckons he can make his own fortune by going beyond this card board making, by going deeper into the wool manufacture. We shall see.' His gaze swept around the tidy yard with its workshops, stables, malting shed, and the wooden cloth drying racks that gave the close its name. 'I've built up my own business from nothing, raised my family up in the world, you might say.' He paused. 'Now, what was I going to discuss with 'ee? Oh yes, you might be useful to my son. You seem to have some bright ideas; if he explains what he wants done, you could be the one to devise ways to make it happen. Hm? What do 'ee say? I often think it takes a fresh pair of eyes to see new solutions, new means of doing things.'

Nathaniel twisted his hat between his hands. 'I thank 'ee sir. If you think I'm up to it, I shall do my utmost to prove you right! I know naught about the cloth trade as you are aware, but I'm willing to learn.'

'Well your next task will be to introduce the new glove to the wire drawers. Strangely enough, you may find some resistance to it. I leave it to you to ensure this change is in my financial interest.' Master Sheppard smiled enigmatically, and walked towards the rear entrance to his home, leaving a puzzled Nathaniel behind him.

Why should the workers object to such an improvement that saved them from injury? He retraced his steps and slipped into the Sun for a meat pasty and a tankard of cider; and there'd be something left for a bit of bread and cheese for his supper tonight too.

The cobbler made short work of Master Sheppard's order and the dozen pairs of strengthened gloves arrived next day. Those wire drawers who were present in the workshop as Nathaniel undid the twine holding the bundle, studied the patched gloves. He could clearly see the scars and cuts that blemished the skin of their palms and fingers.

'Some of you must get real trouble from these injuries, don't 'ee?' Nathaniel asked. 'Deep wounds festering, and blood poisoning, like?'

An older woman in a greasy tattered gown grunted. 'Lost the use of their hands, some folks have. Fingers throbbing fit to bust sometimes. They wires be that sharp, go right through you they do.'

Nathaniel tested the thickness of the patched seam. 'This should be a big help to you then. Save a good few piercings, help 'ee work quicker, do more boards in a day.'

The woman's eyes narrowed. 'Aye, if they don't make us too clumsy we may work faster, but master better not think us'll work for the same payment if he's getting more boards at end of day. That's not right. If we make more, he needs to pay us more.' Her fellow workers were nodding in agreement.

Nathaniel began to understand the problem Master Sheppard had foreseen. 'He pays you what now? Ninepence a day?'

'Nay, that's for you beginners. We gets a shilling as we're more skilled.'

'And you make what, twenty-five boards in a day?'

'Aye, thereabouts.'

Nathaniel thought for a few moments. 'How about if I suggest to him he pays you so much for each board – providing it's good enough – say a halfpenny each. More you make, more wages you get, and with these stronger gloves you should be able to draw faster. He'll be sure to check the quality, so it's in your own interest not to let that fall. It would be a waste of your time if so be it weren't up to standard.'

'We knows what we're doing, my lad.' She gave Nathaniel

a nod. 'Aye, see if he agrees.'

Nathaniel pulled off his hat as he entered the cool gloom of the Sheppards' residence. He'd hesitated to approach the front entrance in Catherine Street, it had felt more appropriate to come through the rear yard of the ancient house and ask the maidservant he saw working the pump, for admission to Master Sheppard's presence.

The girl had smiled as she'd tucked a stray tendril of fair hair back under her cap. 'Follow me. I'll take 'ee to him.'

Nathaniel's mind had still been engrossed with his discussion with the wire drawers, but afterwards he would recall her cheerfulness and self-confidence.

Master Sheppard had removed his coat and hat, but was clearly still involved in business as he turned away from his paper strewn desk to hear Nathaniel's report. His fingers drummed the arm of his chair. 'Pay them by the piece, eh?' He paused. 'So long as the quality remains high . . . I'll need a checker . . . yes, it may be for the best.'

'And perhaps look for more orders from other woollen areas, that would increase your returns, Master Sheppard. Make a name for quality and fast delivery . . .'

'Aye. These are the sort of ideas my son John and I want to hear. He's making time to meet with you. Be back here this evening, sharp on eight.'

Nathaniel's smile was reflected back to him by the maid as he made his way out of the yard, almost skipping with excitement.


John Sheppard the younger held out his hand to Nathaniel later that evening. 'We're agreed then, six shillings a week initially. You'll spend time learning or observing the different processes of the manufacture, then with time, and once you understand the difficulties, you can both offer suggestions for improvements and act as my assistant. I can't be everywhere at once and it will help me to have a second set of eyes overseeing the business.' He raised his pewter tankard to Nathaniel and also to his father seated at the end of the table. 'To our future success! And thank you, father, for finding me a valuable assistant.'

The older Sheppard smiled wryly. 'I think he'll make a better supervisor than a wire drawer. Conscientious enough, but he's too slow with his fingers.' He put his drink down. 'Have you any questions or concerns, young man?'

Nathaniel stared into the candles whose flames were reflected in the highly polished oak of the table. No, he daren't admit his illiteracy to the Sheppards, but it had to be addressed with all speed. 'I thank you both from the bottom of my heart for the opportunity. I promise you that I'll work hard and honestly.'

'Well we can't ask for more. A sober, upright employee is what we're looking for, and God-fearing as well.'

'Aye, sir, and as you know, it's Master Silcox to whom I owe so much and who has shown me the true path, him and his father.'

'Good and worthy men; they have a glowing reputation amongst all of our religious persuasion.'

Nathaniel took a deep draught of ale. It was weak, but of a pleasing flavour. Could the Silcoxes help him attain some book learning, he wondered.

The fair haired maid bobbed a little curtsey to Nathaniel as she showed him out of the front door and he was tempted to ask her name, but desisted. There would be opportunity for that in the coming weeks, he felt sure.

'Reading and writing, and arithmetic too?' John Silcox pursed his lips. 'I'm sure your enthusiasm and commitment will be singular advantages to you in mastering these skills in a short time. I'd offer to teach you myself, but I travel about so much that I couldn't give you a regular commitment.' He shook his head. 'And I'd hesitate to ask my father; he has so many obligations to the congregation already . . . ah! The congregation!' John's eyes held a spark and he raised a finger. 'We have a young woman recently joined us who told me that she is eager to undertake some good works. I did wonder whether she had some personal reason for offering her time . . . be that as it may, perhaps we could engage her services. Dorothea Naish is her name. I know her for an able scribe, and it would be useful to judge her abilities as a teacher, if you don't mind being used as a test piece?'

'Willingly. I'm not sure that I can afford to pay her much, however.'

John clicked his tongue. 'We have a tradition here of giving freely of our time, in the faith that our gift will be returned to us by others in our own time of need. Do not trouble yourself, Nathaniel.' He picked up his hat and led the way out of the Keyford cottage. 'Let us go immediately to ask the young woman.'

It was only a short distance down Rook Lane to the Naishes' home – a gable fronted stone house scarcely larger than the Silcoxes' cottage.

'This is where we Congregationalists, as we call ourselves, were accustomed to meet until recently,' John said. 'It's let to new tenants now.'

The front door opened directly into a large room which

was lit by a briskly burning log fire and a very small casement window. A red and white rag rug covered the flagstones in front of the hearth, and on the rug a white cat stretched languidly, rolled over, and washed itself. The fire reflected from a few copper pans and a row of pewter plates on the dresser; all else in the room was Spartan yet neat, clean and comfortable. Compared with his own dismal home this was heavenly.

The elderly servant who had admitted them returned a few minutes later with a younger woman. Nathaniel sensed that the mistress of the house was older than he, although her clear skin, straight back and slim figure suggested that she was in no more than her early twenties. Her modest black skirt and bodice and spotless white collar and apron set off her pale pink complexion. A few strands of chestnut hair curled from beneath a close fitting cap.

'Master Silcox,' she said, dipping a slight curtsey to John, 'this is a pleasant surprise. I bid you both welcome, but my father is not at home if it is he you wished to see?'

'The object of my visit is in fact yourself, Mistress Naish. But my apologies, may I introduce Nathaniel here, who like you is a new member of our congregation.'

Nathaniel inclined his head as he had seen John Silcox do. 'How do 'ee do?' he managed to say.

Dorothea again dipped in formal greeting and Nathaniel felt that she studied him a shade longer than he was comfortable with.

'It looks as though you have settled into your new home well,' John said. 'Is everything as you would wish?'

'We are truly content to be here,' she replied. 'My father has already secured a number of contracts and is busy engaging craftsmen and labourers.'

John turned to Nathaniel. 'Master Naish is a skilled

mason. They've just moved here – from Warminster I believe?'

Dorothea nodded. 'Yes, there is a growing demand here in Frome for masons. Until now we feared we would miss the fellowship of our old congregation at St Lawrence's, but I am delighted to have received such a warm welcome from your chapel, Master Silcox. I'm sure we shall soon build up a wide number of friends and business contacts.'

'I have no doubt of it,' John replied. 'But let me explain the reason for our call. My friend here is anxious to acquire the skills of reading, writing and reckoning. You mentioned to me that you were seeking an opportunity to perform some good works, and I wondered whether you would consider taking him as your pupil. A more attentive scholar you will not find!'

Dorothea's teeth gleamed in the firelight as she smiled. 'I would be very pleased to do so. I have taught my household in the past and was considering offering to give lessons in your father's school, but this would be the perfect way to start.'

'I'm afraid we cannot commit to financial remuneration at this stage,' John said, 'but maybe in the future . . .'

'Don't even think of it,' she said. 'When shall we start? Would you like to come here for the lessons, Nathaniel? Or somewhere else?'

He glanced around the comfortable orderly room. 'This would be perfect mistress, I thank you warmly.'

As he followed John to the door after taking their leave, Nathaniel became aware of a sensation of warmth on his left shoulder. He turned his head to find Dorothea close behind him, smiling with what seemed to him a strange consciousness in her eyes. He looked away in confusion and stumbled after John, then halfway down the garden path glanced back, but the cottage door was shut and the white cat gazed out of the window.

Over the following weeks Nathaniel spent all his daylight hours observing and attempting to participate in the various processes that went into the manufacture of the broadcloth. One week he'd be using the very same carding paddles that he had made in his early days, combing one against the other to mix and straighten the wool fibres that lay between, and finally peeling off the smooth mass as a neat rolag ready for spinning. The next week he'd be having his ears deafened at a fulling mill down in Pilly Vale, where a waterwheel drove the pounding hammers that beat the woven cloth to clean, consolidate and thicken the fibres. The stench of the mixture of urine and fullers earth used on the fabric, the danger from the moving machinery, the skull-smashing noise both appalled and excited him. He had yet to observe the work of the spinners and weavers, the dyers and finishers, but already he was beginning to see areas for improvement, both to increase efficiency and to make the work more bearable for the labourers. First, though, he needed to understand how all the processes fitted together. Master John, as Nathaniel had been invited to call the younger Mr Sheppard, had explained his vision of an organised process, of one controlling mind organising the manufacture as a linked system of steps to achieve efficiency, consistent quality, and of course profit. Master John intended to invest a large share of his family's fortune in the purchase of raw materials, premises and equipment, and would then closely supervise the movement of the product through all its stages, controlling the stocks, quality and time spent on each process. Nathaniel had never before envisaged such a concept: to be a part of it had become his dearest wish.

Pre-dawn darkness still enveloped Catherine Hill on

a Wednesday in mid October, although occasional flickers of candlelight passed behind dirty windows as folk started to rise for work. As the maidservant opened the Sheppards' back door in Rack Close to Nathaniel, and the light from her lantern fell on him, her eyes widened and she took a step back before laughing at her own surprise. 'Oh sir! I thought 'ee some sort of devil, your face all discoloured like that!'

He pulled off his hat and grinned, 'and good morrow to you too, Mistress Ellen.' He knew her name now. 'Did I startle 'ee? I've been trying to scrub it off but nothing shifts it – look, my hands too. I'm fearful it'll never go. I'll have to wear gloves and a beard.'

'The woad, is it?'

'Aye, Master John sent me to observe the manufacture of the dye yesterday but I got too close, there was a splash, and this is the outcome.'

The Sheppards were right, he thought, to leave this dyeing business to the experts. The drying of the woad leaves, chopping, malting, fermenting, grinding and other steps to create a batch of dye, then the blending and colour matching of dozens of shades of blue was well beyond their capacity; this was a process to be left to the specialists.

Ellen stepped back into the kitchen and held out a basket of white rolls to him. 'They won't miss one. Would 'ee like butter too? Have the scraping from this bowl; don't mark the pat going to the master's table.'

Nathaniel swallowed the roll down with gratitude, as well as the mug of ale she offered. He never seemed to think to get food in, ready for the morning, but at least he could now afford to keep the wolf from the door.

'And how's your book learning going? Is that Mistress Naish still making eyes at 'ee?'

Nathaniel wished he hadn't told Ellen about his tutor's rather demonstrative interest in him. He'd thought a bit of competition might make the girl keener, but she had just used it as a means to taunt him. Tell the truth, he was a bit scared of Dorothea; she seemed very forward for a puritan woman, especially when they were studying alone with the elderly servant busy in the yard. Her eyes were on him all the time and they seemed to carry more than a hint of some offer. If her father or John Silcox appeared she changed her nature altogether and became very prim and proper, and she always seemed to have an intuition of their approach – how did she do that?

'I'd sooner have you teasing me, Ellen.' He grabbed her hand as she reached for the butter dish. 'Will you walk out with me, Sunday after chapel? We could follow the river down to Welsh Mill . . .?'

'Well that sounds exciting, Master Nathaniel.' She pulled a face. 'I'd sooner go and watch the singlestick fighting up on Packhorse Field, the old river's not so much fun!'

Nathaniel swallowed. Whatever would the Silcoxes think of him if he were seen at that sort of entertainment?

'Do you go to chapel Ellen, or be 'ee a churchgoer?'

She turned to put the butter dish on the breakfast tray. 'I told Master Sheppard I goes to church. He thinks I do, but he's at chapel, so he don't really know.' She looked at Nathaniel from under her lashes. 'It would be nice to spend Sunday afternoon with 'ee, so long as I'm back to serve cold supper, and if it's not raining.'

Sunday afternoon proved just about dry enough for Nathaniel to walk out with Ellen. Grey clouds scudded fast beneath a uniform blanket of white, but the breeze was strong enough to keep them moving, rather than stop and drop their burden on the pleasure-seeking folk of Frome. The air was a trifle damp, but she seemed willing to take the risk.

The packhorses, enjoying a day of rest in their pasture, had all been tethered to the side of the enclosure, opposite the tavern where their masters, the coal traders, habitually downed a pint after the trek from Kilmersdon, or from Mells. The larger part of the field had been given over to sporting bouts and Nathaniel could see that a couple of wrestling matches were in progress, while a rope was being laid out to mark the arena for the singlestick contest. In the past he wouldn't have thought twice about coming here, but the sports did attract a rough looking crowd, and now with a young woman on his arm – it was she who had initiated that contact – he felt responsible for her safety.

The two contestants stepped forward, naked to the waist, flourishing the ash staves with which each planned to beat his opponent into submission. Nathaniel felt the mood of the crowd intensify, even as his own pulse rate rose. The gusting wind shook another cloud of dull brown leaves from the trees.

'Who're you backing then Nat?' Ellen's little face smiled up at him – the top of her head only reached his shoulder – but he detected a bloodthirsty glint in her eyes, which unsettled him a little. As his gaze travelled over to the two brawny men, he glimpsed beyond them faces he knew. On the far side of the arena stood his brother Ben, and Joshua Whittock, neither of whom appeared to have seen him, busy as they were with taking bets on the contest from other spectators.

Nathaniel pulled his hat brim lower; the blue woad stains on his face a welcome disguise now, as many of those around him were similarly disfigured. He glanced to left and right.

There were many in the crowd whom he recognised, but none of Mr Silcox's congregation – it was he realised, hardly likely that any would be here, but if his presence were reported to the minister it would look bad for him. More probable was the presence of some of Master Sheppard's workers. This was a stupid mistake. He should never have agreed to bring Ellen here if he wanted to preserve his good name with his new friends and his employers.

He took a deep breath and squared his shoulders. 'I'm sorry. We have to go. This isn't the place for me now.'

She frowned. 'I'm enjoying my outing. Can't 'ee bide here for a while?'

'I've seen some men I'd rather avoid. Let's go before they spot us.'

'Sounds like you're afeard.'

'I'm learning to be careful, Ellen. I'm sorry if it's spoilt your day.' A sudden thought lightened his mood. 'I've some of my wages left. Shall we walk down to try a cup of chocolate at the George? Master John was telling me it's a new drink from the Americas that's come to town. They say it's very good for the stomach.'

She laughed. 'You sound like my old granny!'

Nathaniel grinned. 'Well anyway, it's all the fashion. I hear the gentry are mad about it.

# CHAPTER 12

THERE WAS A satisfying 'chink' as James Baily dropped the leather bag on Richard Yerbury's dining table. The surface of the table was no cleaner, no less sticky, than it had been on their earlier visit some six weeks previously and the justice of the peace's lip curled.

'Please be seated.' The elderly man waved a hand towards one of the dark oak chairs. 'It behoves me to count your payment.' He loosened the drawstring and tipped the coins from the bag. 'Take no offence, sir, but I've no intention of being played for a fool.'

As their host carefully stacked and counted the money, James Baily and Joshua exchanged a glance. Joshua tapped his fingers on the table, but stopped at a further look from Baily. His master had more patience than he did, he thought.

'Yes,' quavered the titular lord of the manor, 'that is the correct sum. You've brought the documents for signature?'

'Of course,' Baily said.

'Allow me to read them through, check there's no alteration to the draft I approved.' Yerbury laid the papers on the table in front of him; there was a sucking sound as he peeled one away and repositioned it. 'Would you gentlemen care for refreshment while I scrutinise these documents?' he asked.

Baily carefully examined the glass in which his brandy and hot water was served before he drank it. Joshua, however, downed his immediately in one gulp: he had no qualms about the finger marks on the surface of the glass, and the provenance of the water was all the same to him.

The long case clock chimed both the hour and also the first quarter before Yerbury finally reached for his quill, dipped it in the pot of oak gall ink, and put his signature to the leases. He took a pinch of sand from a small box and sifted it over his name. 'There, the first of many, I trust. And are you able to speculate when you will wish to take up the next parcel of land?'

'I must see how my men get on,' Baily replied. 'Once the walls of these initial houses are up and the masons released for their work on the next batch, the carpenters and helliers can be left to complete the joinery and the roofs of the first, then I shall be back to you with the next lease for signature.' He drained the last of his brandy and fixed his stare on his host. 'Master Yerbury, may I respectfully remind you of the agreement we made, that you would not admit any other developer to your land, without giving me first option?'

'Yes, yes, I recall. Though there's more than four acres there that's fit to build upon, you wouldn't run short.'

'Maybe, but my concern would be that too many dwellings being built in a short period would flood the market, and the rents we can charge would be driven down due to the excess. I'd sooner release small batches at a time – and that could be in your interest too, sir.'

Joshua had held his peace throughout their exchange, but the warning look he shot at the old landowner was eloquent.

Once he and Baily had mounted their horses to return to town, Joshua leaned closer. 'Those cottages in Vallis Way, they were put up not four years past by a mason of the name of Whymark, engaged by Yerbury himself. He's died since. It don't look like anyone else would plan to develop along there.'

Baily grunted. 'This first section I build will run at right angles to those cottages, down towards us here. What I need now is a master mason who can draw up some designs, lay out the plots, get materials ordered and craftsmen engaged. I've been asking around this last week or two. There's a newcomer to the town, name of Naish. He's been in the trade many years at Warminster, but probably hasn't created much reputation here in Frome yet. I was told he wants to work with stone instead of their local brick. I may be able to secure his services at a good price.' He scanned the sky. 'Rain's holding off. We'll pay him a visit immediately. I mean to press him for a good deal.'

Ten minutes later they were in Rook Lane. A small figure sat on a wall kicking his heels and studying the passing traffic.

'Here boy, hold these horses.' Joshua swung out of the saddle and handed the reins to Billy; Baily did the same, then together they strode up the path to Simon Naish's gable fronted cottage. The elderly servant ushered them inside and left to seek her master.

Baily looked around the room. 'This is bigger than I envisage for my dwellings. What is it, seven or eight paces by six? Six by five will do me, and the chimney stack on the wall shared with the neighbouring house. One room down and one above, plus an attic. That's enough for any labouring family. Smaller they are, the more I can fit in.'

'I suppose if there were a demand for larger,' Joshua said, 'it would be easy enough to add a second room at the side or the back, with a higher rent charged?'

Baily nodded slowly. 'If there proved to be a demand.'

Simon Naish entered the room from the back yard, buttoning his coat as he did so. 'Gi'ee good day, sirs. I apologise for keeping you waiting. How may I be of service?' He brushed a little stone dust from his sleeve.

Joshua adopted his usual slouched pose against the door, his eyes fixed on the master mason. Baily smiled pleasantly. 'I am in need of a business associate. A man with experience in the building trade, who can design small dwellings, organise and oversee their construction. I have in mind erecting more than a dozen contiguous cottages, quite possibly many more. Would this be within your capacity, Master Naish?'

An hour later, Joshua and James Baily recovered their horses from Billy, and Baily signified his satisfaction with his discussion with the builder by parting with not one, but two bronze pennies as recompense. Billy grinned as he headed off downhill for a mutton and gravy pie at the Swan, his brown curls tumbled by the breeze.

Joshua kicked a clod of earth out of the road; it was dry and crumbled immediately. 'We've been lucky with the weather. Driest autumn I can recall, mid November already and no frost yet to speak of. Old Naish's made a good start, look . . .' He swept one hand at the scene before them. More than half a dozen houses had been commenced, but the rough rubble walls of some were still only at shoulder height with gaps left for the doors and windows.

Molly-Ann squeezed his other arm. 'He must have an army working on it. Last time I was round here it was fields and hedges. How many's he putting up?'

'Eight here in this first group. Long Row he's called it. Can'st see those cottages along the road to Vallis that went up a few years back? Master Baily chose to butt these right up to them, then we're going to build all the way down towards old Yerbury's place.'

She nodded, shielding her eyes from the low afternoon sun as she looked back. Joshua glanced down at her; the autumn breeze had brought colour into her pale cheeks. She was looking very alluring today; her bodice seemed fuller than usual. He pulled her closer to his side, his pulse quickening.

'Once these are ready for roofing and fitting out, we'll start the masons on the next batch of eight or ten. Master Baily's got plans to build over the whole of New Close here; lay out roads, put up taverns. He's got it all worked out.'

'And what's your place in all this?' She smiled up at him and stroked his wrist.

'I make sure it happens. I may not know the finer points of the building trade, but I can make sure that we have men who do.' It was pleasing, he thought, to see the smile of admiration on Molly-Ann's lips, for his success to be recognised by the girl. He tightened his arm to squeeze her hand in return. He'd steered their Sunday afternoon walk up here deliberately, and she seemed to be in a receptive mood. 'I thought to ask Master Baily to let me rent one of these houses from him,' he said. 'I believe he'd welcome having me on site to oversee the works and to ensure their security. If he's willing, it would be a fine home for us both. Would you like that, Molly-Ann? Your own place, away from old Grimwade and his customers?'

A broad smile spread slowly over Molly-Ann's face. 'You means it, Josh Whittock? Set up together?'

'Aye, girl.' He held her closer. 'I'd like 'ee in my bed every night: winter coming on, it would be a lot warmer than a fumble in the woods.'

Molly-Ann couldn't return his kiss for giggling. 'But what'll folks think if we're living here and not married? Should we make it legal?'

'Time for that, my dear, the important thing is to get a

roof over our heads. The rest can come later. Anyway, the people taking the new houses up here won't know us, everyone will be strangers.'

'Josh.' She had stopped giggling and her brow was creased. 'Yes. I will come and live with 'ee. It would resolve a coil that's been knotting my thoughts the last few weeks. I . . . I'm going to have a baby. You're going to be a father.'

He blinked. He suddenly felt the weight of his years. It surprised him that he hadn't foreseen this turn of events, considering that he and Molly-Ann had found opportunities to make love many times since the evening of Nunney Fair.

'All the more reason to make a home together, then,' he said, and smiled. Molly-Ann was the woman he most wanted in the town, and it looked likely she would continue amenable whether he married her or not. Yes, this could be a satisfactory outcome. He'd need to put some pressure on the workmen to get their cottage completed in good time.

Molly-Ann picked her way across the trampled soil and rubble to the first of the so far roofless cottages, over the threshold and through the gaping doorway. She turned slowly round, and he could see her taking in the roughly mortared rubble walls; the empty window spaces at front and back of the single room; the broad chimney breast with its massive oak bressumer beam; the space beside it where a staircase would wind up to the floor above. Huge stone flags had been piled in one corner, ready to be laid on the ground floor.

It called for a bit of imagination, Joshua thought, but even he could visualise a roaring fire on the hearth, curtains at the windows and a deal table and chairs for their meals; the night and the rain outside, and warmth and company within. He pulled her close again and kissed her.

'I tell you, Master Baily, the weather has not been fit for working. Water has been inches deep in places for the last week, and before that the frost set in so hard there was no possibility of mixing a mortar that would serve.' Simon Naish stood foursquare in his yard, as solid as one of his own walls, hands on hips and his chin jutting belligerently.

James Baily swept his hand through his own long hair; the curls brushed the shoulders of his fine green coat. 'That's as maybe, but we've lost two months now, both December and January. I'd expected some of the cottages to be ready for occupation by now. With no rents coming in, how can we make progress with the scheme?'

'Aye. There's folks wanting a roof over their heads right now,' Joshua put in. He stepped closer to the master mason. Just a hand's breadth separated their coat fronts, and he towered over the older man. He scowled at Naish. 'If the men aren't at work tomorrow daybreak, come hell or high water, you'll be on crutches for the next month.'

'Don't you threaten me, you bully.' Naish pointed a finger at Joshua's chest. 'I tell you, there's no point working in these conditions. Frost or rain, the work will be spoilt; the masonry will be too weak to stand. I've my reputation to consider. I don't do shoddy work and that's an end to it.'

He jabbed Joshua with his finger, then yelped as the younger man seized his hand and bent the finger back viciously. There was a sickening crack and Naish shrieked.

'You'll do as Master Baily instructs. Next time, it's yer knees. Daybreak tomorrow.'

Baily and Joshua turned to leave the yard by the rear gate, but as they did so the kitchen door of the Naishes' cottage was flung open and Dorothea ran out, her hands to her mouth. 'I saw what you did, you villain,' she screamed at Joshua and put her arms around her father. Nathaniel and John Silcox followed behind her, pulling on their cloaks against the bitter wind and rain. Baily did not pause, but merely glanced around, shrugged and continued out of the yard. Nathaniel grasped Joshua's sleeve. 'What's the meaning of this? Why've you attacked this good man?'

'Clear off yer bugger.' Joshua punched Nathaniel in the stomach. 'Mind your own business, why don't you?'

Nathaniel reeled away from the blow and John stepped forward.

'Oh, there's another of you, is there?' Joshua lifted his fist again but John raised his hands and stepped back a pace.

'C'mon, I'm enjoying this.' Joshua moved closer then paused. He'd never seen an opponents' face with that expression before. The man appeared to have no fear, nor was he narrowing his eyes in an aggressive stare. Rather, he seemed to be glowing with fervour. 'It's you . . . the minister's son.' Joshua scowled even more fiercely. 'I'll teach you to keep your nose out of my affairs. I'll give you the beating I'd like to give yer father.' But the man continued to smile. Joshua couldn't understand it.

'You don't recognise me, do you?' John said. 'More than a year ago you saved my life, aboard the *Old James* at Lowestoft.'

'That's all behind me. It's naught to me now.' Joshua gave him a mighty shove and John staggered back.

'Let us be friends!' John held out his hand. 'Not only do I abhor violence, but I would dearly love to speak civilly with you. Ever since our paths first crossed I've hoped to learn more about you. Come, let us find a place for some private conversation.'

Dorothea and Nathaniel were assisting Simon Naish

into the house and gave no sign of attending to the exchange, they seemed only too anxious to get away from Joshua.

'What do 'ee want from me?' Joshua struck John's hand away. He'd no time for these religious folk; that must be what the fellow was after. He'd probably try to talk him into a sober and virtuous life – ha! He'd have his work cut out.

Joshua spat on the ground, turned and followed Baily out of the gate.


It was late March, and night had fallen before Joshua reached his new home in Long Row. He walked the horse the last hundred yards, reckoning that her eyesight would be better than his in the darkness, and sure enough she paused in her stride twice, once to avoid a large pot hole and then a pile of timbers lying in what would eventually be the roadway. A stable had been constructed in the rear yard and he led the mare inside, lit a lantern, and quickly untacked her. Billy, he saw, had mucked out earlier in the day and left fresh water and a net of hay ready to hand. The boy was building up a domestic livery service for those riders who had neither a servant to care for their horse, nor the time to do so themselves.

The lighted window of the terraced cottage was welcoming and Joshua congratulated himself on his acquisition of the dwelling, as well as on the company of Molly-Ann who waited indoors with, he hoped, a large pot of supper.

The supper did indeed meet his expectations: a stew of dried beans, sage and rabbit meat with crusty bread to mop up the juices. He pushed his cleared plate away, his appetite satisfied, and looked up to find Molly-Ann's blue eyes studying him, rather critically, he thought.

'Is something the matter, girl? Be you feeling alright, now

your time's approaching?'

Molly-Ann piled the dirty plates one on the other. 'I'll be glad when it's all over, and I do worry lest anything be amiss with the baby.'

He could see the anxiety drawn in her face, and nodded silently; childbirth was indeed a time of great danger for both mother and child.

'I went down to speak with old Sarah, about her helping with the delivery, when time comes,' she said. 'She won't be able to get out here, says New Town's too far for her old legs to take her. I'll have to find another to call on. She grows a few herbs down there at the Blue House, but mostly she just cares for the old women that live there, now.'

'How long have you got to go?' Joshua tore off another chunk from the loaf. 'Four, five weeks, is it?'

'Aye. I'm glad we've got settled here in time, it was getting very hard at the Boar, not only Joe making nasty remarks, but customers too when Betty wasn't at hand. I saw Betty when I was leaving Sarah's place, and she gave me some old gowns and lengths of linen as a parting gift. They'll be useful to make clothes for the baby.'

Joshua nodded absently. He didn't see baby clothes were any concern of his.

'She also gave me some information.' She looked directly at him, holding his gaze. 'Something about what you'd stood up and said at Taunton assizes, at the minister's trial last September. It's taken six months to reach my ears, but that don't stop me feeling horror-struck at what you did, Josh.'

'What I did? What are you talking of, girl?'

'When you said you'd seen that banned preacher in company with old Master Silcox, and then they proved you were lying. Why did you say it, Josh?'

'Oh, that.' He scratched his head. He glanced up at Molly-Ann, but the hurt expression in her eyes forced him to look away again. 'Master Baily wanted a witness. He paid well and I wasn't averse to speaking against that minister. What's it to you, anyway?' He stood abruptly, sending his chair clattering on the flagstones. 'I reckon you still got feelings for him.' He leaned towards her, his fists resting on the table between them.

'I've never had what you call "feelings" for Gideon Silcox. He was kind to me in the past, same way as a father would be. It's beneath you to make such suggestions, and it was wicked of you to try to get him convicted.'

Molly-Ann was standing now, but her shoulders shook. Joshua felt a wave of heat rise from his belly, up his neck and into his head; his eyes were focused on her face to the exclusion of all else. He took a deep breath and looked away.

'Don't anger me, Molly-Ann. You keep your criticisms to yourself, or you'll come to regret it. You'd best get away to bed now, before you provoke me further.' He picked his chair up from the floor and reached for his coat. 'I've work to do at the Catherine Hill yard this night. I'll see 'ee in the morning.'

'Master Naish does not have my full confidence.' James Baily placed his tankard on the table and gently rotated it, his eyes on the surface of the chestnut brown ale. 'I suspect he plans to acquire building land of his own and erect dwellings on the same pattern as he is doing for me. I detect a strong vein of ambition in that man.'

Joshua nodded slowly. 'He's a sight tougher than he looks.' He drew on his clay pipe and blew a cloud of smoke towards the ceiling of Baily's study. 'And for one of those puritans, he's damned stubborn.'

Master Baily smirked. 'They're not as meek as they'd have us believe. They know how to make a good return in business, and they're that mean and flinty when it comes to living, they soon amass a fortune.'

'Have you seen evidence of Naish's plans, sir? Do you know if he has secured any land for development yet?'

'No, but I have my ear to the ground, and I want you to see what you can find out, too. I don't want any competitors at this stage.'

'You want me to give him a warning?'

'No, I fear that may only make him more committed in his ambitions.'

Baily put a hand to his short moustache: it resembled the king's, which Joshua had seen in the illustration on a handbill. His patron seemed inordinately proud of the whiskers.

'You've settled into your cottage,' Baily asked. 'Is all to your liking?'

Joshua smiled and nodded. 'Aye, we're very comfortable there. I'm much obliged to you, sir.'

'Well, for the present we shall watch Naish carefully,' Baily said. 'He's proved a good master mason managing the men; he's kept to schedule and budget after that first difficulty during the winter. I notice he still looks sideways at you Joshua, holds tight to his stick when you are nearby. You've got under his skin.'

'Aye. That's where I mean to be.' He drained his ale. 'I have business to attend to, if you'll excuse me, Master Baily.'

Half an hour later his mare was trotting briskly along Keyford, the late March wind snatching at his hat as he rode, his thoughts on the instructions he needed to give Ben for the dispatch of a large quantity of fine Mendip wool that night. With so many ventures underway, he had found the stolid Ben a good deputy for his owling activities; the fellow was reliable and dogged if unimaginative, and now that he was free of that nervous brother of his, he was proving as tough as Joshua himself when it came to handing out threats of violence.

The track down to the crossing of the Adderwell Brook narrowed. A series of stone slabs had been laid to assist travellers crossing the marshy ground and Joshua let his horse choose her own course. He drew rein sharply when he lifted his eyes from the horse's footing. A figure had appeared without warning from a side path and was holding up one hand to stop him. He squinted into the sudden spring sunlight, and recognised the features of John Silcox, son of that interfering minister. Who did the fellow think he was, to try and delay him in this way?

'Master Whittock, do you have a moment?' John's eyes held a steady, serious gaze.

'You again!'

Joshua urged on his horse, but John reached out and grabbed the bridle.

'Get out of my way, or I'll kick you down again.'

'I pray you, stop a moment. I wish very much to speak with you and, I hope, place our acquaintance on a different footing.'

'I've naught to say to you, other than tell you to keep your father away from my Molly-Ann. We've no use for his interference, nor yours neither.'

'Please.' John's expression again baffled Joshua as it had in Naish's yard. Fear, uncertainty, even anger, he would have expected from a man he had previously assaulted, but here he saw intense longing . . . Desire even. The man seemed to be devouring him with that look. Joshua felt a fury grow deep in his belly and surge into his chest.

'What the devil do you want with me?' he shouted, reining

the mare backwards.

John shook his head, the fire in his eyes seemed to have been suddenly quenched. He released the bridle. 'You have no wish for mutual acquaintance, I see that now. So be it, but I had to find out.'

Joshua's horse was anxious to be away, but he held her back. 'I want no further "acquaintance" with you, Master Silcox. I suspect now what you are driving at, and that bain't for me. You approach me again and I'll denounce you to the justices. You know it would be a hanging matter.' He gave the mare a kick and she surged ahead towards Culverhill, forcing John Silcox to step back smartly onto the grass verge.

In the meantime he had fleeces to sort and bag. Ben should be at Cowbridge Farm ahead of him, and with Baily securely in his pocket he had no fear of an unwelcome visit from the authorities.

All the way down Feltham Lane, over the river and up the hill towards Tytherington, he fretted away at Silcox's audacity in this unwanted offer of "acquaintance". He recalled their meeting in the Portsmouth tavern now. He'd dismissed the man's approach as simple gratitude, at the time he'd thought no more of it. But had he given some unintentional look or remark? He was sure he had not. He'd never experienced desire for another man and he didn't now. He couldn't comprehend what this Silcox was feeling, and didn't like to think what he hoped for. He spat into the hedgerow. Next time their paths crossed, he'd leave the fellow with a cracked head for sure.

# CHAPTER 13

MOLLY-ANN GENTLY WRAPPED a woollen blanket around the swaddled baby, pinned it, then enfolded the precious bundle in the shawl she tied around herself, holding him warm, safe and close to her own body. The month of May in this year of 1667 was proving to be chilly and changeable, and she wanted to ensure baby William came to no harm on this, one of his first outings into the wide world.

She could not bide in the house after the news she had heard at midday. Ben had appeared outside in the roadway – she had spied him out of the window, ambling up and down Long Row looking lost. She had gone to the door, called to her brother and invited him into the house, puzzled at his reticence – he had seemed almost overawed, glancing from side to side, not looking directly at her.

'I knew you had one of these new houses, Molly-Ann,' he had said. 'Josh said it was one of the first finished, but I wasn't sure which 'twas. It's been a few months since I've seen 'ee. Is all well?'

'Aye. Josh got us this fine cottage, as you see. And now we have the baby too.' She'd held the sleeping William towards his uncle, and Ben's face had relaxed into a fond smile at sight of him, but then he'd given her some news that had sent a shiver through her.

'You should know,' he'd said, 'Josh is to fight in the singlestick match this af'ernoon, up on Packhorse Ground. It'll be a mighty tough one and he's likely to lose, so he told me. Did he say aught to you?'

Of course he hadn't. Molly-Ann shook her head. 'I'd best come and tend to him, although I hate this fighting. But why's he doing this? A big purse I suppose?'

'Aye. And he's carrying Master Baily's colours. He'll get a share of the wagers too most likely.'

'Will you come with me, Ben? I'd be glad of your company.'

'I don't see as I can, Molly-Ann. I've work to do today, things to move for Joshua. He'd not be pleased if I let him down. Sorry.'

Molly-Ann was still recovering her strength after giving birth. Feeding the baby, the extra laundry, the broken nights, all were wearing her down and draining her reserves. It might have been a five minute walk to Packhorse Ground for most, but by the time she reached it this Sunday afternoon, she felt as though she had walked twenty miles. She drew the checked shawl more closely round the baby. The wind was keen and his little bonnet only covered the top of his head, leaving his neck and cheeks exposed.

Wrestling bouts were already taking place at one side of the field. She watched from a distance but recognised no one among the men participating or those watching the combatants. She turned away. To her left, a rope was being laid out on the ground; she drew closer to see if this was where the singlestick contest was to take place. Ben had not been specific about the time; perhaps it was scheduled for much later in the afternoon.

A young couple stood between her and the fight enclosure. The man half turned to her and she squeaked with relief. 'Nat! I'm right pleased to see you here.' She glanced at the woman:

not a member of Master Silcox's congregation, to judge by the pink ribbons and the profusion of blond curls beneath her cap.

'Sister!' Nathaniel's face broke into the most welcoming smile she could have wished for. 'This is a lucky chance. I've not been up here for more than six months, but Mistress Ellen persuaded me to just walk by, on our way to take tea with the Silcoxes.' His face clouded. 'But what be you doing here in this rowdy place, and on your own too?'

Ellen's eyes had widened and her mouth formed a round "ooh!" as she caught sight of the baby, well hidden by Molly-Ann's shawl. Nathaniel's face drained of colour.

'Come, let's walk to the side of the field, under the trees,' he said. 'I think we've a lot of news to catch up on, Molly-Ann. I didn't even know you were expecting a baby . . .'

'No, I didn't feel able to tell you or the Silcoxes. I know you've a low opinion of Joshua,' Molly-Ann said as she sank with relief onto the stump of a recently-felled beech tree. She untied the shawl to cradle William more comfortably on her lap. 'But he's stood by me and provided us with a good home. Little William here is a blessing to us. Josh is doing well. He has some powerful friends in the town and says he will make a deal of money from his connections, and he has their protection too. He's raised himself up from nothing. I think I made the right choice . . .'

'I pray you did, Molly-Ann.' Nathaniel's serious face suggested he doubted that she had.

'But you haven't introduced me properly to your friend.' Molly-Ann extended her free hand in greeting to Ellen.

'Mistress Ellen, my sister, Molly-Ann.'

Nathaniel's eyes shone as he looked at the girl, his sister noticed.

'Ellen works for old Master Sheppard on Catherine Hill,

as do I,' he said. 'I'm learning all about the woollen trade. I'm to oversee the manufacture for Master John Sheppard.'

Molly-Ann nodded. 'You're doing well then, found your feet?'

'Aye. Well, just starting out. And I'm learning my letters and to cast accounts. I want to make myself as useful as possible to the Sheppards. It was John Silcox that introduced me to them. I attend the Congregational chapel now. Why don't you come along with us, Molly-Ann? We're invited to take a dish of tea with them at Keyford, then go on to the evening service.'

She shook her head. 'I've not seen them since the wintertime, but I'd be awkward in their company now; they're too good for me. And anyway, there's strong feeling twixt them and Joshua. He's told me many a time of his dislike of both the Silcoxes. I'd not want to give him cause for anger at me.'

Nathaniel's eyes were on hers. 'He's a hard man, that Joshua. I hope he's not given you cause for regret, Molly-Ann?'

'No, no. He's kind and caring, mostly.'

'So what're you doing here now?' Nathaniel asked.

'It was Ben. He came to tell me Josh is expected to fight up here this afternoon, and Ben feared it would go hard for him. He seems to think Josh is likely to be bested. I felt I should be here to tend to him if it's needed.'

'You've a kind heart, sister. I hope he deserves it.'

Ellen was gazing across the field. 'I think they may be starting the contest. Look there, Nat.'

Even across the width of the pasture, Molly-Ann could see it was indeed Joshua who was preparing for the bout. The man squaring up to him looked lighter than Joshua, but very agile, and probably quicker on his feet.

'We can see what happens from here,' Nathaniel said. 'No

need to go closer unless we have to.'

Molly-Ann nodded. 'Can you watch, please Nat? I don't want to see it. Tell me what happens.'

Nathaniel sighed. 'As long as these vile sports go on, we'll never be a civilised, God fearing nation. It would have been better if the king hadn't returned, I sometimes think. John and Gideon tell me how much better life was under the Commonwealth.'

He turned to watch the fight. 'Josh has started well; he's driving his opponent back, landed a couple of good strokes.' He shook his head. 'That was a cracker. The other fellow's fallen, no, he's up again.' Nathaniel took a step closer, stood on tiptoe. 'Josh's tripped. How did that happen? He's getting pummelled.' He sucked in his breath. 'That was a nasty blow! Oof! He's not getting up . . . they've stopped the fight.'

By now, Molly-Ann had re-tied her shawl with the baby fastened securely at her hip. 'Come with me. We must see what's happened.'

Together they stumbled across the tussocky field to find Joshua lying on his back, his eyes shut and blood coursing down from a head wound. The match umpires were trying to staunch the flow without much success, and Molly-Ann pushed them aside, anxious to see just how badly hurt he was. She knelt beside him and shook his arm. 'Josh! Josh!' she called but there was no response, although his chest still rose and fell. She pulled the kerchief from her neck and held it firmly to the ugly cut on his forehead, at the same time looking around her at the trampled grass. She reached over and plucked a couple of long narrow leaves, and crumpled them in her hand.

'Plantain. Old Sarah's used this on cuts afore now,' she said as she bound the leaves against the wound with the bloody kerchief. Joshua was a fearsome sight, his face streaked with blood, contusions on his bare chest and shoulders, and one eye closed and swelling up. The other opened slowly. He groaned, rolled over and vomited. Nathaniel helped his sister get him into a sitting position, where he wiped his mouth on his arm.

'My God, Josh, but you're in a state,' Molly-Ann muttered.

She looked up. Two smart buckled shoes, surmounted by a fine pair of masculine legs in white stockings, had appeared beside Joshua. She looked further up and recognised James Baily, having seen him about the town with Joshua a number of times.

'Master Baily.' She dipped her head and Joshua looked up at his patron, who smiled sympathetically and nodded down at him. Molly-Ann was surprised James Baily seemed to have taken the defeat so well. He put a small leather bag into Joshua's hand. Molly-Ann watched as her man sank it deep in his breeches pocket then staggered to his feet. He swayed until Nathaniel held him steady.

'I'll leave you in the care of your . . . friends,' Baily said and Molly-Ann felt a shudder of disgust as his eyes lingered on her, before he turned and strode away to join a group of elegantly dressed men.

Joshua glared at Nathaniel and stumbled groggily away from him. 'We've no need of your help,' he snarled. 'Molly-Ann can get me home. Sight of you fair sickens me. You clear off, Nathaniel, you hear?' He picked up his shirt and struggled to pull it on, wincing as he raised his arm, but rejecting Molly-Ann's offer of help.

Nathaniel lifted his eyebrows at his sister, who nodded. 'I can manage now, Nat. I thank 'ee.'

Back home at Long Row, Joshua slumped onto a chair. Molly-Ann laid William in his crib and filled a bowl with water. With one of the cloths that were piled ready for the baby's use she sponged the drying blood from Joshua's head, neck and chest. 'Master Baily didn't seem upset you'd lost; that's something to be grateful for.' She frowned. It was strange, but Joshua hadn't ranted on about losing, nor the blow to his pride, either. Maybe that would come later once his confusion had cleared. That eye looked bad.

'I'll get some salves from Sarah for your bruising Josh. Let me bandage your head now.'

He held still as she ministered to him. 'My skull throbs fit to burst,' he groaned.

'I'll go and see if she's got some balm I can use.'

After feeding and changing the baby, Molly-Ann laid him back in his crib, made up the coal fire, placed a chair by the blaze for Joshua and reached for her shawl. 'I hope I'll catch Sarah at home. She may still be at chapel. I'll be back as soon as I can.'

It was all downhill from their cottage to the almshouse beside the Boar tavern, and in ten minutes she was tapping on the door of Sarah's room.

'She b'ain't there,' a voice called from the adjoining room. 'She's gone to the meeting with the trustees down in the visitors' hall.'

Molly-Ann called her thanks to the disembodied voice and returned to the ground floor. The meeting had clearly just ended. Two gentlemen and a lady were taking refreshments with some of the old women who were seeing out their days in the Blue House. Sarah tottered across the hall to join her by the door, a steaming cup in her hands: Molly-Ann caught a whiff of peppermint.

'I've come to ask 'ee for some salves and such like. Is it safe to speak of it, here in company?'

'Lord love 'ee, yes. I have my own herb garden here and make up drinks and balms for everyone, they all know about it.' Sarah's smile wrinkled her cheeks as well as her eyes. 'I feel I'm doing some powerful good work for my friends, my dear. And I don't have to trudge the lanes and fields to gather my plants, now they're all growing here in our lovely gardens.'

They moved further into the hall to talk as some of the elderly inmates started to push past to return to their rooms.

'So who is hurt, and what injuries do he have? Is it one of your brothers?'

'Nay, 'tis Josh, my man. He's a nasty cut, a black eye, bruises and grazes. He had a hard knock on the head and lost his senses, he was sick when he came to.'

'In a fight was he?'

'Aye, singlestick. Silly fool, he must have picked the wrong opponent. He came off worst anyway.'

Molly-Ann sensed a movement of the air and glanced around. One of the gentlemen was standing close behind her, his back to her, as he surveyed the choice of cakes and scones on the table before him.

'He told Ben he wasn't going to win. I was amazed at that, he's mighty strong, he could have beaten anyone. Nat said he tripped, which surprised me.'

Sarah nodded.

'Anyway, his patron, Master Baily, he didn't seem at all displeased, gave him a good payment.'

'Good, so all's well. We just need to patch him up.'

The gentleman turned and sauntered back to his companions; Molly-Ann noticed him frowning and talking intently with the other man.

'Who're they, Sarah? What's your meeting been about?'

Sarah sniffed. 'The Trustees. Sons of the Leversedge family

that founded the almshouse, or something. That's Edmund, and his brother I think. Family has a name for rowdiness, even though they be gentry. I'm grateful to them for this place though. Don't know what I'd have done otherwise. They come to see us now and again, I'm told, see how we're doing. We gets a new blue gown every other year, they say. I'll look forward to that, if I'm spared. Now come with me to my little still room – it's just a cupboard really. I think I have the things you want.'

It was Ascension Day, just four days after the singlestick contest, and the bells of the church of St John the Baptist rang mightily, the echoes rebounding from the stone walls of the streets above and below the church. The windows of the adjoining Bell tavern shook in their frames in time with the clamour. The boughs of the horse chestnuts swayed in the breeze, tossing their white and pink candles high in the sunshine. Molly-Ann shielded baby William's ears from the din so far as she could, but he was still crying furiously as she pushed open the door of their home.

She had started to unbutton her bodice to feed the baby even as she came through the doorway, but stopped and clutched William closely when she saw the appalling sight that awaited her.

Joshua stood leaning over the table, one fist on the board. His clothing was in tatters and bloodstained, his face swollen and bleeding – she knew it was him only by his boots. One eye was closed up again, and his left arm hung apparently useless and at an odd angle. The sound of his breathing was audible, even over William's wails.

'What's happened to 'ee now?' Molly-Ann stowed the

baby in his crib and approached the man, her gorge rising. Closer, she could see tooth marks and lacerations to his skin, the blood oozing from ragged bites to his legs and arms. She felt faint, but swallowed the nausea down and took a deep breath. Joshua had lifted his head at her arrival, but seemed unable to speak. She brought a chair and guided him to sit, then gingerly peeled off his jerkin and shirt, exposing the punctured and bruised skin.

'You poor thing, you've been savaged . . . my God, this is cruel . . .' The water in her bowl was soon tinged deep crimson as she washed his wounds, all the time muttering endearments and soothing him as she would a child. He flinched as the cloth touched the raw places on his cheek and neck, and again as she dabbed on the last of the marigold and St John's wort salve that Sarah had provided the week before. She had never known Joshua to tremble at anything, but now he was shaking uncontrollably, and still seemed unable to tell her what had occurred.

Molly-Ann turned to his arm. Was the shoulder dislocated, she wondered. She felt utterly incapable, this was a matter that needed more skill than she possessed. It struck her that such an injury might be caused by a fall from a roof, the feet sliding and the body falling to the hard ground, one that a hellier might suffer. Such an injury as this must be a fairly common sight to Master Naish.

Wrapping a blanket around the shaking Joshua, she left him and set off in search of the master mason, and by chance he was only a few hundred paces away, supervising the installation of roof timbers on one of the new cottages.

His expression was one of concern and empathy as he struggled to pull Joshua's arm back into its socket. Joshua groaned in relief as the shoulder clicked home.

'I know what a dislocation feels like, Master Whittock, as you are well aware,' Naish said, and held up his hand.

Joshua lifted his head and looked coldly at him, then at Molly-Ann. 'This was your doing. The bastards tricked me to their farm at Vallis, set their hounds on me . . . they tried to kill me for their sport.'

She felt a cold wave rise from her chest to her cheeks. 'Who, Josh? Who set upon you?'

'They Leversedges. Supposed to be gentlemen . . . and they use a man like this.'

'But why, what are they to you?'

'It were them we cozened, Master Baily and me. Wagering on the singlestick match.' He glared at Molly-Ann. 'And it was you who gave them to know I threw the match.'

'Me? What do I know of it?' She backed away from the fury that burned in his one open eye. 'I don't even know these men . . .' Her words tailed off as she recalled her conversation with Sarah, the gentleman who had stood so close as he chose his cake. Her hands flew to her mouth. 'I didn't realise . . . how could I know?'

Joshua pushed himself up from the chair and took a faltering step towards her. 'You betrayed me, Molly-Ann. You gave the game away and they've half killed me. I'm minded to do for you an' all.'

He staggered as he came towards her and Simon Naish sprang forward to stop him.

'Calmly, Joshua. This won't mend matters.'

'You back off,' Joshua spat at him, but collapsed back onto the chair.

'You've had a terrible shock,' Naish said. 'Molly-Ann clearly didn't mean to betray you. Think better of it, man.'

Joshua put his head in his hands.

'I thank 'ee Master Naish,' Molly-Ann said as she picked up the now howling baby and tried to hush him. 'We're beholden to you for your help with Josh's arm. I'll tend to him now. We mustn't keep you any longer from your work.'

Naish nodded, picked his hat up and moved to the door. 'I'm along here all afternoon. Shout for me if I'm needed.'

As soon as the door had closed, Molly-Ann sat down to feed the baby. 'Let me get him soothed and settled first, Josh. I can't think straight while he's grizzling and yelling, then we must talk.'

Joshua growled something then hobbled to the corner shelf, where a small barrel lay on its side, a tap projecting from it. He poured himself a mug of ale, sat by the empty hearth and had soon drained the lot. Molly-Ann watched him silently from the other side of the room. His scowl had deepened further and he winced at any movement of his left arm. He refilled the mug amidst much muttering.

At last, William was satisfied. Molly-Ann changed his cloths and settled him into the crib, rocking it gently until his eyes closed and peace fell. She put bread and cheese on the table. 'Will you eat, Josh?'

He glared at her. 'I trusted you, Molly-Ann. I thought you'd know to keep your mouth shut about my affairs. I'd have kept my business ventures secret from you if I'd known you were such a leaky sieve.'

'Honest, Josh, I'd never knowingly give aught away. It were just that I was ignorant myself of the meaning of it all. I won't speak of your doings again, not to anyone.'

'Too late, woman. I've been thinking it over. Reckon I did better when I was by myself. It's like you're a-spying on me. I can't be sure you won't betray me again, whether to my enemies or to the constables.' He shot her a malevolent look.

'It's time we parted. You can pack yer things and go.'

'Go? Go where?' She had visions of herself tramping the streets, William in her arms. She drew closer to him. 'Don't turn us out Josh . . . where would we go?'

'That's your problem,' he snarled. 'I pay the rent on this house, it's mine. You can make your own way. I've no wish to see 'ee more.'

She felt stunned; sight and sound were dimmed. He had always appeared to desire her company; he had been generous in setting up their home. He was not forward in expressing loving feelings towards her, but she had believed he was genuine in his commitment to her – and towards the baby.

'But how can I get by? I can't keep me and William, even if the Grimwades were to give me my old job back. Where shall I live?'

'That's not my concern. I just want you out!' He slammed the mug down on the table; a wave of brown liquid slopped over the side. 'Get out, now!' he roared, half rising from his seat. His face creased up and he slumped back. 'Take yer things, or they'll be on the fire.'

'But the baby . . . how can you treat your own son like this?'

'Is he mine? How do I know that?'

'Look at him! He's the image of you. Of course he's yours. Once I met you, I had naught to do with any other man. I do love you Josh. You know I do . . .' Her voice caught in her throat.

'Don't give me that,' he said. 'I can see through you now. I may have been deceived in the past, but my heart's hardened against you now. You're nothing to me.'

He turned and stared into the cold ashes.

# CHAPTER 14

'I MUST CONFESS,' John Silcox said, 'I do find it more convenient to live here in Keyford with you, sir, than over at Wanstrow. Cherry Tree Cottage was delightful, but the time I had to spend working the land that went with it . . .' He shook his head. 'Better to be nurturing souls here in town than playing the husbandman for the sake of winter feed for my horse and a few eggs on my table.'

'I'm glad you feel that way, John.' His father put down his cup of nettle tea on the garden plank seat. 'It does me good to have your company and support, and with the school rendering a small profit now, the rental of this place is affordable, between us.'

The sun had almost set and it was growing chilly in the back garden of the Keyford cottage. 'Ha! The bats are coming out – look!' Gideon traced the swooping flight of one of the creatures with his finger. 'It'll soon be too dark to see them. I suppose it's the little midges they're catching, hunting on the wing like the swallows by day.'

'God provides them with an inexhaustible supply of food, and we provide them with nooks and crannies in our house roofs and barns. I imagine many people would envy them,' John said.

A rapping at the front door echoed through the house; father and son went inside, Gideon to admit the visitor, John to light candles against the evening gloom. He looked up in pleasure at the sound of Nathaniel's voice. 'You're out late, Nat. It's unlike you if you're working tomorrow . . . and who's with you?'

Nathaniel was followed by a cloaked woman, her hood drawn up over her head, her shape distorted by a burden she bore under the cloak. She pushed the hood back with one hand.

'Molly-Ann!' Gideon's tone expressed his astonishment. 'We've not seen you for months, my dear. How are you, and what brings you out at such a late hour?'

John placed a cushion for her on the settle then caught sight of the swaddled baby in the crook of her arm as she untied the shawl that bound him to her. 'Well, this is a surprise. I had no idea you were to be a mother. I'm sorry, I don't mean to presume, it's just that I did not know . . .'

Molly-Ann covered her eyes briefly with her free hand, then looked up. 'You must think so badly of me, masters, and indeed I've made some rash choices, but I thought all would work out for the best. . .' she swallowed. 'Nat here suggested I come to ask for your guidance. I just can't think straight.'

'My sister came to me this afternoon in a terrible state, sirs,' Nathaniel said. 'That villain Joshua, he's thrown her out, her and the baby. They've nowhere to go and I don't know what to suggest.'

John noticed his father's look of deep compassion. The dear man would try to help anyone in need, but for Molly-Ann, he knew, Gideon would let his heart be wrenched from his chest if it would do any good.

'Let me get you a warming drink first, then you must tell us what's happened, my dear,' Gideon said. 'Sarah left us a selection of her dried herbs when she moved out – I have the nettle for hayfever, myself, but perhaps you'd find chamomile more soothing?'

The candles burned down more than an inch in the time it took Molly-Ann to relate the news of her happy months with Joshua, William's arrival, and Joshua's sudden rejection of them. As she explained, she and the baby had neither a roof over their heads, nor any means of support. Nathaniel had offered them lodging, but his attic room was so tiny and ill-provided, this would be no more than a temporary solution. She refused to go to Cole Hill, not only because the place was virtually derelict, but Ben's presence there could put her in Joshua's path so easily.

John steepled his fingers. 'If you were able to work a few hours, Molly-Ann, and with your progress at Sheppards increasing your wages, Nat, might you be able to rent a bigger home between you? Two rooms would allow you all to live more comfortably.'

Nathaniel nodded. 'Aye, we might find something, I suppose, but what work can Molly-Ann do with a small baby? I'm out all hours, I can't care for him.'

'Two things you could try,' John said. 'Might you take in some work such as spinning? And also I'm sure my father would welcome help with the youngest children in his school – perhaps he'd allow you to take the baby with you?' He looked narrowly at his father. Gideon, he suspected, would be reluctant to make such an offer himself, but if she accepted, her presence at the school would be a great pleasure to him.

Gideon said nothing for some moments and John feared his father may have taken a prejudice against the baby because of his paternity, but John was able to release the breath he was holding as Gideon's eyes took on a glow in the candlelight.

'Nothing would please me more, if it suited you, my dear. I would welcome you both.'

Molly-Ann's face still looked drawn and exhausted, but

a flicker of a smile touched her lips. 'You are both so kind. I doubt I'd be much use at the school though. I hardly knows my letters myself.'

'Well, it's something to think about,' John said. 'Another avenue to explore is to go before the magistrates for a paternity order, get his father to pay towards William's keep.' His jaw tightened. The man who had seemed to him such an image of masculinity, who had provoked such desire in him not a year ago, now appeared a travesty of manliness. John felt both disappointment, and shame at his own misreading of Joshua.

One of the candles was starting to smoke and he trimmed it thoughtfully. 'Tomorrow, we must make an application to the parish authorities, Molly-Ann. Don't worry, my father or I will accompany you for the examination. It may be hard, giving evidence, but it needs to be done. He must be brought to book, and you have a good case.'


John Silcox raised the brass knocker and let it fall. The sound echoed dully from within the fine residence of Master Coombs at Abbot's Farm in Lower Keyford. After explaining their business to a frosty looking servant, John and Molly-Ann were shown into Master Coombs's parlour. 'How do you do, sir?' John offered his hand to the farmer. 'I believe you have been appointed Overseer of the Poor for Frome parish?'

'Aye, last Easter.' Master Coombs scowled. 'And an onerous position it is proving to be; taking up too much of my time. People are coming to the door at all hours of day and night. I'll be glad when my tenure is over.'

'My apologies then, sir, for adding to your burden. I am John Silcox, a lay preacher and servant of the Congregational chapel.'

Coombs nodded.

'I bring with me a young woman who has been abandoned by her child's father. She is here to submit to an examination by the parish to establish the child's paternity and the father's responsibility for his maintenance.'

Coombs waved his visitors to seats at the paper strewn table. Molly-Ann held William on her lap.

'Very well,' Coombs said. 'I have the form of the examination by heart.' He turned to Molly-Ann. 'Your name, mistress? What is your place of settlement, and the child's birthplace?'

Molly-Ann gave the details.

'Yes, this matter falls within my jurisdiction,' he said. 'And now I must ask about the circumstances of the child's conception. The father is known to you? What has been your relationship with him?'

Molly-Ann gave as clear an account as she could of Joshua's courtship of her, their time living together on Long Row, and Joshua's acceptance of William as his own, even to choosing the baby's name with her.

'And you say he has abandoned you? How did this come about, and when?' Coombs noted down her description of Joshua's behaviour and words, then asked about her financial position. At her response he tapped his teeth with his pen. 'Unless your brothers can help you, it does appear you will be destitute. It further seems that there is no doubt that this Joshua Whittock is the father of the child William.' He laid down his pen. 'The father is liable to maintain the child until he is old enough to be apprenticed. I will require him to enter into a bastardy bond and the parish will remit these funds to you for William's maintenance.'

Molly-Ann smiled her thanks, but there remained a

haunted look about her eyes. 'Sir, what if he resists?'

'If he refuses to pay, we can apply for an affiliation order and threaten him with prison. Don't worry, it's clear cut, it's his responsibility.'

'I thank you for your time and patience, sir,' John said. 'We shall look forward to hearing of your success.'

But success was not forthcoming. Coombs sent John a note the following week asking Molly-Ann to appear with him before the magistrate at the next petty sessions. The Overseer of the Poor would be applying for the order on behalf of the parish, but Molly-Ann would be required to give evidence in support of the application.

Her face fell when John told her the name of the magistrate before whom they were to appear: James Baily JP.


John Silcox felt a shiver pass across his shoulders. What was it they said? Someone walking across your grave? The last time he'd had occasion to pass through this doorway was in support of his father, when they had attended old Sarah's hearing before the magistrate. That must be nearly a year ago now. Baily had proved to be the bane of his life in many ways, and it looked as though the justice of the peace was about to have power over Molly-Ann's future as well now. He sighed deeply and offered her his arm to enter the gloomy hallway of Baily's townhouse. They were shown into an anteroom and told to wait.

'I trust Master Coombs has prepared the case for the parish well,' John said. 'It is in his interests to do so, to avoid the charge falling upon the ratepayers.'

'I don't care who pays, Josh or the parish, so long as I get something to help me out,' Molly-Ann said. 'I won't be a burden on my brothers, but I can't yet see how I can support myself and William. I was foolish to trust in Josh – why ever didn't I listen to Nat and believe him?'

'We can all look back and wish we'd done things differently,' John said with feeling. 'But I can understand how you were attracted to him.' He passed his hand over his face, and Molly-Ann gave him a puzzled look.

'Joshua is a very persuasive man, and he inspires a strong fascination. In spite of, or perhaps because of his disreputable reputation he has a strange allure. There's no shame to you in having been beguiled by him, Molly-Ann.'

'I wish I'd never met him, now.' She looked out of the room's single window, down onto Master Baily's stable yard. 'It can't have been love between us. It must have been something more shallow, more easily destroyed. It just seemed to evaporate. He said I'd betrayed him, and that was that. And as soon as he turned away from me, I knew I didn't want him anymore. I was truly a'feared for my life. I'd lost all trust in him. William and I couldn't have bided there, even if he'd let us.'

The door opened and Master Coombs beckoned to them. 'Come in now, please. The magistrates are ready to hear the case.'

Again, James Baily sat with his back to the window, his attention focused on the papers before him. The garden behind him shone with raindrops as the sun appeared briefly from the clouds. Beside him, Joseph Glanvill, the vicar, replaced his coffee cup in its saucer, and stared at the three claimants. Master Coombs was given a seat across the broad table from James Baily; Molly-Ann and John stood behind him.

'So, Master Coombs, yet another paternity case, I believe?' Baily's eyes were still fastened on the documents.

Coombs twitched. Had he been a bird you could have said his feathers were ruffled, John thought, then dismissed the passing notion as too flippant; nonetheless, the Overseer of the Poor seemed to have taken offence at the perceived implication that he was the instigator of these cases. John frowned. This was not an auspicious start to the hearing.

'Sir, I have conducted a full examination of the mother's case, and it appears well-founded. However, the father has refused to enter into a bastardy bond, and I come before you now to seek an affiliation order for the parish.'

James Baily sighed and finally lifted his eyes from the papers on his table. They skimmed over first Coombs, then John himself and finally came to rest on Molly-Ann. John observed that it was several heartbeats before the magistrate ceased his scrutiny of her, let his eyelids drop, and looked again at the paperwork. The man's breathing had grown faster. Molly-Ann, he saw, was frowning and her cheeks had become quite pink.

Glanvill cleared his throat. 'We have read your account of the examination, Master Coombs, and it does indeed appear a persuasive claim.'

Baily raised one hand imperiously. 'Not so fast, sir. I have yet to be convinced.'

'Of what element are you doubtful, sir?' Master Coombs sounded perplexed. 'I cannot believe I have come across a more cogent case in all my experience.'

'Which, I believe, is not very long,' Baily sneered, and again looked Molly-Ann up and down. 'The alleged father has himself informed me that he is certain the child is not his, that this woman, Molly-Ann, was already pregnant when he first met her. He states that he will not be held responsible for another man's child.'

'Well where is he?' Coombs snapped at Baily. 'Why doesn't he appear here and give us evidence himself?'

'He's away, working on important business.' Baily waved his hand dismissively. 'I obtained a full statement from him before he went. He has signed a declaration, sworn on the Bible.'

'But that bain't true, sirs.' Molly-Ann stepped forward and John noticed Baily's eyes light up. 'It's his baby, no doubt of it. I was *not* expecting when we met.'

'He tells me you were not a maiden either, and he'd heard it said that you had borne a baby three summers past.'

Molly-Ann shook visibly with frustration. 'Yes, that was true, but not that I was pregnant when I met Joshua. He acknowledged William as his own when he was born, chose his name with me. He's a liar and a cheat if he thinks to disown him now.'

The justice of the peace and the vicar exchanged a look.

'I find the case not proven,' Baily said. 'You must seek again for the child's father's identity, Master Coombs. Joshua Whittock is not liable.'

Molly-Ann started to sway on her feet and John put out a hand to steady her.

'How am I to support my baby?' she asked plaintively, her eyes on Master Coombs.

'You could place him at the baby farm. He'd be cared for by the guardian with the other little ones of the parish. That would free you to get employment.'

'The thought of that place . . . it horrifies me. So many die.'

'I can see no other recourse, mistress,' Baily said, smiling. He paused. 'If you require employment, come back later once you have considered our ruling. I may be able to offer you something.'

John scowled at the magistrate. 'I had thought you to be a gentleman, sir. I can see what you are after.' He turned on his heel. 'Come Molly-Ann. I'm sure we can find you more honourable employment elsewhere.'

They trudged away from the magistrate's house in Hill Lane, heading for the Silcoxes' cottage, where Gideon had been left to mind baby William. The upper Market Place was busy. Half a dozen cows – some with calves at foot – were being herded down to the livestock sales in Brownjohn's Mead, as dogs snapped at their heels and growled. Molly-Ann squeezed against the houses and shop fronts to avoid their trampling feet.

When the beasts had passed, John turned to her. 'You understood the way Baily's mind was running, I've no doubt?'

She nodded. 'He thinks I'll sell myself cheaply now I'm in this situation. Well I won't. If he's determined to have me, he can damn well pay through the nose.'

John looked up sharply. 'You can't mean that, surely? You'd take his money after the way he's cheated you today?'

'Josh always said he had powerful friends. He's proved it now.'

'Please don't acquiesce in their evil plans. The injustice of refusing the bond was bad enough, but for Baily to prey upon you when you are so vulnerable is truly wicked.'

Molly-Ann paused to give way to a horse and rider trotting out of Rook Lane; she drew her skirts aside as the hoofs threw up a spatter of mud from the wet roadway. 'I'm too tired to think, Master Silcox, too dispirited. I'll take William back to Nat's place now and try to work out what's to be done. Maybe the Grimwades would take me back at the Boar of evenings, if I could leave William with Nat.'

John shook his head.

'Rook Lane gets steeper every time I walk up it,' Molly-Ann said, 'how can that be?'

He offered her his arm. 'You're probably going hungry Molly-Ann. You need feeding up after all you've been through. Please come and share our meal; my father would be delighted to have your company, and we can talk about you helping out at the school.'

He glanced to his right as a door opened in one of the cottages and Dorothea Naish emerged, her expression unusually cold.

'Good day to you Master Silcox.'

He raised his hat. 'Mistress Naish. I hope we find you well?'

Dorothea looked pointedly at Molly-Ann. 'I don't believe we have been introduced.'

'This is a young woman whom my father and I have known many years: Molly-Ann.'

'I don't recall seeing you at meeting, mistress?' Dorothea said.

'No, I don't attend,' Molly-Ann faltered. 'Master Silcox and his father have been good friends, but I've never been drawn to the chapel.'

'Molly-Ann is sister to Nathaniel,' John said.

'Ah! Of course, I thought I detected a resemblance.' Dorothea's lips formed a smile, but her narrowed eyes were still cold. 'Your brother has been very assiduous in his studies; he has little more to learn from me. I shall be sorry to lose such an apt pupil.'

'I am glad if he has profited from your instruction.' Molly-Ann's tone was unusually flat, and John looked from one young woman to the other. There seemed to be a distinct chill that he could not account for.

'Please give your father my compliments,' Dorothea said to John as she set off down the hill towards town.

He again lifted his hat, but she had turned away.

'A fine gentlewoman,' Molly-Ann said. 'I'm sorry if my presence brought down her scorn upon 'ee, Master Silcox.'

John gasped in surprise. 'Is that what you think? I'm sure she had no such feeling, Molly-Ann. Surely not?'

Molly-Ann simply nodded.

# CHAPTER 15

J UNE BROUGHT A radical change in the weather after a cool, damp May, and hot sunshine had baked the mud of the roads rock hard. The delightful summer weather had inspired James Baily's wife to propose a visit to her parents' home in the cathedral city of Wells, giving the elderly pair an opportunity to see their grandchildren, and providing a change of scene for herself.

'Sadly, business affairs and my judicial responsibilities preclude my involvement in this pleasant excursion,' Baily said to his wife Sophia over the breakfast table. 'By all means, do you go, and take the children with you. You haven't seen your mother and father for a long time, I know. Don't concern yourself about me; I've plenty to occupy my time here.' He took another slice of toast. 'Why not stay a month? You may as well make the most of your journey.'

His wife's grey eyes studied him for a few moments. 'You seem mighty keen that we should go, James. What is your reason for this, I wonder?' She buttered her own toast aggressively. 'Are you perhaps planning to invite your drinking cronies, or hold a gambling session?' Her teeth tore into the slice and Baily flinched.

'Business, as ever. I need to agree more leases with Yerbury, hurry the works forward, take full advantage of the season. I can't leave it at this juncture. The returns are starting to come in. They give me real hope for our future financial position.'

Sophia tutted. 'Not before time. I trust any profits will not be frittered away on horses and dice.' She dabbed her lips with a white linen napkin and gestured to the servant to refill her cup with chocolate.

'Of course, my dear. Now, why don't you write to your father this morning? Propose next Monday for your arrival and see what he says.' He signalled an end to their discussion by directing his full attention to a copy of last week's *Public Intelligencer* which had recently become available in Frome. He rustled the pages assertively.

An hour later and alone in his study, Baily gazed down at Hill Lane. The street was relatively quiet, but to his right the noise and bustle of the Market Place was building steadily and the cries of the traders could be heard quite clearly. His marriage to Sophia had grown stale of late. They now met over the dining table and little more. She had her interests and he had his; they had a reasonable number of healthy children: why should he not seek amusement outside the home?

Since the day of that last bastardy case, he'd had almost constant thoughts of the young woman. Not for her welfare, her means of support, or the health of her child, but rather thoughts of her pretty face, her strong young body, and how easily he might attain some measure of control over her. Most of the mothers that came before him were drab, miserable creatures who seemed devoid of spirit or self-esteem. Molly-Ann was in a different class altogether. He had seen her about the town, sometimes with Joshua, and most recently up at Hell's Corner on Packhorse Ground, at the singlestick competition. Whittock was a fool, he thought, to cast her off, but his rejection of her certainly made his own path smoother. He pondered what was the lowest amount that would secure her services to himself, exclusively. It wouldn't cost much, he was pretty confident. He liked the prospect of a mistress at his beck and call. It wasn't as if he wanted to be seen in society with her; he'd just install her in some convenient place and take his pleasure whenever he wished. He chided himself. His thoughts were running away with him. She had not returned to see him and he had yet to strike a deal with her.

Now that the development of New Town was underway he could anticipate having access to more ready funds. His inherited land holdings were let on long leases to established tenants, and generated a regular but modest return which barely covered his normal household expenditure. Once the loan from Singer was taken into account, the rents from the dwellings on Long Row would enable him to live a more entertaining life without falling further into debt. Yes, this seemed an opportune moment to indulge his desire for Molly-Ann.

But where, he wondered, might he house her? One of his new cottages was out of the question; she couldn't be left in Joshua's vicinity, that would be sure to end badly, and it would be a waste to let her have the use of a whole dwelling anyway. Maybe a couple of rooms somewhere in town would suffice, somewhere he could easily call upon her without attracting undue attention. He tapped his fingers on the window ledge. Perhaps a chamber at a local inn . . . he would look into that without delay.

The rent of two attic rooms at the Sheaves was reasonably modest, he discovered. If he gave Molly-Ann a further five shillings a week to keep herself and the baby it would, he thought, be well worth the expense to have exclusive and unlimited access to her. It would not excite real censure if he were seen entering the main door of one of the foremost taverns of the town, and it would be easy enough to continue up the busy staircase and so to the top floor. The silence of the landlord and his servants would have to be bought, but he could see no other risks to his scheme. Striding down the street from the Sheaves, he fingered his neatly trimmed moustaches and contemplated the pleasures that awaited him. His pulse was quickening in anticipation.

He threaded his way between the people who thronged the Market Place – you could hardly move for people and animals today. Few would have the means to buy the merchandise before them, but it cost nothing to look and dream: he jingled the coins in his own pocket. Stalls selling second quality broadcloth and the cheaper kerseys were doing brisk business and he recognised one trader as the man whom Joshua had punched in Naish's yard some months before. His attention shifted to the young woman speaking to the fellow. She had her back to him but Baily would know those dark curls anywhere – at last he'd run her to earth. But was there a connection between her and this man, he wondered. Did she have someone other than Joshua in her past? The young man was smiling very familiarly at Molly-Ann, then reached out and patted her arm. It was the same fellow he'd seen after the singlestick match, he recognised him now. He felt the blood rise to his head: had he already lost the opportunity to take her for himself?

He hung back in the crowd that constantly shifted around the stalls, until he saw her move away from the woollens and walk slowly out of the Market Place. She carried a small cloth bag as well as the baby, as though she had been purchasing some few things at the market. He followed her, adjusting his pace so that he very gradually caught up with her after she had turned into Cheap Street.

'Good day to you, Molly-Ann.' He nodded to her. A fierce emotion that he struggled to interpret lit her eyes, and she took a step back. She seemed to be undergoing a struggle, as though she wanted to speak but was determined to restrain herself.

'I'm glad to have the opportunity of a private word with you, my dear.' He allowed himself a few seconds to study her face and neck, and was gratified to see a distinct blush rise up from her exposed collar bones to her forehead. 'You did not return to hear my offer of employment after,' he paused, 'after our previous encounter. I am in a position to do much to help you, albeit on a private basis. There will be no further legal steps you can take – you will *not* be receiving support from Joshua Whittock.'

The silence that fell between them was emphasised by the purling of the water that ran down the gutter in the centre of the street. Baily glanced around. There was no one within earshot.

'No, he will not be your provider, but *I* might.'

Baily noticed the muscles in Molly-Ann's jaw working then her words poured from her as if from an upturned bucket: 'You're as black hearted as he. I want nothing to do with either of you. I'd rather be as poor as I am than be beholden to a villainous hypocrite such as 'ee. How can you claim to be the king's justice here when you twist the law to suit your friends? What an example do 'ee set when you let men like Joshua get away with ruining a woman – and his own son?'

Baily struck his cane on the ground. 'You show some respect, young woman, or I'll have you put in the pillory. I'm minded to offer you a roof and support and you have the impudence to call me hypocrite! You're on the way to a whipping if you don't mend your manners.'

Molly-Ann scowled at him but said no more. He looked her over from top to toe and she stared at the ground but did not move away. She really was a fiery creature, he thought, and his breathing deepened as he sensed her acknowledgement of her vulnerability and her resentful submission.

A pair of soberly dressed women approached; he dropped

his voice. 'You come to my house on Monday at noon, and I'll tell you what I have in mind and how you could benefit from my goodwill.' He glanced at the bundle in her arms. 'Leave the child with someone. Come alone. Noon on Monday.'

He strode away, back to the Market Place, and turned into the shady archway of the Angel. A glass of something cool and strong was needed to restore his self-possession.

His self-possession was not, however, immediately regained. As he sat at his favourite table, the one in the window looking out onto Apple Lane, who should he see emerge from the adjoining taproom, but Whittock. Baily had already debated with himself whether or not to mention his plans for Molly-Ann to him. The fellow would learn about their connection from Frome gossip in a very short time and it would, he thought, be politic for him to pre-empt the tittle tattle.

'Take a drink with me,' he hailed the younger man, simultaneously pouring a second glass of fruit and brandy punch from the jug before him.

Joshua nodded. 'Just a quick one, as you've poured it. I'm on my way to Mells. I have further business with the landlord of the Greyhound, so can't stop long.'

Baily nodded. 'You're a busy man. I trust you've had no further trouble from Coombs? He's not pressed you further for that bastardy bond?'

'Nay. And I thank you for taking my part in the matter.'

'You've washed your hands of the woman, then?'

'She's nothing to me.'

'You'd have no objection then, if I were to have a passing acquaintance with her?'

Joshua's harsh laugh rebounded from the stone walls. He drained his glass. 'Do as you like with her. She's water under the bridge as far as I'm concerned.'

Late on Monday afternoon James Baily showed Molly-Ann to his front door himself, his servants having been given an unexpected half day's holiday. 'You've made the right choice, my dear. I'm looking forward to our next encounter.' He fondled her hastily laced bodice. 'I have a key to those rooms at the Sheaves, so I may appear there at any time, don't forget. Though I'm sure you wouldn't dream of entertaining any other man there.'

He put a door key and two silver half crowns into her hand. 'Your first payment. Oblige me and serve me faithfully, and it won't be the last.'

The bright sunlight dazzled Molly-Ann and she stumbled down the steps of Baily's townhouse. She felt nauseous, not only because of the indignities she had undergone in that place, or the glasses of apple brandy he had plied her with, but also her disgust at having sold herself to the justice of the peace. Nathaniel and John had begged her to spurn his offers, but she could see that the alternatives they had proposed would never furnish her with sufficient income. She had started to help with the very youngest children in the mornings at Gideon's school, teaching them their letters and to count, before they moved on to the minister's own instruction. Nathaniel brought her wool to spin, as he did to so many of Sheppard's outworkers, but the occupation was new to her and she lacked the skill others had mastered in their earliest years. She had promised to try to improve, but her output was small and Nathaniel had been obliged to tell her that the quality was unacceptable. No, there had seemed no alternative to taking Baily's silver.

While baby William was still in Gideon's care, and as she was passing the Sheaves on Eagle Lane on her way to collect him, she thought she would look at the attic Baily had taken for her.

The landlord, Jem Davies, was stacking tankards on a shelf at the back of the public room; she recognised him and introduced herself. The slow look the man gave her revealed his understanding of her position in society. She fought down her sense of shame.

'I used to work at the Boar,' she said.

'Aye, I thought I knew you.'

'Would you take me on for evening work here, if so be I haven't other commitments?'

His raised eyebrows indicated his grasp of her meaning. 'Why not? A few casual hours, you being here already, that could work well.'

'I'll move my belongings into the attic today, then. I'm sure the baby won't disturb you or the customers.'

Davies grunted. 'Better not.'


A few weeks later, James Baily's initial ardour had waned a little and his visits to his mistress were becoming less frequent. Baby William slept soundly through the evenings and Molly-Ann had a few hours available to work in the inn's public room. Even as she carried brimming tankards to the customers, and responded automatically to their tedious banter, she was alert to Baily's possible entry into the tavern. Other than making a few ribald remarks, Jem the landlord seemed resigned to her sudden disappearances to the attics.

Tonight was busy. The August day had been a hot one and working people had flooded into the Sheaves to slake their thirst as the sun went down, some drawn perhaps by the jaunty fiddle notes of a Cornish jig. Molly-Ann was serving pints of beer, ale and cider as fast as she could go. The tavern had gained a reputation for the quality of its beer due, Jem had boasted, to the steady, cool temperature of its cellars. Not only was there a commodious cellar immediately below the public room, but another existed beyond the first, delved deep into the layers of clay and limestone. Barrels could be raised by a rope and pulley system through a hatchway to the bar, from where the drink could be served in tankards – pewter for the better class of customer willing to pay a premium and wooden for the ordinary sort.

And then the cider barrel was down to the dregs and customers complained about the sludge in their drink. Jem had bellowed for his son to come and help him raise another cask from below, rolling it into the rope cradle and hoisting it up to the floor above. No sooner was it done than new customers arrived. Jem's wife was growing red in the face with the heat and the exertion, her apron was stained and her cap coming loose. She thrust a quart jug into Molly-Ann's hands. 'Get down to the cellar quickly. These new uns want apple brandy, 'tis in the smaller barrels, the ankers. Fill this jug full then we shan't need to get more for a bit.'

Molly-Ann hurried to the back stairs, picking up a lighted candle as she went. The wooden steps turned a corner as they descended, and immediately she was in near darkness, only the little pool of light from her candle showing the lower stairs and finally the stone flags of the cellar floor. A dank, beery smell pervaded the place. She shivered a little in the suddenly cool air, raised the candle and peered about. She had been down here before, but always found it an unsettling place and completed any errands there as fast as she could. The ceiling rafters were festooned with cobwebs; it looked as though they had been built up by generations of spiders over centuries, they were so dense and dark. Along the opposite wall was a rank of huge barrels, with a space where the most recently raised had left a gap like a missing tooth. The ropes up to the now closed hatchway continued to sway slightly.

To the right of the stairs the ankers lay on their sides, a spigot already inserted into the nearest one. Avoiding the dangling cobwebs, Molly-Ann approached the barrel and opened the tap; the distinctive aroma confirmed it was indeed the apple brandy and she filled the jug. As she twisted the tap to shut off the flow, she was conscious of a growing rumbling noise. She lowered the jug to the floor and lifted her head to listen; the sound seemed to come from below her feet and she could swear there was a sort of vibration in the stone flags. Gradually the noise stopped and instead of the rumbling there was a distinct grunt, followed by heavy breathing. She looked about her anxiously; the sounds were muffled but now appeared to be ahead of her. The hairs at the back of her neck gave a prickling sensation, as if a finger had passed over them. Peering beyond her candle, she noticed a flicker of light from a low opening in the wall beside the cider barrels. She crept closer, and tried to shield the light of her candle from falling on the little doorway.

She gasped and jumped back a step. A man's head and shoulders were emerging from the hole. He raised his head and his expression was one of shock, his eyes round, the whites visible; his forehead was creased and his mouth agape. Molly-Ann brought her candle forward, and as his features relaxed she gave a self-conscious laugh. 'Ben! My God, you frightened me. I feared you were a evil spirit or something.'

'Well, you near terrified me too, sister. What're you doing there? You're the last person I expected to see. I thought Jem would be here, not you.'

'Do you want him? He's busy, but I can call him if he's needed.'

'Don't draw attention, Molly-Ann. Tell him quietly he's needed here.'

She looked narrowly at her brother. 'What's this all about, Ben? What're you doing so late at night and breaking into the cellars?'

'Never you mind. You get Jem down here quick as you can. I've work to do that'll take all night at this rate.'

'Work? Is this some scheme of Josh's? Be you moving stolen goods?'

'Nothing's stolen, Molly-Ann. It's all Josh's own. Just making a delivery for him, but it's not easy in the dark and by myself. I need Jem to give me a hand.'

'Oh, so Jem's involved is he? Is it contraband from France you're bringing here?'

'Less you knows the better. You'd best forget you've seen me, Molly-Ann. Stay out of it and keep your mouth shut. I know you've split from Josh. He won't be minded to protect you if you cross him now, girl.' Ben looked beyond her into the upper cellar. 'Do you forget this altogether, Molly-Ann. If you don't, you could be putting yer head in a noose, one way or t'other.'

His own head disappeared as quickly as it had emerged, and Molly-Ann stood a moment, unsure whether to look deeper into the doorway or retreat to the light and company of the bar room. She raised her candle and took a quick look into the chamber beyond, the flame dancing in a strong draught. Ben's shape was visible on the far side of the dingy place, but close to the little doorway rested an anker barrel, just like the one from which she had filled the jug.

James Baily made no appearance at the Sheaves that night, for which Molly-Ann was truly thankful. Her past, she knew, was already morally tainted, but her relationship with the magistrate had brought her even lower in the estimation of her family and acquaintances. Everyone in town would soon know her disgrace, yet the man, she suspected, would suffer only at the hands of his wife. A threat to reveal his iniquities to the lady might be a useful weapon, she mused.

She had already checked on the baby, fed him and settled him down, and returned to swab down the tables in the public room when Jem ushered out what looked to be the last of the evening's customers. Her weary progress around the room showed her that these were not quite the last, however. Nathaniel was ensconced in one of the high backed settles, nursing a half pint of cider and looking tired and miserable. She collapsed onto the seat beside him.

'Didn't know you were in tonight, Nat.'

'I've not been here long. I don't seem to have the inclination for taverns anymore. Knowing you were living and working here, Molly-Ann, I hoped I might get a word with 'ee, now the folk have all gone.' He sipped his drink. 'He's not about, is he? Baily I mean.'

'No, thank God.' She shook her head. 'I know it's no way to live, but what could I do? He's a powerful man in the town. I'm truly in a bind.' She said nothing of the feverfew she had obtained from Sarah, to try to stave off a pregnancy.

'I don't look to criticise you,' Nathaniel said. 'I'll do my best to rescue you from this, but it may take time.'

'Nat, you've your own life to consider. Don't ignore your own future. Don't let me cast a blight on that.'

'Aye, well.' Nathaniel looked morosely into his tankard.

'I did need to speak with 'ee. This very night I found out about Ben bringing apple brandy here through the tunnels. I suppose it's part of Josh's smuggling racket?'

'Keep your voice down, sister.' Nat glared about the room

which was quite empty now, save for Jem clearing away the dirty drinking vessels.

'I'd dearly like to turn Josh in to the excise men,' she muttered. 'It would serve him right for the way he's treated me and the baby, and for giving false witness against the minister. I was so stupid to fall for him. I can't even think now what I saw in the brute.' She looked up. 'I'd be sorry to see Ben suffer along of him, though.'

Nathaniel looked darkly at her. 'You don't know what our brother's got himself caught up in, nor how deeply mired he is. He's done far worse than shifting some illicit brandy.'

Her eyebrows had lifted.

'I daren't say what he's done, but it would be a hanging offence of the worst kind.'

'Not our Ben?' Molly-Ann had her hands to her mouth.

'Aye, and in Josh's pay, he was.'

'This will eat at our consciences if we don't reveal it, Nat, but who to tell? Baily will surely protect his own; look how he twisted the law against me to save Josh a few shillings.' She laid her head on her arms on the table. 'I'm too tired to think about it. You think for me, Nat . . . What should we do?'


Nathaniel was again manning the Sheppards' woollen stall in the market the following Wednesday. Molly-Ann stood to one side and watched, the baby asleep in her shawl, as he measured out a length of the deepest blue broadcloth for a customer, marked the place with his thumb and took the shears to sever the required piece. She brushed one hand over the display of fabrics; the nap was smooth and soft even on these second quality pieces. The customer had selected the darkest of the blue shades, but the range was huge, through twenty or more gradations to a light blue that was almost grey. All were neatly pressed and turned onto flat boards to be stacked across the stall. Her brother looked the part too, in breeches and jerkin that she had not seen before, and with spotlessly clean linen at neck and sleeves: Master Sheppard's salesman.

The customer's coins were tucked carefully into a moneybag before Nathaniel beckoned her closer. 'I'm wondering if we should take Master Sheppard's advice about . . . about those matters we discussed,' he said. 'It may reflect badly on me, but t'would look far worse if it all comes out and I've said naught. It would put a clear line between you and Josh too, save you being incriminated.'

Molly-Ann nodded. She could see his reasoning, but she feared any betrayal of her own family. 'But what can Master Sheppard do?'

'I don't know yet, but he has contacts in London, and he uses local lawyers. Maybe he could get another magistrate to investigate Baily. I've no idea how it could be done, but he deserves to be shown up, and Josh too.'

Molly-Ann stroked the top of baby William's head. 'Perhaps Master Silcox – Gideon - could advise us. He'd look at it all wisely and steadily. Then maybe Master Sheppard would be the person to actually take steps?' She looked into Nathaniel's eyes. 'I feel so guilty about Ben though.' Her thoughts went back to the naughty yet loving little boy he had been. 'Mother would turn in her grave if she could see us now. No, we mustn't say aught against our brother.'

# CHAPTER 16

THE MEMBERS OF the congregation always left Rook Lane House in ones and twos and family groups, to avoid the attention of the authorities. A gathering of five or more for religious purposes outside of the Church of England was proscribed by the Conventicle Act, as the dissenters were well aware, yet their numbers grew steadily as the people of Frome resolved to assert their independence. Today, those that waited talked quietly about the minister's words: others were silently digesting the content of the prayers and the sermon. All were modestly dressed in grey, black or brown attire, with covered arms and necks and snow white linen. All that is, except for a young couple who attended the meeting occasionally, whose slightly more colourful clothing and choice of headgear marked them out as relative newcomers.

At the door of Master Smith's parlour, Nathaniel handed his hymn book back to Dorothea with a shy smile. 'I am beholden to you, Mistress Naish. Without your patient instruction I could never have read these words and received the joyful message they contain. I thank 'ee from the bottom of my heart.'

Dorothea placed the well-worn volume beside a dozen others on a shelf. 'It is a great joy to us to see you both here today.' Her eyes moved to Ellen; she winced slightly and looked quickly away from the younger woman's low cut bodice and loosely dressed hair. She drew a deep breath. 'Would you both like to call in and take tea with us on your way home? I believe John will be joining us also.' Her gaze moved across to the minister and his son, busily shaking hands with the departing worshippers. 'Master Gideon Silcox has other commitments, I think he plans to visit some of the poor, but John said that he would stop by for refreshment.'

The gusting breeze picked up dust and russet leaves from the roadway and created a truly autumnal feel as the group followed Rook Lane the hundred yards or so from Richard Smith's house, down to the Naishes' cottage. The white cat was watching from the window, and came to the door to greet them. Nathaniel ran his hand from nose to tail.

'I hope you enjoyed the meeting, Mistress Ellen?' Simon Naish put his head on one side, questioningly. 'I think this was not your first attendance?'

Ellen nodded. 'That's correct, sir, I have been once or twice before with Nat. I found it very . . . uplifting, and all the folk very welcoming.' She sat on the edge of her seat, her eyes darting here and there about the Naishes' cottage. 'I still feel a little out of place, but Master Silcox's address is always both clear and instructive.'

Nathaniel noticed a slight sheen across her forehead and smiled at her encouragingly. 'Ellen and I are still finding our way in matters of belief.'

The elderly servant offered a plate of small curd tarts around and Naish took one. 'Of course,' he said 'it always takes time to adapt to new ways, new ideas. Please don't be alarmed if some of us appear very earnest, or perhaps intrusive, in our conversation with you both. It's become our manner, and we forget it may be off-putting to newcomers.'

Nathaniel shifted his weight to his other foot. 'And how is the building project proceeding, sir? I notice more and more dwellings every time I pass through that part of Frome.'

'Ah yes. We are commencing the thirtieth this week I believe. More than twenty have been completed and occupied. There is a huge demand for these small cottages.'

'You're still working for Master Baily?' Nathaniel reminded himself to be cautious in his remarks, recollections of the dispute between Naish and Joshua last winter still alive in his mind.

'I may take a step towards independence in a couple of months,' Naish said. 'I have found the connection with Master Baily a little ... trying at times. I trust this will go no further?'

'You have my word upon it, sir.'

'I could acquire land from other owners than Yerbury, build to a better design and quality. We shall see. It would be a welcome change to be free of Baily and his thug.'

John Silcox joined them, stirring his tea. 'What is the latest news from Sheppards, then Nat? Have you completed your circuit of all the stages of manufacture? I see the woad stains have finally come off.'

Nathaniel smiled wryly. 'I thought I'd be painted like an Ancient Briton forever. I tried growing a beard to hide it, but Ellen said that was even more alarming. I've been taking wool to the spinners and yarn to the weavers in their own homes. I've seen the conditions they have to live and work in, and even with a master like John Sheppard who is much less grasping than most, they have to work all hours with no certainty of future employment and very little money to show for it.' He took a gulp of tea. 'I've been hungry myself, and it was hard to take money from them for the hire of the spinning wheels and looms, the very tools of their trade. It didn't feel right. However, I've been fortunate in having the Sheppards' favour, they've put a lot of faith in me, and I hope to repay them for it by long and loyal service.'

Simon Naish excused himself from the conversation and John turned towards Nathaniel again. 'And how is Molly-Ann faring?' he asked, quietly.

'She's mortified at the situation she's in,' Nathaniel replied. 'She says it's the only way to keep the baby with her, and both of them fed. If I can afford a bigger place, I'm hoping to be able to get her out of this fix and restore her spirits. That Joshua and James Baily have a lot to answer for.'

John's vigorous nod in response surprised Nathaniel. 'Anything I can do to help, just let me know,' the minister's son said.

Dorothea offered a plate of warm buttered griddle cakes to her guests. Ellen took one then paused, her head on one side as if listening intently.

'What is it?' Nathaniel began but was hushed with a gesture of her hand.

A moment later she resumed her normal posture. 'Five of the clock by St John's bell, I could hear it.' She ate the cake in two bites. 'Quick,' she mumbled through the crumbs, 'I've to be back to serve supper at six, or Mistress Sheppard will flay me.'

Nathaniel grinned. 'I doubt she'd do that.'

Dorothea looked from one to the other. 'You work for the Sheppards, Mistress Ellen? Just like Nathaniel?'

'Aye, 'tis how we met,' Ellen said, dabbing her lips with a napkin.

'First time I saw her at their house, I knew she was the one for me,' Nathaniel added and Ellen smiled fondly at him.

'We've been walking out together best part of a year now, but only on Sundays,' she said to Dorothea. 'Rest of the week we scarce see one another. I do like Sundays.'

Dorothea looked from one contented face to the other and turned away abruptly. Nathaniel watched her carry the cakes across the room. 'I fear we've offended her, but I don't know how. Are we too immodest for these good folk?'

Ellen pursed her lips. 'I think she may have just had her own plans overturned, 'tis all.'

The cat jumped onto the window ledge, and Nathaniel tickled it under the chin.

'Come on, Nat. I need to get back soon. We'd best take our leave.' Ellen started to gather up her belongings.

'I must just speak a word to Master Silcox.' He approached John and Dorothea who were standing close to the hearth, their backs to him, and waited for a pause in their conversation; both were speaking very low and appeared oblivious of his proximity. Dorothea's complexion, he noted, had grown very pink.

'Your father did speak with me,' John was saying, 'but I confess I had to tell him immediately that I was not looking to be married. Please do not be offended, Dorothea, it is not personal at all. I am simply not at all inclined to seek a wife, whether someone known to me or a complete stranger. Forgive me for disappointing you both. I was honoured to receive your father's enquiries . . .'

Nathaniel stepped quietly backwards and wished he had not overheard John's words. He felt ashamed both for having done so, and also for his friend's discourtesy to Dorothea, though he knew he would also have sought to avoid such an involvement with Mistress Naish were he in John's position.

Ellen was tugging at his sleeve. 'Nat, we have to go. Please,' she hissed. Nathaniel's thanks to Master Naish for his hospitality attracted John's attention and he turned away from the fire. Dorothea did not do so, and appeared to be fumbling in her sleeve for a handkerchief.

'You're both off?' John looked from Ellen to Nathaniel. 'Perhaps we could meet one evening, Nat, to discuss that matter relating to your sister, further? Might you be able to visit me at Keyford? Tomorrow would be best; I travel to Chapmanslade and Westbury on Tuesday, I hope to see some folk who may join us in the emigration.'

Nathaniel nodded, and wished the company farewell as he and Ellen left the cottage. Again, the cool breeze was sweeping the fallen leaves down the road.

'I like Sundays too,' Nathaniel said with a smile as he walked her back to Catherine Street. 'Much as I enjoy my work the rest of the week, 'tis a pleasure to walk out with 'ee Ellen, and today a double pleasure, having you accompany me to the chapel. Were you moved – as I was – by the minister's words?'

'I could certainly feel the power of them, and it did seem that much of what he said was spoken to me directly . . .' She hesitated. 'I found a greater meaning in what he said than in what I've heard at St John's. That's more for the richer sort, I'd say, or for those that just want tradition and routine instead of being made to think for themselves.'

'I think Master Sheppard would be pleased to hear we've both put our feet on this path. I hope he's no objection to our doing so in company together.' He tightened his arm to gently squeeze the hand tucked inside his elbow.


Nathaniel shook the raindrops from his heavy broadcloth cloak before he entered the Silcoxes' cottage the following evening. The rain had only started ten minutes ago and had been largely repelled by the densely woven fabric; with luck, it would have stopped before he left Keyford. The cloak had been secondhand, but he was thrilled to own such a useful and respectable garment. He blew out the flame of his lantern to conserve the candle for his return journey. The nights were dark earlier now, and the rain merely thickened the gloom. John placed a chair and cushion for him beside the fire, facing Gideon. The elderly man appeared tired and quite downcast.

'My son has kept me informed of these infamous actions by Joshua Whittock and James Baily against poor Molly-Ann,' Gideon said. 'I am deeply distressed on your sister's behalf, and also because of the way these men are undermining the local administration of justice. This magistrate should be upholding the law, not warping it to his own ends.'

John put a cup of hot thyme and honey into Nathaniel's hands. 'But what can we do when he is the supposed embodiment of justice in the town? To whom can we complain about his actions?'

His father shook his head. 'To the judges at Taunton?' he suggested.

'They will hardly listen to us, who have appeared before them in the dock, and have been identified as dissenters from the state's religion.'

Gideon nodded slowly. 'Maybe it is time to enlist the help of Master Sheppard? As you have said before, John, he is a respected manufacturer, a model of the new middling sort, and he has contacts in society. Yes, I endorse your suggestion that we seek his help in this righteous cause.' He threw a log on the fire. 'And what of Molly-Ann? Are we able to extricate her from the claws of this Baily?'

'I am indeed seeking new and bigger accommodation,' Nathaniel said. 'I plan to ask Master Sheppard if he will increase my wages and, if he does, I think I will have sufficient to allow us to take a lease on some larger rooms together.' He looked into the glowing embers and grey ash. 'I am hoping however, that Ellen and I may be marrying before long, and that may make for some want of space in the one household.'

'I see your difficulty,' John said, 'but we must do what is possible at the present time and let the future bring what it will.'

The internal wooden shutters at the windows of the Sheppards' counting house had already been closed for the night. It was late October and the evenings were closing in, dusk had fallen early under the lowering clouds and there was no point in hoping for more daylight to penetrate into the offices today. Instead, candles and lanterns had been placed on the high wooden desks to illuminate the pages of the ledgers, and their bright flames dazzled Nathaniel as he resumed his seat and picked up his steel pen. He dipped the nib into the ink and was about to make the next careful entry into the inventory when there was a clatter of boots on the bare wooden stairs and the office door was pushed open.

'Not finished yet, Nathaniel?' Master John Sheppard the younger strode into the room, brushed the ubiquitous dust off one of the high stools, picked up the open accounts ledger, and ran his eye over the most recently entered figures.

'Almost done, sir. I have the last few items to enter then the stock list's complete.'

His employer grunted. 'It's not too bad this quarter, but we must be careful to hold the minimum of stock, and of goods in progress. How did you find the warehouse, on your inspection, was it all kept orderly?'

'Yes fairly good. All tidily stacked, no evidence of damage

from rodents, or the weather coming in. All the tags were in place on the bales and the rolls of fabric; that was a big help to me as a novice.'

'Aye, but you've applied yourself well to learning the business. You know a lot more now than you did a year ago.'

Nathaniel steeled himself. This was the perfect moment to ask the question. The matter had been gnawing at him for a couple of weeks, but he'd felt the time was not right – until now. He looked steadily at his employer, took a deep breath and tentatively asked for an increase in his wages.

'Ah. I was wondering whether you were going to raise that with me.' John Sheppard smiled wryly. 'I said to my father the other day, he's either going to ask for more money, or for our agreement to his marrying your maid Ellen.'

Nathaniel's expression must have been one of shock, as John chuckled.

'It's been pretty clear to us all that you've taken a liking to her, and I dare say it's reciprocated.'

'But . . . but I've not broached the idea of marriage to her yet, sir!'

'Well, well, perhaps I've run too far ahead there. So tell me what your plans are. I hope you mean to continue as my assistant for some time to come?'

'Indeed I do sir, if it pleases you. I thoroughly enjoy my work and can think of nothing I'd rather do.' He ran his hand through his hair. 'I am very much in your debt for taking me on and for teaching me so much. I want nothing more than to repay you with faithful service.'

'Good. Yes, I think we can justify a modest increase. And in the fullness of time, maybe you and Ellen will be asking for our agreement to another matter.' He cheerfully thumped Nathaniel on the back.

'Sir, I wonder if I might ask your advice on quite a different problem?' Nathaniel couldn't resist pushing his luck with young Mr Sheppard, he appeared to be in such an obliging mood.

'And what's that then?' John Sheppard leaned forward, his hands clasped together on the desk.

'Some friends – the Congregational minister Master Silcox and his son – and I have become aware of criminal activities, some of them involving a very important and powerful local gentleman – a magistrate. We don't know to whom we should deliver our evidence, seeing as who this man is.'

John Sheppard nodded slowly, a slight frown furrowing his brow.

'We wondered if you or your father might advise us?'

'The Silcoxes, eh? My father and I have a lot of respect for them, men of great integrity and kindliness, hardworking too in the Lord's name. Their beliefs may differ slightly from my own, but nonetheless they are a force for good in the town. Tell me, what have they uncovered?'

Nathaniel outlined Baily's failings as a magistrate in refusing to order the bastardy bond and affiliation order against his protégé Joshua, and Joshua's smuggling of wool and illicit spirits. For the present, he said nothing about his brother's crimes: he still cherished some hope for Ben and could not yet reconcile himself to turning king's evidence against his own brother.

'Nat, these are truly serious matters,' Master Sheppard said, 'and it seems to me that you are the principal witness, against Whittock at least. I'd advise you to take precautions; you stand in some danger if word of this gets to his ears.'

Nathaniel could feel the blood drain from his face, his cheeks felt suddenly cold as if a scarf had been removed. 'I see.

Could these men be taken up before the news is spread abroad, do you think?'

'We must take care the charge is kept as private as possible. Say nothing to anyone else for the time being, except for my father. He'll doubtless have wise advice. I'll go over it with him then perhaps we and the Silcoxes could all meet to plan what to do. In the meantime, you finish that inventory and get off home – with one eye over your shoulder, Nathaniel.'

Nathaniel put a consoling hand on Molly-Ann's shoulder as she hesitated at the corner of Hill Lane. 'I know it's going to be a trial for you, entering his house, and then telling him to his face, but you must make clear to him that he can have no further control of 'ee, that you reject him altogether. Don't be swayed if he cajoles or if he threatens; you stand your ground, Molly-Ann. You're not his to be bought and sold. I can support you and protect you. You'll soon be free of him, think of that.'

His sister forced a smile onto her lips; she looked terrified as well as thin and tired out, he thought. He patted her shoulder gently, and turned towards Baily's front door. 'Come on, let's get it over.'

The streets were quiet now in the early evening, the market place empty of stalls, a few folk making their way home to supper or out in search of an evening's entertainment. His sister's stance, Nathaniel noticed, was growing more lopsided as William grew larger and heavier astride her hip. The baby was awake and watching the scene around him, his eyes drawn especially to the gold and grey of the sunset sky.

Brother and sister were shown into the justice of the peace's parlour. A few moments later Baily himself came through the door, wiping his lips and moustache with a napkin. 'What the devil . . . I was told there were callers on an official matter. Why are you here?'

Molly-Ann took a step forward and shifted William to her other hip. 'Master Baily,' she said firmly, 'I return your key to 'ee.' She dropped it on his desk. 'I've no need now of your money. I don't wish to see you ever again.'

Baily's eyes were fixed on Molly-Ann and glared furiously. 'You wish . . . you've no need . . . That's all very well, but I've laid out money here, I've supported you and your brat for months. I don't agree to you just walking away and dropping me like this.' His voice was rising angrily. 'And who's this fellow? I've seen you together before – what is he to you?'

Nathaniel squared his shoulders. 'I'm her brother and I'm releasing her from this devilish trap you've held her in. You should be ashamed, using your position to drag her down to the gutter like this.'

Baily took a few steps towards Nathaniel, who stood his ground, breathing heavily but holding the magistrate's stare. 'I'll have you taught a lesson – respect for your betters, the pair of you. Get out of my house.'

Nathaniel had started to leave, but whirled around, his finger pointed at Baily. 'If you retaliate in any way your wife will be told of your doings. Your name will be despised by the whole town and your authority will be held for naught.' He slammed the parlour door behind him as they left.

The confrontation had upset the baby, and he was still crying inconsolably as Molly-Ann and Nathaniel reached their new lodgings on Hunger Lane. The narrow thoroughfare was still busy with carts and pedestrians as folk made their way out of town after their day's work, some towards Keyford and the south, others to turn left or right along Portway or Behind Town. A post boy had just ridden up to the Waggon and

Horses and several people were heading towards the tavern to collect the letters and packets they anticipated. Nathaniel and Molly-Ann skirted around his powerful horse, its flanks still steaming in the chill evening air. William's screams made the horse back away and young Billy had his work cut out to hold it steady.

Nathaniel pushed open the front door of the adjoining gable fronted property and led Molly-Ann into the hallway. To the left were the two rooms he had taken, and he fitted the key in the lock with a sense of satisfaction. 'I'm sure you'll want to reorganise things to suit yourself, Molly-Ann. You do as you please. It's your house now, too. I set your bundles in the back room, that's for you and William. I've a pallet here in the kitchen, so that chamber is yours entirely.'

She looked all over the rooms, into drawers, up the chimney, out of the windows. 'It's a real home,' she said. 'Thank you, Nat,' and gave her brother a hug. 'But if so be Ellen agrees to marry 'ee, we'll move out, William and me. We don't want to cause you problems.'

He smiled. 'It does me good to see you here and free of that man. I trust we can destroy him and his wicked servant, Joshua Whittock, before much longer.'

Molly-Ann looked up from the baby whose soiled cloths she was changing. Neither brother nor sister noticed the cessation of the tuneless whistling that had been going on in the rear yard, Clavey's Barton, just beyond their open window.

'What chance have we of doing that? Baily is so powerful here in Frome, and Joshua would fight tooth and claw against any sort of attack. He'd be mad as a stung bull if we tried to get the law on him.'

'Even so, old Master Sheppard has said it's worth the attempt. John Silcox and I are to meet with him and his son tomorrow morning to discuss what we can do, and they will help us draw up our statements about what Baily did. Master Sheppard knows a lawyer at Shepton who is acquainted with the sheriff of Somerset, and he reckons this is the authority to whom Baily answers. The information coming from the Sheppards, it would have a better chance of being believed and acted on than if it came from us or the Silcoxes. And once Baily's out of the picture, we can lay charges against Joshua, hopefully have him dealt with by the law and taken out of our lives forever.'

'And Ben?'

'I've said nothing to the Sheppards of Ben's crimes.'

Molly-Ann's eyes were again fearful. 'Perhaps we should confront him with them?'

'But it's Joshua we most need to bring before the law.'

Nathaniel scarcely noticed the noise of boots scrabbling on the cobbles outside the back window, or the resumption of Billy's tuneless whistle.

# CHAPTER 17

THE AUTUMN WINDS howled in the chimney of the Silcoxes' cottage and blew a billow of smoke back into the room. Rain spattered down and hissed to steam on the glowing logs, startling Gideon as he sat beside his hearth, lost in thought.

'Consider the bees.' John Silcox turned to Nathaniel. 'Once their hive grows too full, they seek abroad for new dwellings. This is one reason why so many folk want to emigrate from England. Here, all the land is taken; there is not sufficient employment for all; not enough homes for everyone.'

Nathaniel nodded attentively.

'The New World offers the poor the possibility of an improvement in their lives,' John continued. 'The great majority hope to be able to make a decent living for themselves and their families through farming, trade, or fishing.'

'I've heard tell many expect to find gold and precious stones in the soil there.' Nathaniel took a sip from his cup. 'They hope to make a fortune with little effort.'

'Then their hopes will be dashed.' John shook his head. 'Hard work, fortitude, careful planning; these are the only things that will bring success. And many will still fail, beaten by the harsh climate, crop failures, even the unpredictable natives.'

Gideon threw another log onto the fire. Sparks flew up the chimney and the wood crackled as the embers settled again.

The flames that licked around the apple wood lit up his son's eager face on the opposite side of the hearth. Gideon remained silent.

'Have you thought further about that point I raised, father? You and the congregation were going to consider whether our group should comprise only those who attend our chapel, or if we should accept the inclusion in our project of those of different persuasions.'

Nathaniel put his head to one side. Gideon pursed his lips. 'My initial thought was to take people with homogeneous views. It would be simpler, cause less friction.' He shrugged. 'Possibly. But on reflection, I have come to question this. I am minded to open it up to any God-fearing people.'

'But surely, sir, you'd want all your adherents there together, practising the same style of worship, not bickering and arguing,' Nathaniel said. 'I understood this was why so many dissenters had emigrated, that they wished not only to follow their own religious path, but to do so without the annoyance of alternative practices around them and . . .' he smiled uncertainly, 'also to be free to persecute others who held to different creeds.'

Gideon laughed. 'That was certainly the case a generation or more ago. Now so many have settled on the eastern seaboard that everywhere there seems to be a real mixture of religious groups. The elders of the chapel discussed this matter and we concluded that we could not hope to form an unadulterated society even if we wished to do so.' He nodded at his son. 'You were right to make me see this, John. We ought to be more accepting of different views, more tolerant of others.'

'Plenty of the earlier colonists would disagree with you. Some are positively fanatical about preserving the purity of their doctrine.'

'As I grow older,' his father said, 'I find myself not doubting my own beliefs – indeed they grow stronger - but perhaps questioning why mine should be superior to those of another person. Surely every thinking being has an equal right to their own convictions, and if they mean no harm to others, to the rest of society, should they not be respected equally?'

'Well, well,' John nodded. 'It's encouraging to me to learn what an open mind you have, father. I just hope that this attitude can be maintained amongst our congregation here and the emigrants also.'

'I hope that we can generate toleration towards all who dissent from the Anglican religious orthodoxy and from other social strictures, in the future,' Gideon said. 'For instance not shunning those who have fallen on hard times like that family, the Greens from Stoke St Michael, that I have been sponsoring, or indeed Nathaniel's sister our own dear Molly-Ann.' He looked into the leaping flames. 'I wonder whether she would find it easier to build a future in the New World without the stigma that at present hangs over her, here?'

John and Nathaniel both looked up questioningly; John's brow furrowed.

'In what capacity would you see her travelling, father? Most of the people are going as families. Would you see her as an indentured servant? She has no knowledge of farming, couldn't be expected to till her own land. Or perhaps you're thinking of some other occupation – a teacher or shopkeeper perhaps?'

Gideon paused a moment. 'I confess I hadn't really thought it through. I just felt it would be a good place for her and the baby.' If only I were twenty years younger, he reflected.

'The Americas will be a refuge for many of us nonconformists, away from the interference of the present ungodly government,' John said. 'I feel sure that these new colonies are what God wills. His power is universal; His church can exist anywhere in the world. We have only to take the Bible, the divine spirit, and a group of devout people, and we can form our own domain.'

'I admire your courage, John,' Nathaniel said. 'I'd be sorely a'feared, not only by the sea crossing, but by the thought of settling in a strange land with no neighbours, no history. Not knowing what to expect would be my greatest worry.'

'I believe God has created room in these western lands for His people. Inertia would be a sin, a sign of sloth and lack of the divine spirit. We must push ahead with this project.'

'What's holding you back?' Nathaniel asked.

'We have received no word yet from the governor of our chosen colony – Newfoundland. We have asked his permission to bring our pioneers to establish our own settlement. I have spread the word throughout the West Country and, once his assent is given, it will not take more than six months for us to implement the plan. Next spring, I hope.'

Gideon nodded. 'Let us all pray that word comes soon. Then each must determine his future.' He closed his eyes. Could he bear to part from his son and remain in Frome, close to Molly-Ann and William, or would he resolve to go with John and leave her behind? His own suggestion that she travel with the group was wishful thinking. She would know nothing of the colonies, he reflected, and she would certainly find little in common with her fellow travellers. He could not suppress the sigh that burst from him.

The stove made a regular clicking sound as the iron cooled. The last shovel of coal had been thrown into it in mid-afternoon and now, as the green glazed windows darkened with the dusk, the last of the glow was turning to ash. Billy riddled it fiercely with a poker. Gideon wondered which the boy enjoyed more, the last wave of heat on his skin, or the noise of the business. He watched as the lad dexterously scooped the ashes and cinders with the shovel and carefully carried them out of the school hall.

Molly-Ann entered the room as Billy left it, having seen the last of the smallest boys off the premises at the end of the day. She walked across to check on the baby. He was sitting now and would soon be starting to crawl; a guard of some sort would be needed to keep him away from the stove, Gideon realised. She started to gather up the pupils' hornbooks and load them into a basket, humming a lilting tune as she did so.

Dorothea looked up from a pile of slates on which the older boys had chalked their sums. She laid down the last of them and cleared her throat loudly. 'Is that an entirely appropriate song for a place of education? The children may have left, but it is hardly seemly to bring tavern songs into the school, Molly-Ann.'

Gideon raised a hand. 'I have no objection, mistress. Let Molly-Ann sing if she wishes.'

Billy returned and started sweeping the floor. His eyes darted between the two women as if he could sense an imminent squall approaching; he worked his way towards the back of the schoolroom.

Gideon shuffled his papers into a neat pile. 'Dorothea, Molly-Ann, I need to speak with you both about the school's future.'

The young women looked anxious at his words. Molly-Ann bit her lip. 'I hopes you're not going to close it, sir? I've really enjoyed looking after the infants and I'd hoped William could join the class in a few years.'

'Aye, well, with God's help I hope it will continue into the future, but I may not be able to run it after next spring. What I need to ask you, Dorothea, is whether you would consider taking on the responsibility from me at that time, and with Molly-Ann's help?'

'Are you ill, sir? Do you find it too much to manage?' Dorothea asked.

Gideon frowned. 'No certainly not. I feel hale and hearty, in spite of my grey hairs. No, I may be travelling with my son and the colonists to the New World, leaving Frome altogether.' He glanced at Molly-Ann. Her eyes were on the floor, her expression one of distress.

'But sir, I shall really miss you and Master John. You've both done so much to help and guide me over the years . . .'

'It will be a wrench for us all,' Gideon said quietly. 'Mistress Dorothea, I should have asked, do you have the intention of travelling to Newfoundland with the congregation? I was perhaps wrong to assume that you would remain here.'

Dorothea sank down onto the pupils' form. 'No, I will not be going. Had my hopes not been sadly disappointed, I might have accompanied the group, but no, there's no point in me joining the project. Furthermore, my father needs me to remain here and support him as he may be extending his business affairs in the coming year, and he'll need me to keep his ledgers for him.' She smoothed her skirt and looked up at him. 'I'll be very willing to take over the school, Master Silcox.'

'Is Nat going with 'ee sir?' Molly-Ann asked. 'He's said nothing to me.'

'No, I think he's well settled at Sheppards', and hoping for a future with that young woman he brought to chapel,' Gideon said.

Dorothea looked up, her eyes glinting in the last of the daylight. 'They're well suited. She's a frivolous creature if ever I saw one. He may be a fast learner when it's in his own interest to master his letters and accounts, but he disappointed me in not making the most of my friendship. He could have done a lot better than that little maid.'

Molly-Ann looked stricken, Gideon thought, at Dorothea's condemnation of her brother. Jealousy, hurt feelings, he couldn't find it in himself to condemn Dorothea's outburst, but something in his chest ached for Molly-Ann's upset.

Gideon became aware of Billy's broom raising a small cloud of dust just behind him. 'Right, now lad well done, off you go!'

The broom was returned to its place and Billy had trotted off to his next job before Gideon could think of any further task for him.

A week later, Gideon pulled his tall hat firmly over his ears, picked up a stout walking stick and left his cottage to walk the three miles or so to the village of Mells. The November morning was crisp and sunny, a light frost overnight had encouraged the last leaves to turn colour and finally to fall from the trees. As he stepped out he pondered which trees he most admired: the stately beech, its leaves now a glorious russet; the shapely elm whose green leaves were edged with lemon yellow; or maybe the tall horse chestnuts beneath whose bare boughs he passed on the westerly road out of town. By the time the floral candles on these trees were lit next spring, he might be more than a thousand miles away, about to commence on a very different stage of his life. Doubtless the trees would remain, following their annual cycle, long after he had departed both from Frome and from this world altogether. He shivered, conscious of his own insignificance in time and space.

The view across Vallis Vale was as glorious as ever, and Gideon paused a few moments to drink it in, the dark green of Selwood far to his left, the arable fields below him, and the rich pasture running up the hill towards Buckland Denham on his right. He passed the turning to Elm Lane and Master Singer's house quite unconscious of the connection between the clothier and James Baily, then took the next turning to cut through the edge of the Mendip Hills to Mells.

Mells: presumably the name derived from the numerous mills along the fast-flowing Mells Stream, he mused, some for the grinding of corn, others the fulling of cloth. The monks of past centuries would perhaps not recognise the village now, with its gravitation towards an industrial economy of woollen cloth and coal mining. The sunshine still had a little warmth in it. Gideon took out his handkerchief and wiped his face before resuming his walk. Once in the village, he crossed the old wooden bridge over the tumbling stream, passed the almshouses and made his way onwards and up the valley side to the area they called Mells Green. The common land had been built upon here and there over the years; poor people had seized the opportunity to raise tiny cottages, often a single room with an attic above and a sturdy stone chimney stack, which looked as if it held up the building by itself. Some of the houses had become so tumbledown they had reverted to grassy lumps and bumps in the ground, their stones and timber robbed out for the construction of newer places.

He soon found the humble home he sought, that occupied now by the Greens. The door was pulled open as he approached and a woman dressed in several layers of worn and patched clothing greeted him.

'I fear you've had a wasted journey, Reverend. My man is from home. He's been taken on at the coal pit yonder,' she indicated across the valley. 'He's in charge of the 'oss that winds up the rope, he tells me. Raises the tubs of coal, and the colliers too, up and down.'

'I'm only pleased he has work,' Gideon said. 'I just wanted to check all was well for you, and I hope it will continue so all winter.'

'Aye, well folks will want even more fuel then, won't they? Or so he says.'

'That sounds promising then.' Gideon turned to make his way home. 'Send me word if any problems arise. Otherwise, I hope to see you all at service sometime in the future.' He raised his hand as he walked away across the wet grass.


'And will 'ee be going to the Americas, sir, with your son and the congregation?' Molly-Ann added a sliced onion to the soot-blackened pot suspended by a chain over the fire. 'Nat said you were discussing it between you the other evening. You'd be sorely missed in the town. Many of us owe a great deal to you and to John – Nat and me more'n most.' She added some chopped root vegetables, and gave the pot a stir. 'It'll leave a hollow inside of me, to think I'd never see you again.'

She raised her eyes from the fire to look directly at him and Gideon felt as though a page of life had been turned. The silence between them lasted just three heartbeats before William started to grizzle. Gideon rose from his seat and took a step closer to Molly-Ann. He took her left hand, and swallowed. 'Parting from you, the thought of being thousands of miles away across the ocean, I'm not sure I can do it, you know.'

William's cries were becoming more insistent, but his mother made no response to the baby. Had he said too much, Gideon wondered. Would she think him too forward?

Molly-Ann squeezed his hand then released it. 'John will need you beside him in this great adventure. I'm sure it will all be far harder than he expects, especially keeping the peoples' spirits up in the face of adversity, preventing petty divisions and jealousies – all the things you are so good at, sir.' She stirred the pot again. 'I'll think of you all every night, and you above all, who have been a second father to me. I will think of you starting a new life in a clean place, with no harsh laws or corrupt and powerful people to oppress you, and I shall rejoice for you.'

She sniffed and Gideon could see tears glistening on her cheeks as she turned away from the fire. William was fairly bawling now and Molly-Ann scooped him up and buried her face in his wrappings.

Gideon sat down again on the bench. Her reference to him as a father figure should have come as no surprise, but he was a little winded by it. Her tears though gave him reassurance of the depth of her love for him – even if it was that of a child for her parent. He lifted his hands and took the baby from her onto his lap, and started amusing him with a series of strange faces; William was soon chuckling.

The pot was now bubbling away, sending up an aroma of thyme and onions. Molly-Ann added some floury dumplings she had prepared earlier. 'Will you stay and share this rabbit stew with us? Nat will be here shortly and he'd be glad to see 'ee. There's plenty for all, now he's doing so well.'

Gideon was torn. Would he be taking the food from their mouths, when their recent poverty had been so profound, or would Molly-Ann be gratified more by his acceptance of their hospitality, something she had previously been unable to extend?

'I'd like that very much, my dear. John away, I'd be going home to a cold hearth.' Her smile told him it was the right decision.

With the windows shuttered against the cold and dark of Hunger Lane, the three of them sat to the table on Nat's arrival, and Molly-Ann shared out the stew and dumplings. Silence fell as their spoons ladled up the savoury meal. Gideon's thoughts reverted to John's words as they had discussed the roles of the settlers heading for Newfoundland, and without thinking he said 'You'd be a welcome addition to the colonists, Molly-Ann. Your skill in cooking up delicious meals from anything available would be just what we'd need.'

'What do they have there – do they grow vegetables and crops such as we have here in Somerset? Or are there plants and animals such as we've never seen?'

He cast his mind back to his earlier trip to the New World. 'There's abundant fish, especially cod. The seas are teeming there. Grain doesn't do so well, but root vegetables, peas and beans, they grow well enough. And the forests are full of game. The settlers will be taking sheep, cows, chickens to raise. It will be a more generous land than here in many ways, although very hilly and with dense forests to clear.'

'It sounds almost like paradise. A new land with food, and space, and work for all.' Her eyes had a dreamy look, before snapping back to Gideon. 'But I'm sure there's problems too. There's bound to be some fierce animals or monsters or something!'

He smiled. 'Well, the winters can be long and hard, and the soil is not as rich and deep as we have. I suppose there are dangers in the forests too, but no monsters, I'm sure!'

Her interest in the venture surprised Gideon. He pushed some parsnips around the last of the juice in his bowl then looked carefully at her. 'Molly-Ann, would you wish to join us in this colony? It would be a radical undertaking for you, leaving behind all you know and setting out across the ocean, but you would certainly be with friends, with good people, and your worth would be recognised.'

Her eyes lit up and stared at him. 'I'm mightily drawn to the idea, but how could I go when I'm not a member of your chapel? Indeed I'm not very godly at all! And I'd be seen as a fallen woman by the others – they all know my story and little William here would remind them of my past – they'd despise me, I'd be scorned and condemned, especially in such a small group.' Her face had fallen as she'd gone on visualising the reaction of strict puritans to her past life.

'You'd do better biding here, sister,' Nat said firmly. 'I can imagine what unkindness you might face in such a settlement at the back of beyond. Better to stay here where folk know your merits as well as the hardships you've faced.'

Her forehead creased. 'Yes . . . now that I'm free of both Josh and that swine Baily. Life is a lot better for me now in Frome, but I still find myself looking around, making sure they're not about . . . it would be better still to be right away from the pair of them.' She offered a spoon of the stew liquid to William, sitting on her lap. 'I'd like to raise my son in a land without people like them, even if there were hardships too.'

'It's a big decision, sister,' Nat said, sadly. 'If you go, there's little chance you'd return. We'd probably not see each other again in this life.'

Her eyes shone in the candlelight, and a tear streaked her cheek again. 'I see that, but then we could any of us be struck down at any moment, and gone beyond all hope of recall. Mr

Sheppard gave you a second chance to make something of yourself, Nat. Maybe this would be my second chance.'

William had seized the spoon from her and she absentmindedly prised his fingers off it, to give him some of the mashed parsnip.

'I'd like to think carefully about this, Master Silcox. Maybe there'd be a school set up in the new colony and I could look after the little ones, like here?' Her brow clouded. 'But where would I live? It would be hard and lonely if it were just me and William.' She suddenly brightened. 'Perhaps I could keep house for you and your son? Now that would be a godly purpose in life!'

Gideon felt his heart beat harder. To share a roof with both Molly-Ann and John . . . he could wish for nothing more.


'It's come! It's here! The Lord has heard my prayers!' Gideon waved the pages of a letter in front of his son. 'They've agreed to accept us! The governor has confirmed!'

John's smile was wide as he steered his father to a seat in the kitchen of the Keyford cottage. 'Father, I pray you, be calm. You'll give yourself an apoplexy with too much excitement. Oh but this is joyful news. Let me read it, will you!'

Gideon shut his eyes and breathed deeply to restore his equanimity, while his son read the letter twice through – the second time out loud.

'Marvellous,' John said. 'All our questions answered, everything seems to be as we had hoped. I must busy myself with spreading the word to those who hope to join us, charter a ship, order supplies for the journey, and equipment and stores for the settlement. Praise the Lord, we can at last start our preparations!'

He spread the letter out on the table in front of him, sat, and read it through for a third time. 'The governor seems to have taken account of our request for a site close to both sea and forest, with flat land to clear for crops and building. It sounds as if it is virgin land, so the soil should be quite fertile, but there'll be poor access overland. A harbour will be our first priority, and clearing ground to sow seed, also. We may have to pass the first summer under canvas – leave building until the autumn.'

'John, John, calm down. You are right that planning is needed, but we should do it as a group and in a more measured way. Let us call a meeting of all those involved and reach agreement – you might draw up proposals that all can discuss and vote upon.' Gideon was delighted to see his son's enthusiasm; his greyish blue eyes were fairly dancing with excitement. It had been a long wait for the letter of consent, a real test of John's commitment and patience, but at last action could be taken.

Gideon swung the old kettle over the fire. A cup of chamomile flower would calm them both while they sat at the table to plan for the meeting, and to schedule John's travels around the West Country. A stray sunbeam lit up the last of the marigold flowers on the window ledge; truly a blessed day, he thought.

# CHAPTER 18

T HE MUD OF Pilly Vale was several inches deep after the heavy rains of early December. Molly-Ann's wooden pattens were thick with it, the raised soles completely caked with the filth. All the town devoutly wished for a hard frost, to freeze the claggy surface. She knocked the pattens off against the doorstep of the Sheppards' counting house, holding Nathaniel's arm for balance. He drew his own boots across the scraper to remove the worst of the mud and silently followed her up the steps and into the building. Inside, he led the way up the wooden staircase, his sister following carefully in the gloom. For once, the baby slung in her shawl slept quietly.

Brother and sister had exchanged hardly a word on their way down from Hunger Lane to the Sheppards' warehouse and offices. Young Master Sheppard had asked Nathaniel to bring Molly-Ann after their noonday meal to a meeting with his father and himself, and each was anxiously thinking about the significance his news would have for their futures.

John Sheppard rose to greet them and placed a chair for Molly-Ann in front of his father's desk. The ledgers were closed and put to one side, and old Master Sheppard brought out a letter from his writing chest. He unfolded it and smoothed out its creases. Nathaniel could see the official seal that had secured it, broken now that it had reached its destination. The scarlet wax seemed to glow in the dark room, brought to life by the flame of the single candlestick. It seemed to him that time was running very slowly as the four of them gathered around the desk and stared at the letter. Molly-Ann was trembling, he noticed, and he put his hand on her shoulder. Rain pattered briefly against the grimy window panes.

Master Sheppard cleared his throat. Nathaniel thought he looked particularly grave.

'This letter brings us no cheer,' he began. 'My friend at Shepton has made representations to the sheriff of Somerset, as we requested, but to no avail.'

Molly-Ann's shoulders drooped.

'The sheriff acknowledged that he has authority over the magistrates, that he is responsible for their appointment and governance – I specifically asked my friend to check that – and claims to have investigated the allegations.' Master Sheppard ran his hand through his untidy grey hair. 'He goes on to say that Baily has refuted the accusations that he was partial towards Joshua Whittock in the judgement and that he sought personal benefit from his office; that Baily presented persuasive evidence in his defence – he doesn't say what it was – and that the magistrate has been vindicated and confirmed in office.' He shook his head. 'I fear the county gentry are looking out for one another. They have scant concern for the law or the honour of their position.'

Nathaniel looked at Molly-Ann; her face was ashen as she stared at the blood red seal of the letter.

'I should never have hoped to get justice,' she said. 'He's probably going to make real trouble for me now – and for you too Nat, if ever either of us gets brought afore him.'

'And Baily's grasp on power means that Joshua has free rein for his crimes. No one's going to disrupt his smuggling activities, and any who incur his displeasure will be in danger.' He put his hand on his sister's shoulder again. 'Maybe you and the baby would be safer out of Frome, Molly-Ann?'

'Surely he'd not use violence on you, mistress?' John Sheppard frowned. 'You have friends here. We will do everything to keep you safe.'

She shook her head. 'My friends can't be beside me all the time, and they could do little against that evil man anyway. I must simply keep out of his path and avoid his attention.'


The Swan served a decent drop of ale, Ben thought as he stared into the wooden tankard before him. Charged a reasonable price too, unlike the inn where Joshua met with his wealthier friends. And he could smell the pies baking out the back. Helen would soon be in the bar tempting her customers with the sight of that steaming, golden pastry.

Joshua joined him with his own mug of cider and sat with his back to the window. Ben studied the scarred face, the intent eyes of the man for whom he'd worked, how long was it now? Coming up two years he supposed. He still felt nervous in his presence, that latent streak of violence, the coiled energy, his single-minded drive for his own ambitions. My God, Ben thought, the man must be wealthy by now. What did he do with the profits from his "ventures", his payments from Master Baily, the money he creamed off the rents and bribes he collected for his patron? Ben had seen him pocketing any amount of cash. Where was it all hidden, he wondered?

'You're thinking, Ben.' Joshua was staring at him as if he could read his thoughts. 'I don't like it when you think.' He frowned. 'I find it leads to trouble.'

'Sorry Josh.' Ben averted his eyes. 'Just a bit tired, is all.' He shifted his gaze to the street outside, where who should he see but his brother Nathaniel, in a fine coat and breeches, with a new hat and a nice looking girl. Ben blinked, but said nothing to his drinking companion. He looked away and scowled at the ring marks on the table. Nat seemed to be going up in the world, while he was still struggling with the misery of dank, muddy Cole Hill. He'd no one to make a future with, no one to take an interest in him, no one who cared if he lived or died. He drained his ale and called for another. It was threatening snow out there. He'd bide here in the warm for a few more pints yet.

His eventual trek back to Cole Hill was eased by the loan from Joshua of one of the pack mules. Ben was not in a fit state to walk the three miles, but provided he kept his seat on the animal he'd be able to find the way.

He couldn't face the climb up those near vertical steps to the bedroom, though, and instead lit a fire on the kitchen hearth and huddled himself in blankets on the settle. It was perishing cold in the house; he could see his breath as it left his mouth. He'd keep awake a while to feed the fire as it caught, he thought, but his eyes kept closing in spite of the chill.

And with a start, he was awake. Accustomed to the utter silence of the house at night, something had penetrated his drunken doze. He lay still, his ears straining to hear the sound again. A deep sigh came from the passageway where the stairs led up to the first floor, then silence. He could hear his own heart beating. A second profound sigh sounded from behind the closed passage door. He had stopped breathing, the better to hear. A scratchy, dragging noise followed; again it came, and again. His throat ached with the strain of repressing a scream. The sigh was repeated then slowly, slowly, the door latch lifted and the door swung towards him.

Ben scrambled into a corner of the settle clutching the blanket, his feet up on the seat. The last of the flames leaped and flickered in the draught and clearly illuminated a huge toad, lying flat on the floor in the passage doorway; its pale yellow skin covered in warty brown splodges glistened in the firelight. Across its back a deep indentation, scratches and splinters marked where it had forced the door up on its hinges, releasing the latch. Ben expelled the breath he was holding, staggered to the doorway, gathered the toad in his hands and placed it outside in the yard.

Shutting the doors firmly behind him, he returned to the heap of blankets. His hands still shook from the tension and fear as he settled to sleep again, but this time sleep would not come so easily. Instead he found himself imagining what meaning this toad's appearance had for him. Try as he might, he couldn't recall that he'd heard what a toad was a sign of, apart from the fact that it was poisonous. Folks around seemed to drag out a superstitious meaning from every natural event, but what a toad portended he couldn't fathom.

It was mid-morning when he awoke. The ashes were stone cold, as were his feet and nose, but he had to get outside to relieve himself before he could do anything about the fire. As he turned back to the house from the midden he looked around for the toad. Naturally, there was no sign of it and he wondered whether he had imagined it. The sound of hoofs on the stony track through East Woodlands was not in his imagination however, and he raised his head sharply. Horse riders were heading in his direction. He moved inside and shut the door quickly. With luck, they'd pass the house and disappear down the lane. He stood with his back to the door, his forehead beaded with sweat, yet his body shivered.

There was a clack as the gate was unlatched; voices in the yard. He stumbled down the passage and into the kitchen, then crept along the wall to squint out of the window. Two men, their backs to him, were poking about in the log shed. They moved into the hay store briefly then peered into the pig's sty. He froze as they looked towards the house. One glanced away up the slope of the hill then drew his companion's attention to what he had seen. Ben followed their gaze across the grass to the two wells. There was a footfall behind him at the back door.

'Ah. Here you be. We do want a word with 'ee.'

Ben swung round and shut his eyes in exasperation. He'd not thought there'd be more of them, that they'd have put men at the back of the farmhouse. His plan had been to creep out the rear door, the one the cattle used to use, through the hedge and into the lane then head off into the woods. The two men who barred his way carried staves and looked as if they knew their job, and would relish doing it. He shook his head and allowed his arms to be seized. They frog marched him out to the yard, and their seniors. One of his captors was then detailed to search the house.

'What do 'ee want here? By what right have your men taken me?' Ben stood stoutly in the yard, his hands now tied behind him, scowling at the intruders.

'We are investigating a very serious crime indeed: the suspected murder of two excise officers,' the older of the horsemen said. 'I am the parish constable of Maiden Bradley, and have a warrant from the Wiltshire magistrates authorising me to inquire into the matter throughout the area, including in parts of Somerset.' He removed a folded paper from an inside pocket and shook it in Ben's face. 'You are obliged by law to answer my questions and to render me all the assistance I require.'

'What's it to do with me? I know nothing of excise men or whatever 'tis.' Ben jutted his chin truculently.

'Whether you're involved or not is for me to judge. You can start by telling me what's going on there in your field.' He pointed up the slope to the new well. 'What's all that digging in aid of?'

'It's a new well I've sunk.' Ben shrugged his shoulders; there was no denying that, it was pretty obvious to all.

'And why did you need a new well?' The man glanced down to the disturbed patch where bare soil studded with loose rocks had not yet grassed over.

The other rider nodded to the untidy area. 'Is that yer old well?'

Ben could see where their questions were leading.

'It's a trial digging. I started there, but it weren't suitable. I started again up a bit.'

The constable's mouth twisted to one side. Not a smile exactly, there was certainly no friendliness in it. 'Dig it out,' he nodded to his two men. 'Deep as you can go. Untie his hands, he can help you.'

Ben looked up the slope of the hill towards Roddenbury and down towards the lane, but there was no chance of escape, he was well outnumbered and the constable and his men looked to be ready for a fight if need be. He swallowed. It might have been a lucky chance on their part that had brought them to Cole Hill, but it looked as though his own luck was about to run out altogether.

The handle of the wooden spade was smooth and hard, reassuring almost, in his hand. The two had fitted together often enough in the past: the one wearing away with use, the other growing calluses to counter the friction. Ironical, Ben thought, that this old tool was now pressed into service to expose its owner's crime.

The two men who had accompanied the constables dug

beside him, turn and turn about. There was no rest for him though; they were keeping him at it continually. The infill was still soft, hadn't yet compacted, so before the two guards had had their first changeover, the well had been dug out some four feet. Ben took a breather while he could still see out of the shaft. He looked around the field, the yard, the woods. A movement by the gate caught his eye. Looking carefully he made out the crouching figure of a boy, watching what was going on. Billy? Ben looked in the opposite direction. Word of his arrest would get back to Josh then. And arrest was inevitable: it was just a matter of time before the bodies were revealed, unless he could persuade the constables to call it off.

The afternoon light was going fast. Heavy grey clouds moved quickly from the northwest, bringing an early end to the day. The constable must have realised at the same moment that time was pressing.

'Get on with it. We'll be here all bloody night at this rate.'

Ben scowled at the man. Despite the physical effort, he was growing colder, his hands and feet numb. Something soft tickled his face and he groaned; it was starting to snow.

'Fetch lanterns.' The constable waved his riding crop at the guard and pointed back at the farmhouse. 'There must be some in there.'

The feeble light shone into the old well, flickering across the stone lining of the shaft.

'Dunno what you're hoping to find,' Ben growled. 'Bain't nothing down here as I knows of.'

'We're hardly going to believe anything you say,' the constable responded. 'Your lie about this being a trial digging has already been exposed. This is clearly the farm's original well, and I want to know your reason for filling it in.'

Blisters had formed and torn on Ben's hands. He couldn't

see the wounds, but the stickiness of the blood was a different consistency to that of the mud on his skin. One of the lanterns had been lowered to the level of their working and the guard beside him had, for some time now, been carefully studying the spoil they dug out. A powerful cloying smell had been building around him, and it was almost impossible to breathe without gagging. Ben's spade now seemed to be entangled in something: he couldn't pull it out or push it further. The guard's attention was on him immediately.

'Dig carefully, there. A little at a time,' he said then turned his face up to the top of the well where the light caught a dense flurry of snow. 'There's something here. Clothing. Give us a hand.'

The second guard lowered a ladder he had brought from the log shed and descended. 'My God, that's a powerful reek now. I'd say it's growing worse.'

Ben stood aside as the two men dug into the soil to loosen the fabric and expose what else was in the well shaft. Their attention was on their work; tired and cold as they were, they might not be alert enough to stop him . . .

He moved quietly to the ladder and began to ascend, slowly at first then he scrambled rapidly up. As he stepped onto the grass above and drew his first breath of clean air, he reached down and grabbed the ladder. The guards were shouting in alarm and one had started to climb up behind him, but by twisting it to and fro, he was able to dislodge the man and jerk it out of the well.

Candlelight dazzled him. There was a great crack to the back of his head. He sank to his knees and another blow to his skull plunged him into pitch darkness.

'Visitors for 'ee.' The gaoler stood aside to admit first Nathaniel then Molly-Ann.

Ben struggled up from the heap of dirty straw where he'd been sitting on this, his second day in prison. He took his sister's hand, but noticed a passing reluctance in her face – it was gone in an instant, but it had been there. 'I know, I'm filthy, I smell, I've got lice . . . best not to touch 'ee, Molly-Ann.'

'I didn't bring William for fear of gaol fever – he's with Master Silcox.'

'P'raps you should both have stayed away. There's naught 'ee can do for me. Leastways, not to stop them convicting me – they'll do that whatever comes.'

Nathaniel shook his head. 'Will you plead guilty and beg for mercy?'

Ben laughed sharply. 'What good can come of that? Nay. I'll make them prove it. A guilty plea won't win me any favours.'

'Are they . . .' Nathaniel paused. 'Are they looking for anyone else for the murder?'

Ben squeezed his shoulder. 'I've told them I was alone that night. That I thought I was being attacked by robbers and struck in self defence. I was just a benighted traveller fearful for my own safety.' He looked steadily into his brother's eyes. The less Molly-Ann knows the better, he thought.

'Could you not turn king's evidence?'

'Give them Josh in return for my own skin?'

Both brothers had lowered their voices. Who knew what spies might be listening at the door.

'If I dropped Josh in it, all the other owlers would be taken, like as not. It wouldn't be him alone,' Ben said.

There was a rustling in the straw. Molly-Ann drew her

skirts closer about her. 'We've brought you blankets, another coat, some food and money, Ben. What else do 'ee need?'

The rat ran across the cell and down a drain hole in the floor.

'That's all I need, thank 'ee. The trial's this Thursday.'

'Aye we heard.' Molly-Ann put her hand on his arm.

'If it's a guilty verdict, I'll hang next week. They don't waste time. Don't come to see me before the execution, I'm not worth it.'

'I will, Ben,' Nathaniel said. 'I'll be there for you.'

There was an unholy noise as the key grated in the lock. 'Yer time's up,' the gaoler growled.

'Molly-Ann.' Ben grabbed her hand. 'I need to tell you I'm sorry. About Josh I mean.'

'Come on, I said yer time's up.' The gaoler stepped towards them.

'I shouldn't have encouraged him to court 'ee. I knew he was a bad man. And he's a mean bastard, he should at least have given you money to support the baby – he could afford it, the wealth he's got.'

The brawny turnkey was pushing them out through the doorway.

'Goodbye Ben. God keep 'ee.' Molly-Ann's voice was raw.

The door slammed and the key was turned.


A week later, Nathaniel hitched the horse he had borrowed from John Sheppard to the iron ring set into the wall outside his home in Hunger Lane. Unaccustomed as he was to riding, the twenty-five miles to the place of execution at Fisherton then back home again, had left him sore, stiff and tired, but this discomfort was nothing to the emotional storm he had undergone as he stood there and witnessed the judicial execution of his brother. And now he would have to relate the day's events to Molly-Ann, reliving the horror as he told her.

He loosened the girth, patted the horse and pushed open the door into the common passageway. The kitchen he shared with his sister and nephew was quiet; William sat on a rug before the fire, playing with his toys, while Molly-Ann stood close to the window looking out into the street. His sister's face was frighteningly pale, while her eyes were red and sore, her cheeks thin and sunken, and her trembling lips were tinged blue. She held her hands in front of her, the fingers twining around each other.

'It's done,' Nathaniel said, hollowly. 'He went bravely.'

Molly-Ann swayed a little and put one hand out to the edge of the table. 'Poor Ben. Was he the only one?'

'No, a couple of others, for theft. There was quite a crowd; they weren't abusing the prisoners, or mocking. Just there to see the spectacle I suppose.'

'And was it quick for Ben?' Her voice caught on his name.

'Aye. I'd paid the hangman. He did what was needful to make it fast.'

Molly-Ann swallowed and looked away. 'He was guilty of the murders, then?'

Nathaniel nodded. 'Oh yes. I pray that he repented while he could. But yes, he was guilty.'

'Why did he do it, Nat?'

'I truly think he feared for his own life. But perhaps there was no need for him to go so far as he did.' He shook his head. 'He would never have done that in the past. Joshua's influence, I fear.'

'Dear God, that man has so many crimes on his head. Yet

I doubt if he'll ever be brought to book.'

'Probably not in this life, at any rate.'

'I'm only glad our mother never saw this day. It would have broken her heart.'

Nathaniel glanced up as a slight scuffling sound came from the passageway – he'd not quite shut the door to the room – and the street door opened and closed.

'I must return Master Sheppard's horse to him. It was good of him to allow me time off, though I was able to perform some errands for him in Salisbury while I was there.'

'You might see Ellen while you're at the house. Give her my compliments.'

Nathaniel picked up his hat and gloves.

'And you could invite her to visit on Sunday afternoon, if you like? I'd be glad to know her better.'

# CHAPTER 19

H E MISSED BEN. The man might not have had wits as sharp as his nor yet his own boldness, but he'd certainly had his uses. Joshua flicked the reins on the horse's neck. If the idiot hadn't allowed himself to be taken up for those murders, or if he'd made an escape from gaol, Joshua could have found him some place to hide away till the fuss died down. He'd been a useful pair of hands, a reliable deputy in both the smuggling of wool and the running of the untaxed spirits. As it was, Joshua had to do much of the transportation himself now.

He pulled his coat tighter and tucked his muffler in. The frost hadn't melted all day and the wind was bitter. Ben would have done this delivery to Mells with barely a moan, had he been here. Now it was he who had to drive the cart laden with anker barrels beneath a layer of straw and a horse blanket.

News of Ben's arrest and subsequent hanging had reached him through Billy. The lad had also seen with his own eyes the retrieval of the corpses from the well. Joshua had feared Ben might name him at the trial, or under pressure in gaol, but the fellow had proved loyal and held his tongue. Not like his sister. Joshua swore at the very thought of her. Conniving with her brother Nat to incriminate Master Baily like that; if the magistrate had fallen he'd have brought Joshua down with him. Billy had relayed all he had heard them say as he sat beneath their window, in Clavey's Barton round the back of the Waggon and Horses. Molly-Ann and that snivelling brother of hers: they made his blood boil. The more he thought about it, the more he'd like to teach them both a lesson they'd never forget. He'd give that woman a real beating if he ever got the chance, and as for Nathaniel, he'd leave him dead in a ditch. Sneaking chapel goer.

And that was another pair that deserved punishment: that old minister and his degenerate son. The recollection of John Silcox's attempted advances at the ford over Adderwell Brook made his gorge rise. He swore again, even more volubly, as his cart rumbled over the stone bridge into Mells.

He glanced down at the stream on his left. The early winter rains had fed the water so that it was at the top of its banks. As he watched, little surges sent waves breaking over and into the grass of the water meadow; the level was rising, and there'd be more to come. Just here the stream bed was rocky and the river ran fast and wide, white water crashed between jagged black stones slippery with moss and slime. Fifty yards upstream a tributary joined the Mells Stream, the two flows mingling with many eddies and whirlpools as they met. A wooden footbridge led across the main channel to give access to the old almshouses and beyond them to the higher part of the village. Above the ramshackle bridge the water flowed silently, strong and fast – as fast as a man could run. Fallen leaves floated on the surface, some gliding slowly, others rushing down towards the tumbling white water where the rocks cut into the velvet smooth depths and lacerated the surface.

The horse had come to a standstill as her master's attention was held by the water; as Joshua came out of his reverie, his thoughts on revenge, he shook the reins more fiercely and swore at the mare. 'Get on, will you. Sooner we drop this lot, sooner we can get in the warm.'

It took less than ten minutes to unload the cart and roll the barrels of apple brandy into the outhouse at the Greyhound Inn, the landlord Isaac Watt standing by to count them all.

'Come in and I'll mull some ale for 'ee,' the man said. 'It's cold as a witch's kiss out here.'

Josh tethered the horse, with a net of hay to hand and a blanket thrown over her, and followed Master Watt into the taproom. A poker was heating in the fire; the landlord knocked the worst of the ashes off it then thrust it into a quart jug of ale. Steam rose in a great cloud amidst much sizzling and spitting, and Josh's mouth watered at the smell. The tavern was empty of customers and he stretched his boots out towards the blaze of logs.

'That's six ankers I've brought 'ee today, Master Watt, if you'd be good enough to pay for those now, and let me know when you need more. Give me a day or two's notice and I'll have 'em delivered right away.'

'I'd just like to sample these you've brought, Master Whittock.' The landlord removed the poker from the jug and poured the ale into two tankards. 'I'll sup this, then bring in a flask of the brandy so as we can taste it together. Not in a hurry, are you?'

Joshua sighed. He did have other tasks to do today, but he recognised the importance of serving his customers well; he'd oblige the man for now – and it *was* a miserable afternoon out there.

By the time he'd helped Master Watt finish the flask of apple brandy and a second pint of mulled ale, Joshua realised that the light was fading and the December afternoon was drawing to a close. The landlord counted out the sum he owed, but the calculations and the counting had to be performed three times before both parties were satisfied. Once he'd pocketed the coins and untied the horse Joshua was fair fuming at the delay. He draped the horse blanket over his own shoulders and shook the reins. The horse turned out of the inn yard and into Selwood Street, and was soon trotting through Mells in the direction of home. Joshua belched. The combination of brandy and ale was making him feel nauseous and his eyes were not focusing too well. He'd be glad to be back in Long Row.

He struck the seat beside him with force. Six months ago, he'd have returned home to a fine supper, a roaring fire and Molly-Ann in his bed; now it would be a cold hearth, bread and cheese, and a solitary night. Damned woman! Why'd she have to go and ruin everything? The furious resentment he'd built up in the morning simmered again and he felt like smashing his fist on something.

He drew level with the old footbridge over the river, and a light on the track beyond it caught his eye. He pulled the horse to a standstill. Daylight was going fast and a light rain – or was it sleet – had started to fall, but he could make out the shapes of two men approaching the bridge from the other bank, one carrying a lantern. He made an effort to focus on them, and as he recognised John and Gideon Silcox it felt as though his nausea and bleariness fell away instantly. Nobody else was about. The Silcoxes appeared to be unarmed and were at his mercy.

He swung himself down from the cart and groped among the straw for a stave he'd hidden there in case of trouble on the road. The noise of the river downstream of the little bridge masked his footsteps on the planks, and he could see the two dissenters were unaware of his approach until he was halfway across, when they both raised their heads sharply. He was gratified to see the alarm in two pairs of eyes as they broke off their conversation and stopped dead in their tracks.

The old man had been about to step onto the bridge, but seemed to shrink back in fear. Where was his faith in God's protection now? Joshua sneered. John Silcox pushed past his father however, and stood defensively in front of him, his fists at his side and his eyes blazing. A smile twisted Joshua's lips; it looked as though the preacher had found guts enough to confront him.

'You're a disgrace to the town, Joshua Whittock. You deserve a thrashing for your treatment of Molly-Ann.' John shook a fist at him and took a step forward.

Joshua smiled more broadly; the stave was hard against his palm.

'You'll be held to account for your conduct one day. Bringing a fine young woman down, abandoning her and your own son . . . you'll face God's judgement for this and all your crimes . . . you'll pay in the end.'

Joshua brought the stick forward and struck John in the chest. The man doubled up and staggered backwards.

'Your God will ignore *your* activities, then?' Joshua's bellow was accompanied by another blow, this to the side of his ribs. 'Making propositions to me, wanting more "acquaintance" – you never picked a more dangerous target for your lewd attentions.' He jabbed the stave into John's belly. He was enjoying taunting the fellow and, as he had hoped, he'd raised a cry of horror from the old man. He assumed Gideon had known nothing of his son's predelictions, let alone the identity of the man who had been the object of his desire.

'How does he know?' Gideon shook his son's arm. 'Have you . . . you didn't?' The old hands, knuckles swollen, were pulling John off the bridge as he struggled away from Joshua.

He raised the staff higher and delivered a cracking blow to the side of John's head. The man slumped to the ground and lay on his side in the mud of the riverbank, insensible, vulnerable. His blood pounding in his ears, Joshua felt the heat of anger spread through his body, galvanising every part of him. A good kicking would settle their account. He took a step closer, but in the narrow confines of the bridge one end of his stave caught on the upright of the handrail, pushing the other end between his ankles and tripping him. He staggered, his feet slipping on wet leaves, then crashed against the flimsy rail. The wood snapped under his weight and he teetered momentarily above the rushing stream before tumbling into the icy waters.

John rolled to his knees, his hands pressed into the mud and leaf litter. The smell of the earth, the wet leaves, the dank darkness around him, where was he? He shut his eyes again. His head seemed to be full of black clouds through which red lightning tore, scratching at his skull and splintering his senses. He couldn't breathe. Every movement of his lungs sparked an appalling pain that shot from one side of his chest to the other then tied an excruciating band around him. He forced his eyes open. The clouds in his head obscured much of what was before him, all he could see were shadows and flickers of light below him – were there stars down there? He became aware of the gurgle and splash of waters, mingling with the roar of blood in his ears. Weaving through it all, his father's voice calling, calling - but not his name; Gideon was calling Joshua. He lifted his head higher and narrowed his eyes. The shadows coalesced and he could see Gideon stooping at the river's brink. The next breath he drew sent a spasm of pain coursing around his chest. How he could get to his feet was beyond him when every movement, every gasp of air, caused such intolerable sensations. He brought the back of his hand across his eyes; it came away wet and sticky, but his vision was a little clearer.

Gideon seemed to be leaning forward over the river bank, poking a branch into the water. John blinked to focus his eyes. Yes, he was sweeping the stick to and fro. It made no sense. What was his father doing?

The groan as he straightened his knees could not be suppressed. His stomach and back were bruised from the blows Joshua had inflicted, and his head was pounding. Slowly standing, he recollected Joshua's attack and glanced quickly round in case the villain remained nearby. It was hard to see here, the gloom beneath the trees was deepening all the time. His father had placed the lantern at the river's edge, and he made his shambling way towards it.

'John! The Lord be praised! I feared he'd done for you. But where he is now, I know not,' Gideon said, continuing to prod the branch into the fast flowing current with both hands.

John tried to stand upright but the pain doubled him up again.

Gideon raised the lantern and looked further down the stream. 'Oh, good Lord! There, do you see?' He pointed. 'A hand . . . raised from the river. It's carried him right down to the bend.' He stooped for the lantern. 'We've got to get him out. Can you walk John?' His father tugged his sleeve.

'I'm not . . . I can scarce move or see.' John's breathing was too shallow for him to say much.

'Follow as you can. I'll see if I can reach him.'

Gideon hurried away, splashing through the rising waters on the muddy riverbank, while John struggled behind him, one slow footstep after another. A beam from the lantern picked out a crooked elbow, rising, turning, falling under the tumbling water again. John could see his father ahead of him, trying to catch the arm with the branch, but Joshua was in the centre of the stream and out of reach.

John's foot caught in a hole and he fell again on the wet grass, his ankle wrenched sideways. He struggled on all fours, his hands scrabbled in mud and gravel, the icy rain soaked his hair and stung his head wound. He'd lost sight of Gideon. The lantern still cast a dim light, standing on the sodden ground some ten yards away, but there was no sign of his father.

There was a cry, and his throat tightened. He reached the lantern to find a pair of shoes lying beside it – he recognised them by the modest buckles as his father's. Had he entered the water? John raised the lamp and shone its beam to and fro across the churning stream. The dark angular rocks that broke the surface confused him: was it a knee, an elbow, a shoulder he had spotted? The immobility of the stones destroyed his hopes. Movement would indicate a body, whether floating or immersed, but the solid objects he could see were unmoving; only the water surged and crashed between them.

'Hoy! Who's there? What's amiss?'

A second light was weaving a path towards him on the opposite bank, alternately lighting an arm and half a chest, then a pair of breeches.

'Help us!' John cried. 'Two men are in the water.' He gasped as the pain seared his chest. 'I'm injured. I can't get them out.'

'Lord 'a mercy,' the stranger groaned. 'River's so high they'll be swept off and drowned by now. I fear 'twill be their bodies we recover. Stay here. I'll rouse up the village.'


Joshua's horse and cart were pressed into service next morning to transport back to Frome two bodies, decently covered by the horse blanket. It would have been an awkward job to retrieve them from the river, but at daybreak they were found, mangled and torn, caught amongst the trees and other debris that had wedged in the arches of the stone bridge.

'He tried to save that villain,' John said. 'All the harm the man had caused, yet my dear father didn't hesitate but jumped into the flood to try to rescue him.' He put his hand to his bandaged head. 'A frail old man, he didn't stand any chance of success. I should have done it, not him.'

Molly-Ann touched his hand gently. 'You were in no state to help, Master Silcox. From what I hear, your injuries would have prevented you from doing any good – there'd have been three bodies, not two.' She offered him a mug of sage and honey tea. 'Sarah says this'll help your head feel clearer. It was a sad chance you ran into that man at Mells, 'specially with night coming on. What had taken 'ee there?'

'My father was determined to call on the Greens – the family he supported. He'd heard that morning that the man had had an accident – broken his leg at the coal pit – and wanted to see what was needed. I'll take over his pastoral duties now, maybe I'll get them to join the colonists, seek a new life with us.'

Molly-Ann stared into the embers and ashes of the log fire. 'Your father's death will be felt by very many in this town. I can't say the same for Joshua's.'

Baby William screamed as his mother wrapped him in his blanket and fastened him to her hip with her shawl; she guided his thumb to his mouth and he gradually calmed down. At seven months he was becoming quite a weight and the cunning way of tying the shawl was helpful in supporting him. 'I imagine the members of the congregation will want to come and visit you later today, Master Silcox, pay their respects.

I'll get along, out of your way, if you feel well enough now? Mistress Naish and I can see to the school today.'

John nodded. 'Thank you, yes. But tomorrow I'll be there; I must try to keep it going in my father's place. I'll talk to Dorothea about her taking over altogether in the coming months; she seems to be willing to do so.' He ran his hands over his face. 'Of course, there's the chapel also. Once I leave for Newfoundland someone else will have to lead their worship. I'm not sure what my father had planned to do. He was still in two minds whether to come with us.' He could scarcely finish the sentence and Molly-Ann nodded sadly.

'He'd have thrown himself into that project,' she said, 'if he had decided to go, but at the same time, he'd have been sad to leave Frome.'

John smiled wryly at her. 'Yes. I believe his heart would have been here still.' He took a sip of the sage infusion. 'Molly-Ann, would you consider joining us in this sacred adventure? You and William would be very welcome, even if you do not feel drawn to our chapel yet.'

Molly-Ann felt her pulse quicken.

'It would get you out of the reach of Baily, give you the chance of a new life in a place that's free and open.' John was gazing into the flames.

'But I don't have a skill or trade to offer the colony, no money to put into it either. I don't want to be a burden to them.'

John frowned. 'Let's think about it in the coming weeks.'

Molly-Ann trudged along Keyford towards the school hall, turning John's suggestion over in her mind. A six or seven week sea voyage with a baby; a strange land with possible dangers from wild animals and strangers; to be a member of a religious colony where she would be very much the outsider;

on her own without the support of either Nat or Gideon Silcox – it was a daunting prospect. On the other hand, it was a new start; William could grow up with greater opportunities; and it would certainly be exciting. But as she had said to John, what did she have to offer? She could work as a servant, and that was about it. She had no means with which to start a business, knew nothing of farming, lacked the skills to run a school or nurse the sick properly. No, she and William would have to bide with what they knew, and Joshua being gone, it might not be so fearful as before.

It was strange to think of him gone. It was as if a weight had lifted from her, yet a hollow place had opened inside as well. She mourned the loss of dear Master Silcox. His lined face would bring a smile to hers whenever she thought of him – and that would be often. Perhaps in Joshua's case she regretted what might have been – if he hadn't turned against her, if she could have made a better man of him. She cuddled the baby closer. His father had been precious to her at one time, made her heart beat faster, sharpened her senses, but she and William would be better without him. She didn't want his shadow to fall over their son.

She had reached the turning into the schoolyard before she saw Simon Naish hurrying up Hunger Lane towards her. He raised his hand in greeting; the steep slope up from the church must have taken his breath from him.

'Good day to you Mistress,' he panted. 'I've heard the news about the tragedy at Mells and I needed to speak with you. Thank heavens you're here.' He drew a couple of deep breaths. 'I can't say as I'm sorry about Joshua Whittock,' he continued, 'but I'm mightily sorry for Master Silcox's death – his loss is a sad blow for us all.'

Molly-Ann nodded. 'Indeed it is. The whole town will feel

it.' She frowned. 'But why were you seeking me so urgently, sir?'

Naish took her by the elbow and walked a little way off the lane and closer to the school hall. 'I want you to come with me to Long Row, to your old cottage. I think I may be able to help you, if we can get there before Master Baily.'

She pulled back a little. 'Long Row? I'm not sure as I want to go there. It would bring back some bad memories.'

'This is in your interest, and the baby's.' Naish looked at William meaningfully. 'I'd feel wrong doing this on my own, but you have every right. We must go now, please trust me.'

She studied the master mason's face. As ever, she saw an honest, open expression, with a new urgency about his eyes. She nodded. 'As you wish, Master Naish.'

The back door was easy for Simon Naish to open, forcing the lock with a metal blade from his tool bag. Once inside, he closed the door behind them. Molly-Ann looked around the kitchen in disgust. There was a stale smell and it looked as though nothing had been done to tidy or clean it since the day she had left in early summer.

Master Naish had gone directly to the chimney breast. Taking a chisel from his tool bag he crouched inside the fireplace and worked away at one of the large stones at the base of the side wall. In just a few moments it came free. Molly-Ann bent closer to see just what he was doing. He levered the stone out and she could see a deep opening that had been concealed behind it. He grunted. 'He asked me to create this hidey hole when we were building the place.' He reached into the void and withdrew a large metal box. 'Yes, as I thought. Here you are, Molly-Ann, open this. It's yours by rights, I'd say.'

The lid was jammed on tightly, but with two hands she managed to prise it off. Inside lay a heap of coins, mostly silver: crowns, half crowns, shillings. Amongst these she found twenty-two golden guineas. She had never seen such wealth before.

'It's Josh's?'

'Was Josh's. Now he's dead and gone there'll be people coming looking for it – James Baily for one, others of his associates. They wouldn't know where to find it, I'd say, but they'd ransack the house till they did.'

'What am I to do? Is it theft if I take it?'

Naish shrugged. 'Like I said, you're the one that ought to have it. I'll say nothing and I'd advise you to keep it secret, perhaps go to another town and start afresh?'

He started to replace the stone, but Molly-Ann put out a hand. 'If we leave the box with just a few coins in it, it may serve to mislead any others.' She emptied the hoard from its container then replaced a few of the shillings. The higher value coins she tied up in a cloth bag. The box – now so much lighter – was hidden again and the stone eased back.

Naish smeared wood ash on the surrounding mortar to hide the scratches. 'All done. Now, let's hope no one sees us leave.'

Molly-Ann took a last look around the room; it was the bad memories that predominated. She shrugged and left. One hand supported the sleeping baby, the other held a small fortune: now she felt she had the freedom to choose her future.

# AUTHOR'S NOTE AND ACKNOWLEDGMENTS

THIS NOVEL IS entirely a work of fiction; the events and characters it depicts are the work of the author's imagination. Dr Joseph Glanvill, Dr John Humfry, the Sheppards, James Baily and Richard Yerbury are historical figures of seventeenth-century Frome, but the characters and actions I have attributed to them are wholly fictitious. Any other resemblance to actual persons, living or dead, events or localities is entirely coincidental.

My thanks to Professor Steve Poole of the University of the West of England, whose talks to the Frome Family History Group gave me some of the very first ideas for *Dissenters*. I also owe a great deal to the historian Dr Ian Mortimer, whose wonderful book *The Time Traveller's Guide to Restoration Britain* resolved so many practical questions for me. This fascinating book and many others are listed in the Bibliography. Historical errors and deliberate distortions are of course my own responsibility.

Members of the Frome Writers' Collective and Silver Crow Books have done much to encourage and support me in the writing of *Dissenters*, and my special thanks go to the Wednesday writing group of Brenda Bannister, Debs Dowling, Gill Harry, Mary Macarthur, Wendy Worley and Sue Watts.

I am very grateful to Steven Jenkins for the wonderful cover illustration of 'Hunger Lane' in Frome. And last but by no means least, my thanks to John Chandler and Hobnob Press for saying 'yes', and for their help in bringing my book into the light of day.

## BIBLIOGRAPHY

Belham, Peter, *The Making of Frome* (Frome Society for Local Study, 1985)

Chatterton, E Keble, *King's Cutters and Smugglers 1700-1885* (Leonaur, 2008)

Christian, Garth ed., *A Victorian Poacher – James Hawker's Journal* (Oxford University Press, 1978)

Davis, Mick & Pitt, Valerie, *The Historic Inns of Frome* (Akeman Press, 2015)

Evans, James, *Emigrants – Why the English Sailed to the New World* (Weidenfeld & Nicolson, 2018)

Goodall, Rodney D, *The Buildings of Frome* (Frome Society for Local Study, 2013)

Griffiths, Carolyn, *Woad to This, and the Cloth Trade in Frome* (Frome Society for Local Study, 2017)

Leech, Roger, *Early Industrial Housing, The Trinity Area of Frome* (HMSO, 1981)

McGarvie, Michael, *The Book of Frome* (Barracuda Books Ltd, 1980)

Mortimer, Ian, *The Time Traveller's Guide to Restoration Britain 1660-1700* (Bodley Head, 2017)

Nozedar, Adele, *The Hedgerow Handbook – Recipes, Remedies and Rituals* (Square Peg, 2012)

Lightning Source UK Ltd.
Milton Keynes UK
UKHW020621120520
363135UK00006B/199